Starting New Lives

JAMES DE LA BOULLAYE

Translated from the French by JULIE SAPPA

Cover by CHRISTOPHE VENOT

CONTENTS

*Ce n'était pas l'heure des bilans mais l'heure terrible du présent
où l'on constate l'étendue des dégâts*

It wasn't a time to take stock, but a terrible moment for
observing the extent of the damage

(*Au revoir là-haut* (Goodbye up there), Pierre Lemaître,
Prix Goncourt 2013, France)

1

NEAR TORGAU, GERMANY, MAY 7, 1945

Wilhelm Steimer is exhausted. He is walking slowly and with some difficulty, and he hasn't eaten anything for two days. The Russians are hot on his heels, or, more precisely, on those of the rest of the German 12th Army. The troops are under the command of General Wenck, who was supposed to go and fight in Berlin. But the Russians were too strong, and the Germans had to retrace their steps back to somewhere near Potsdam.

They are now beating a retreat towards the west. Anything rather than being taken prisoner by the Bolsheviks! They say that the Russian soldiers rape women, send soldiers to Siberia and pillage the countryside and towns. Wilhelm has been to this region before and he knows that the Elbe, a river that flows into the North Sea several hundred miles further north, is nearby. The Elbe is their lifeline. On the other side of the water, American troops, who generally treat their prisoners well, are waiting for them.

Wilhelm is a sergeant in the *Wehrmacht*. Despite his fatigue, he is carrying a backpack that he refuses to put down. For the last three days, even when he has stopped to rest, he has kept his backpack on, refusing to be separated from it. At the bottom of this bag is something precious that could change his destiny if he can figure out how to use it wisely.

He isn't the only one walking. The scene is extremely chaotic, with tens of thousands of civilian refugees of all ages, and *Wehrmacht* soldiers of all ranks fleeing from the Russians. These soldiers no longer have any faith in a German victory. The best they can hope for is to fall rapidly into the hands of the Americans, even if it means being prisoners for a while, because they believe that the conditions in which they will be detained will be bearable.

As for Wilhelm, he has other ideas. He was forced to join the German army almost five years ago. Until the middle of 1942, he was one of the lucky ones, having a great time occupying France. What wonderful memories, that period spent occupying a French village! He hasn't been able to stop reminiscing about it for the last two years. If only he could go back there! Then the nightmare had begun, being transferred to Russia, the Russian front, the battle of Stalingrad, rats everywhere, thousands of deaths every day, and then the cold, always terrible. And then a miracle happened, thanks to his linguistic talents. Wilhelm is 29 years old. He speaks German, the language of his father, English, like his mother, an American born in New York, and French, which he learned at school and university and practiced during the years of occupation. Fortunately, at the end of 1943, he was transferred to the intelligence services in Germany, to help decode the American messages intercepted by his unit. At last an escape from Russia and its many horrors!

The road along which Wilhelm is walking runs along the edge of a dense pine wood. The trees are planted very close together and it's difficult to see much beyond the edge of the wood. The sergeant takes a few sheets of newspaper out of his pocket and leaves the road quickly, as if to satisfy an urgent need, and he disappears into the greenery. In the army, there are many cases of dysentery. The food is often rotten and food poisoning is only too frequent. Very soon, Wilhelm considers himself to be sufficiently out of sight of the others. He takes a razor, a pair of scissors, a looking glass, some soap and a bottle of water out of his backpack. He doesn't want to be recognized and is more than willing to sacrifice his moustache, which he trims closely with the scissors before attacking it with the cut-throat razor. He takes his uniform off and takes some civilian clothes out of his bag, and rapidly puts them on. A blue shirt, a nicely cut suit, some smart black shoes, a hat with ear protectors, and a stained raincoat that is a bit too big and hides the rest. However, a closely shaved individual would look a bit out of place in these times, with all the German civilians fleeing down the roads, sleeping outside and no longer washing. He rubs some dirt over his face. Transformed, he cuts a branch from one of the pine trees to use as a cane and puts his backpack back on. He hides his uniform under the branches of the trees around him.

Wilhelm then rapidly returns to the tide of refugees and starts to walk along, limping and using his cane. Some would be surprised by the sight of a young man in civilian clothing in the middle of this crowd, and would suspect him of being a deserter. But with his attire, no-one can tell if he is 30 or 50. The people walking alongside him are far too tired to be surprised by his presence. Some are moaning and crippled with pain due to the many miles they have already covered, and others are out of breath and on their last legs.

They got up early. They have been on their feet since dawn, after only a few hours of sleep. Wilhelm is sure that the Elbe is not far away now. He wonders what he will find when he gets close to the river. It will be vital to avoid being identified as a *Wehrmacht* soldier, but he doesn't want to find himself lost in a sea of civilian refugees either. He has other plans entirely.

Wilhelm is feeling weaker with every step. He is feeling nauseous and terribly thirsty. He has been trying to conserve his water supplies since the night before, but, at this stage, he senses that he must drink a little to make sure that he doesn't faint. He dips into his reserves and takes a few mouthfuls. He now has only about half a pint of water left. He keeps walking, limping more and more. The walkers perceive the sound of voices from somewhere ahead, growing louder as they approach. The vegetation changes. The road is no longer bordered by woods, but by poorly cultivated fields covered with soft green grass. There are apple trees in flower, the great tits are singing and there are many sparrows in the sky. But in the convoy, everyone is too anxious to enjoy these spring-tinted pleasures. The refugees march every more slowly, and the convoy eventually comes to a halt.

Wilhelm wants to know what is going on. He leaves the road, clambering over a fence to the right, and carries on across the open ground, tracing a large loop, hoping to gain time and arrive sooner at the river. Several other refugees follow him. But Wilhelm doesn't talk to them, and instead tries to scatter them so that he can stay on his own. He has hidden some identity papers in his undergarments that he is counting on using, at the appropriate time, to invent a new life for himself. He can now see what must be the River Elbe, but he is still too far away to determine whether there are any American soldiers there waiting for them. Another five minutes of walking slowly and he will know either way. These minutes are long and stressful. The difficult part will soon begin. He is so desperate for his plan to work, but for that, he will first need to find a boat.

Wilhelm has reached the banks of the Elbe. The river is wide at this point. On the right, a bridge has been damaged by the bombing and is missing two arches. In the fields, he can see several carcasses of German light armored vehicles that were hit several weeks ago. No sign of any boat that might get him across the river though. He walks along the right bank of the river towards the south, where the river bends, making it impossible to see what lies further down. Wilhelm carefully makes his way to the point at which the river starts to bend. A few hundred yards further on, he can see a crowd, a mixture of soldiers and refugees. On the river, several boats are ferrying people from one side to the other. Wilhelm joins a group composed mostly of civilians dressed like himself. He tries to go unnoticed, pushing his hat down hard onto his head, and stands in line with the others. The boats are small, each able to take only about a dozen people. A boatman goes back up the river in his boat and then crosses the Elbe again, continuing the transport. There are no GIs on the right bank, but a heavy concentration of troops and armored vehicles on the left bank. He can also see some large tents towards which the new arrivals are being herded.

It's almost midday by the time Wilhelm finally manages to get onto a boat. In a few moments, he will be asked about his identity and his activities, and he is going to have to be very careful. When he arrives on the bank, he and his fellow passengers are met by two American soldiers, one black and the other white, each armed with a gun. They tell the passengers to follow them, after separating out two *Wehrmacht* soldiers from the same boat. They walk for a few minutes, until they reach a tent set up next to a fence. They are told to sit down in line and wait until it is their turn to be interrogated. If they want to, they can use the nearby latrines. Water and bread are distributed to the new arrivals, who literally throw themselves on this frugal meal. Wilhelm is shocked by the number of people waiting. Civilians gradually trickle out of the tent and are accompanied to a destiny unknown to those still waiting.

After about a quarter of an hour, Wilhelm hears a noise, like murmurs, snatches of conversation coming from the throng. He's too far away to be able to make out what is going on. A German civilian comes out of the tent looking very excited and says a few words to some of the people sitting close to the entrance. A rumor starts to spread. Some of the faces tense up, whereas others relax at the news, as if relieved.

The rumor reaches Wilhelm. During the night, the German General Jodl signed an unconditional surrender in the presence of Eisenhower. This is enormous news. It's the end of the Nazi regime. Germany is totally occupied. Wilhelm is German. He has fought hard in the last few years, but he is serene. He didn't like the Nazis, despite being violently anticommunist. As a soldier of the *Wehrmacht,* he had done his duty like any other young German man, but without enthusiasm, particularly as his mother was American and, thus, on the other side. He thinks about his parents now. He hasn't heard from them and he doesn't know whether they survived the bombing of Dresden.

The news changes the atmosphere in the refugee camp. The American soldiers start shouting and running around, congratulating and hugging each other, ignoring the civilians waiting for them. Wilhelm watches carefully and analyzes the situation. Maybe it would be a good time to execute his plan?

He is already at phase two in his plan and he has no choice, it's now or never. A one in ten chance of success, but he has to try. Wilhelm is afraid, but he pulls himself together. He looks around him, searching for a secluded corner, but he can't see one. He gets up to walk around the tent. No-one thinks to stop him. The tent has been pitched against some shrubs. If he can penetrate into these shrubs, he will have a few instants of calm in which to act. He does this, terrified at the thought of being discovered. He still has his precious backpack with him.

Wilhelm takes off his raincoat and recuperates the identity papers from their hiding place in his undergarments. He wets a piece of cloth with his remaining water and wipes his face and hands to clean himself up. He puts on an armband bearing the word "PRESS" and then grabs the camera hidden at the bottom of his bag. He comes out of the shrubs and heads towards a group of American soldiers drinking and singing a few tens of yards away.

When he gets to them, camera in hand, he shouts out gaily in English, with a perfect American accent, "Hey guys, how's about I take a picture of you? A souvenir of the day of victory. I'll develop the photo straight away."

The soldiers assume he is a reporter from an American newspaper. Wilhelm is perfectly bilingual and has no trace of a German accent when he speaks English. The GIs are delighted and pose, bottle in hand, for Wilhelm.

He leaves them, assuring them that he will be back within the half hour. He walks towards another group and does the same thing all over again. Little by little, he gradually edges his way towards groups of Americans closer to the camp exit, right next to the Elbe. He loiters near the barrier, just inside the camp, taking lots of photographs of American and German soldiers. He then approaches the GIs posted at the camp entrance, with his camera still hanging round his neck, and politely asks, "Hey guys, I'd like to take a few shots of the people arriving in the boats. Will you let me back in in a few minutes?"

"We're letting all the Germans in, we're hardly likely to turn away one of our own journalists! See you in a jiffy."

Phase two of Wilhelm's plan, undoubtedly the trickiest part, has worked perfectly. He is outside the camp, in civilian clothes, and people think he is an American journalist! But he's not out of the woods yet. Just over six hundred miles to go to reach his destination. Guarded borders to cross, with soldiers hunting down SS officers terrified by the idea of finding themselves in prison.

For the moment, all he has in his possession is half a bar of chocolate given to him by a sergeant delighted to have his photo taken, and a few dollars in his pocket. But, he has got away from the Russians and the Americans, and none of the *Wehrmacht* soldiers have recognized him. He now feels the need to be on his own for a while to focus on the next part of his adventure. The woods will serve as his refuge today.

Wilhelm checks his identity papers whilst hidden in a beech wood, and goes over the events leading him here. He isn't German anymore. He has become an American journalist working for the Washington Post. A war correspondent! A few days ago, he heard some moaning whilst walking alone in a wood. He approached the source of the sound and found an American in civilian dress who had clearly parachuted from a plane in flames and landed badly. The man was in a great deal of pain and was bleeding heavily from a wound on his right side. Wilhelm initially spoke to him in German and then, realizing that he was American, continued to speak to him in his own language. The man had explained, with some difficulty, that he was a journalist sent to report on the fall of Berlin and the Russian invasion. He had lost too much blood, and he died less than half an hour after Wilhelm's arrival. Without scruple, Wilhelm recuperated the American's identity papers and carefully altered them, adding his own photo and forging an official stamp. He also took some of the American's clothes. The result was convincing enough for Wilhelm Steimer to become William Clark, age 32.

2

MEKNES, MOROCCO, MAY 7, 1945

"Right, that's it! I've had it up to here! Enough is enough."

Maggy can't help shouting out loud, even though she is on her own. She is beside herself due to a letter that she received yesterday from her son, Phil, Lieutenant Colonel and Commander of a heavy bomber base at Gaitford in England. In his letter, he explains once again that the war is not over and that, even if it soon will be, he won't be returning immediately and those at Meknes will have to wait a bit longer before returning to France. And yet, Paris was liberated more than nine months ago and, prisoners aside, the Germans have long since departed from France!

It's been four years since she arrived in this godforsaken hole with her grandchildren, Paul and Claire. It was fine at first. Phil was there, even if his behavior left something to be desired! But life has been hell since he left for England at the end of 1943. Many other airmen have left Morocco too. The only Europeans left are their wives and children, and, at close to 71, she is older by far than any of them. Half the time, the heat is unbearable. And as for food, they might not be starving, but it's hardly a feast. Maggy dreams of cooked meats, ham, garlic sausage, black pudding and nice fatty pork chops to replace the starved chickens and mutton she has to eat here. There are days when the children tire her out. They are teenagers now, and they often answer back. They're nice kids really, but they aren't very easy to raise, especially Claire, the youngest, who tends to be very stubborn.

Maggy misses her family in Bois-Colombes, Asnières and elsewhere in the Parisian suburbs. She has continued to write to them of course, but the mail is so very slow! Maggy is in a really bad mood, and she's hungry, which only makes things worse. She woke up early this morning, at half past five, and got up for some coffee with bread and butter. She feels the need to talk to someone and she decides to visit her friend Ginette, who runs a clothes store nearby. Maggy pays considerable attention to the way she looks. She's not the mother of a lieutenant colonel for nothing and she must keep up appearances. She paints her face discreetly, and puts on a pretty pink floral dress in cotton. The children are at school and she has a bit of free time ahead of her. She is just about to lock the door of her little house when the sirens suddenly start blaring as if to warn the inhabitants of some imminent danger. What on earth is going on? There haven't been any Germans or Italians in North Africa for ages. The sirens have already been going for almost a minute when the bells of the neighboring church chime in with a more melodious touch.

Maggy realizes that the blessed moment, so long awaited, may finally have arrived. She needs to find out and she runs along the street, rather than walking, despite her age. She soon arrives at a large road, where Moroccans and French people alike are streaming into the street, shouting joyfully. She runs into the wife of an officer, who tells her, excitedly and almost yelling, "Maggy, it's the armistice! The Boche signed last night! The war is over! We'll be able to go home soon. Isn't it wonderful?"

Maggy had almost given up hope and the news comes as a shock to her. She doesn't know what to say and has to walk over to a bench to sit down and rest for a moment, breathless. She wants to talk to someone, but who? One name suddenly comes to mind,

Slimane[1], her only Moroccan friend, a man very different from herself. They are complete opposites, in terms of their nationalities, cultures and lives. But Maggy likes talking to Slimane, and he seems to like her too, even if she's much older than he is. Where would he be now? Surely not at home in the middle of the morning. Telepathy or pure chance, Maggy hears a voice behind her.

"Hello, Mrs. Colonel, how are you? So it's the armistice. You must be happy. You've been here four years now, haven't you?"

Slimane is quite a sight. He is tall, with a handsome gray moustache. He was awarded the War Cross in 1917 and he and Maggy use the familiar "tu" form when they speak to each other. The Moroccans have never really got used to the more formal "vous" form, which has no equivalent in their language, but that doesn't bother Maggy, who doesn't see herself as superior and doesn't care for airs and graces. What does it matter whether he calls her "tu" or "vous"? Slimane often calls her "Mrs. Colonel", as a term of endearment and respect. He also calls her "Mrs. Maggy" or "Mrs. Destivel", as the mood takes him.

"Ah, Slimane, I was just thinking about you, and I turned round and there you were! What a pleasure to see you! Six years ago this war was declared! So many people in the road! I think I'll go home soon. Would you like to come to my house in an hour to celebrate? I made a cake for the kids yesterday and there's some left over. Would you like coffee or tea with it?"

"OK, Mrs. Maggy, I'll be at your place in an hour."

Slimane leaves Maggy to rest and cogitate for a few minutes on the bench. What is most important to her, especially now, it to get back to Paris. But, for that, she is dependent on the army to provide her with a means of transport to France. Plane? Boat? She doesn't

---

[1] *See chapter 11 of "A French Pilot in Gaitford"*

know yet, but what does it matter so long as she can leave this country as soon as possible?

Meanwhile, Paul and Claire, her grandchildren, aged 15 and 14, have been let out of school early with their classmates, to join the parade in Meknes. Paul has met up with his friends from the scouts. They went looking for their troop's pennant, which they are now bearing as proudly as if it were the national flag. Claire is marching in the street with her friends. They had heard over the last few days that it was looking very bad for the Germans, who would soon lose.

Back at home, Maggy is preparing a snack for her friend from the Atlas Mountains, Slimane, a road-mender. When she was little and living in the countryside close to Orleans, her parents also offered the road-mender a drink when he was working nearby, and he never refused. She is perpetuating this tradition. She had been pleased to meet Slimane and there is something a bit exotic in their relationship. They are friends, they help each other, and they enjoy talking to each other. Maggy gets him to talk about his childhood, when he lived with his parents in a village in the high Atlas Mountains. Slimane asks her questions about her youth, her parents, who were vintners, and her husband, who took her to live close to Paris and died a few years ago.

Time flies and Slimane is soon there, ringing the doorbell. Without waiting to be asked, like the frequent visitor that he is, he enters the small house inhabited by the Destivels in Meknes and finds Maggy in her kitchen.

"So, Mrs. Colonel, the Germans are beaten then? Are you going home or do you like Morocco so much that you are going to stay with us forever?"

Maggy really doesn't want to upset him. She replies diplomatically.

"Morocco is a beautiful country, but I have my family waiting for me in France. I'll have to go home soon, but not straight away. I'll have to talk things over with my son first."

"And what are you going to do in France Mrs. Maggy? Do you have your own house? Or are you going to live with your son and continue to look after your grandchildren?"

"Good question. Not sure I know the answer yet though. I'm not sure what would be best."

"Mrs. Colonel, wouldn't you like to get married again? Your grandchildren are getting big now."

"Get married again? Are you out of your mind? I'm an old woman, way past all that!"

"You're still beautiful, elegant. I'm sure that you could find a widower who would love to look after you. I miss that. Wouldn't you like to stay here and marry me?"

"Slimane, you're teasing me, and it's not nice of you!"

It's not the first time that Slimane has asked her, with a broad, tender grin on his face.

Maggy starts to prepare some tea, not the very sugary mint tea they usually drink here, but French-style tea. But, suddenly, she changes her mind and opens a bottle of *vin gris* from Guerrouane, from which she fills the two bowls she had prepared for the tea. She cuts several portions of the plum tart she made the day before and returns to the living room with Slimane. She doesn't tell him that it is wine in the two bowls. They toast the victory and start to drink. Slimane is surprised. As a good Muslim, he has never tasted an alcoholic drink before. Maggy notes his surprise.

"Slimane, you can't celebrate an event like today without wine. You have to taste it. Do you like it?"

Slimane drinks the wine in little gulps and seems to like it. Maggy refills their bowls several times and they drink to France, Morocco and the end of the war. The alcohol soon works its wonders, making them more lively than usual. They sit on the floor, on either side of a copper tray that Maggy bought recently.

"Mrs. Colonel, my head feels funny. Your ceiling is spinning."

Both of them laugh. Maggy draws closer to him and kisses him on the forehead. Slimane pulls her even closer. Surprised, Maggy laughs even more. She's a bit taken aback when she notices that her Moroccan friend has started to undress her, but she doesn't protest. She's a bit too tipsy to be reasonable and tells herself that she probably won't live to see another armistice! She whispers to Slimane that they would be better off in her bedroom. They rapidly end up in bed. Before he died, her husband had been ill for several years, with a heart condition that had left him very weak. Her last experience of carnal love was years ago and she didn't believe she would ever again experience such strong pleasures.

Suddenly, Maggy hears a noise. It's the garden gate, which someone has just opened. Then the door to the house makes its characteristic grating noise.

Someone has entered the house. Slimane makes a sign indicating to Maggy that she should remain silent. Shh! Shh! Maggy is anxious. What would she say if one of her grandchildren came into her bedroom, which they often did without the slightest hesitation? Maggy holds her breath. She sweats it out over three long minutes that seem endless. This woman usually so in control is, for once, at the mercy of the gods. There is no lock on the bedroom door. Maggy feels like she is trapped. The house door creaks again and then all is silent. The alert is over. Phew! Maggy thought she was done for! What an escape!

Slimane takes advantage of the situation to stoke the flames of passion, and Maggy doesn't resist. She enjoys taking his manhood in her hand and caressing it. When their frolics are over, she can hardly believe what has happened! They go their separate ways, grinning, half an hour later. Maggy remains in the house and is delighted that she can still please a nice, good-looking man who must be 10 or 15 years younger than she is.

Slimane's words have given her food for thought concerning her return to France. What is she going to do with her life now? It's true that there are small adds from people seeking a spouse in one of the magazines she reads regularly, *Le chasseur français*. She regularly comes across women of her age who would like to get married again. Her son will undoubtedly remarry. That's only to be expected. He is in the prime of life and needs a companion. But maybe he'll get mixed up with some little tart who will give him the runaround? She will have to look out for him!

Maggy ends up falling asleep on her bed. No-one disturbs her because her grandchildren stay late at the celebrations in Meknes.

That evening, when Claire returns home with her brother Paul, it is late, but, given the circumstances, Maggy doesn't yell at them. Claire isn't sleepy. She knows that she has just lived through a historic day that she will always remember.

She decides that today would be the ideal time to start writing a diary, an activity that she will continue for many years. A way for her to immortalize the key moments in her life and to reflect on the high and low points. She senses that it will do her good to keep a diary. One of her best friends started writing a diary three months ago and already sees herself as a feted writer and candidate for membership of the *Académie Française!*

First entry in the journal of Claire Destivel, age 14 years[2]

Monday, May 7, 1945

At long last!!! The armistice. I've been waiting for this blessed day for six years. The world has changed. What a joyous atmosphere, it's like a dream. I've seen people hugging and kissing and, wonder of wonders, the Meknassi (the inhabitants of Meknes) running, which they don't usually do. It must be amazing in Paris. I can't help thinking about Grandad and Dad, whom I love so much and hope to see again soon.

But I'm straying from the point. Let's come back to the events of this memorable day. Since Friday, the whole school has been in disarray and, of course, we haven't been doing anything. We've all been waiting for the sirens to go off and, at the slightest hint of a noise, we're all of a quiver. I will never forget the moment when the sirens went off, the poor old church bells started ringing and the ancient canon, the only one in Meknes, was fired. The whole school charged out of the gates under the severe glare of the Deputy Head, who was completely overwhelmed by events. We paraded throughout the town, singing and shouting.

When we go back to the airbase, I will have to say goodbye to Ginette, a dear friend of mine who is going away. I wish she were staying. I've known her for three years and she's a great girl, even if she can be a bit childish sometimes. It's a good job that it's the armistice today, or else I'd be feeling really down. I'm very sensitive, too sensitive even, and extremely sentimental. How much I've changed! I used to be so happy before. It must be because of the war.

This evening, after dinner, I went into town with some friends and we had a wonderful time. Yvette was in a delightful mood and we went up and down the avenue hundreds of times. We kept bumping into people. We went to the Benoist family's house close to midnight to eat some bread and butter and a chocolate mousse that we ate in the garden by moonlight. We danced "La Bohême", otherwise known as the "danse macabre" when danced at midnight surrounded by ghosts!

---

[2] *Text based largely on an excerpt from a real diary*

I have a secret to confide to my diary. Etienne, Yvette's brother, was in the garden. He made eyes at me and tried to kiss me in the shadows until Yvette arrived. I was all butterflies, and I still am, but shh! No-one is supposed to know!

3

BOUGIE, ALGERIA, MAY 7 AND 8, 1945

It's the middle of the afternoon of May 7 and it's hot at Ferme Saint Jacques, an agricultural holding run by Jacques Canot. It is located close to the sea, just over four miles from Bougie and about 140 miles east of Algiers. Françoise Dumaine has been invited to spend three days in this haven of peace. The Canots have become fond of her and have been helping her since the death of her husband almost two years ago. Jacques drove her here with her three children, Agnes, aged 11, Michel, aged seven and Romain, who is almost two. All three kids love coming here, to the country.

Jacques Canot divides his time between Bougie, where he oversees the management of his land, and Algiers, where he sells his produce: lots of fruit, especially oranges, grapes and dates. Cereals too, wheat, rye, barley and oats, which are often lacking in Algeria. Yields are good here, because the farm is located in Kabylie, a region that is quite rainy in the fall and winter.

The farm is composed of several buildings arranged around a very green courtyard full of shrubs and other plants that perfume the air. The lilac is in flower and the rosemary bushes are filling the air with the aroma of Provence. Two magnificent fig trees, with large complicated leaves, stand on either side of a well-pruned carob tree. On the eastern side of the courtyard, there is a large irrigation basin that is particularly useful in the spring and summer, when there is no rain and the crops are in need of water. The noise of the fountain is enticing, inviting the visitor to bathe in the water. On the western side, the courtyard gives way to an orchard and vegetable plot, providing oranges and lemons, black radishes, carrots, potatoes and cauliflowers. Jacques comes from the Rhone Valley, and he has tried to get the fruits and vegetables local to that area to acclimatize to the conditions here.

Jacques Canot is 50 years old. His wife, Henriette, was supposed to come with them, but she ended up staying with one of their two children in Algiers because she is becoming increasingly car sick with age and often ends up vomiting during journeys. Her eldest son, Georges, has come along though. Jacques is not unhappy to find himself with Françoise and the children. He has promised them a tour of his land on horses and donkeys, like cowboys in the prairies of the Far West. Romain, who is still a bit too young for that kind of adventure, must stay at the farm, where he will play with a local nanny and the children of Jacque's staff. Françoise appreciates the protective side of her host and friend, who is very attentive and constantly concerned about their well-being. The interior decoration of the house is very sophisticated, with many locally made objects. Pottery painted with brightly colored geometric motifs, finely crafted silver jewelry set with precious stones, mostly red, with various inlays.

They look majestic on their mounts when they depart. Françoise's husband was initially in the cavalry before becoming an airman, and he taught her how to ride. She is wearing pants for the occasion. The estate manager, Pierre Hernandez, originally from Spain, accompanies them. Agnes, Georges and Michel each have a little stick with which to prod their donkeys forward. The estate is vast and it takes more than an hour to ride round it. The estate manager tells his boss about the problems that have arisen recently, such as obstructions in several irrigation channels and certain diseased trees. Midway round their tour of the property, they stop to refresh themselves by drinking cool water from a porous pot and eating a few figs and very sugary pastries. Françoise is enjoying this peaceful ride. The Kabylians they meet, mostly agricultural workers employed by the estate, exchange friendly greetings with Jacques Canot, who is very cordial with them. Hernandez is more authoritarian and often contemptuous.

The riders are exhausted when they return at seven in the evening. Shortly after their return, one of Jacques' friends, a man with an agricultural holding a couple of miles away, arrives in a state of agitation.

"Jacques, Jacques, I've just got back from Bougie. Have you heard the news? The Germans have capitulated. They signed an unconditional surrender in France during the night. We knew it was coming, but it's finally happened! The fucking war is over in Europe! Can you believe it? Over! My son is alive and he will come back from Germany."

All the adults present are stunned by the news, even though the Allies have been in control on the ground in North Africa for more than two years. Françoise Dumaine is undoubtedly the most affected, as this news means that she will be able to return to France. She is delighted at the news, but disconcerted too. She will have to start again and build herself a new life. When she left France, she was married to an attractive man that she loved. Now, at the age of 32, she is a widow with three children to raise, the youngest not yet two years old. Like most middle-class women, she doesn't work. Both her parents are dead, as are her grandparents. The only place she could go is the village of Morleau in Burgundy, where she has a house. But what state is it likely to be in after five years away, with the village occupied by the Germans until 1944? She wants to go home, but the very idea fills her with anxiety. In Algeria, she gets lots of help from her Algerian maid, Zora, who is sweet and often funny. Returning to France will be a leap in the dark.

The evening passes in high spirits. To celebrate, Jacques has opened two bottles of Champagne that he had ordered from France. He asks the estate manager and his wife, Jeanne, to join them. Exceptionally, the children are allowed to eat with the adults. The mood is joyful.

But Françoise has a fitful night. She wakes up towards two in the morning. She knows that she must go home to France, but she realizes that she has grown attached to Algeria, a beautiful country where life is easy for her despite the hardships linked to the war. Why not stay another year? Her eldest, Agnes, could go to a boarding school run by nuns in Algiers. Michel could continue going to the local primary school, and Romain is very fond of his nanny. Here, she can afford a full-time maid, which makes her life much easier. She has made a few friends among the French people who have settled here. In fact, she is afraid that she will feel isolated when she does return to her village in Burgundy. She finally falls asleep again, telling herself that it is too early to make a decision.

The next morning, the children play in the internal courtyard while Françoise prepares a French-style lunch. The war has taken its toll on food supplies. In the towns, even in North Africa, food is scarce, but things are much better on the farm. Only coffee remains rare, but they have found a substitute in the form of torrified barley. A pig was killed the night before and a black pudding was rapidly prepared from its blood. Some apples fried in oil will make the perfect accompaniment. The children are helping Jacques to prepare some bread from maize flour, to be baked in an ancient clay oven. Jacques opens a bottle of Volnay 1938 to continue the victory celebrations.

After lunch, the children have a little nap or some quiet time in their room. Françoise takes advantage of the calm to read. A friend recommended she read *"L'Etranger"* by Albert Camus, a writer who lives in Algiers. Françoise has just started to read it. Towards four o'clock, Jacques suggests that they go for a walk, with a planned game of hide-and-seek in the carob tree wood about half a mile from the farm. The children are very excited. Even Romain can come along this time, in an old cart pulled along at breakneck speed by the other children.

After they have been playing for about half an hour, Farid, a young farmhand, suddenly appears out of nowhere, looking haggard and asking them, with poorly coordinated gestures, to stay hidden and remain silent. He explains in whispers that a group of Algerian demonstrators has arrived at the farm demanding to see the boss. They are armed and very aggressive. The estate manager, Hernandez told them that the boss was away for a few hours and that they shouldn't wait. They hit him when he told them they shouldn't be there.

"That's when I left the farm," says Farid, "I knew I'd find you here. Mister Hernandez yelled at them! Don't go back boss! They're completely mad. They've got an Algerian flag and they're from the Algerian People's Party."

"Farid, we will wait here for an hour. Go and see what's happening and then make your way back here without being seen and tell me. We'll go hide in the cave. Got that?"

Farid leaves and Françoise starts shaking with fear, not so much for herself as for the children. Jacques tries unsuccessfully to calm her down.

"Jacques, I want to leave this place right now. I want to go back to Algiers. Those people are terrible. They are capable of doing the worst things you can imagine."

"No. Don't worry. It will all be all right. We'll go a bit further into the wood while we're waiting. There's a little cave hidden in the vegetation."

Jacques is also scared stiff, but he is trying to look brave. They all walk to the cave, a crevice in the rocks that is difficult to see, where they sit on the ground in silence. They have understood that it is vital not to speak. Romain has fallen asleep in his mother's arms. After about a quarter of an hour they hear the sound of voices approaching. Clearly, a group of men has come looking for them. Jacques has a quick look outside, well camouflaged by a bush. He sees five men, two carrying guns, the other three armed only with daggers. They aren't heading in the direction of the cave and, if they keep going, they should pass about 80 yards to the left of its entrance. But they stop, because another man who has run to catch up with them seems to be telling them to go back quickly the way they have come. They rapidly retrace their steps. Jacques decides that they should stay another quarter of an hour in the cave. Then they all go back together, making as little noise as possible. When they are about 300 yards from the farm, Jacques turns to Françoise.

"Stay behind this little hill with the kids. I'm going to see what's happening. I'll come back for you."

Jacques takes a circuitous route, following an arc back to the farm via the kitchen and flower gardens, so as to arrive as discreetly as possible. He can see Farid alongside several other farmhands. The atmosphere seems to be tense. He walks up to Farid.

"Have they gone?" he asks.

"Yes, they didn't stay long, but there's a problem. Come and have a look."

Farid takes Jacques to a room on the ground floor, at the back of the house in which Hernandez lives. The room is a bit dark and there is a putrid smell. It takes Jacques a little while to adapt to the lighting before he can make anything out, but he is rapidly horrified by what he sees. At the place where they hang up the pigs before killing them, he can see his estate manager, hanging by his legs.

"They cut his throat before hanging him up there. They were annoyed when he yelled at them to leave. They are monsters that lot. They said they would come back for you. You must leave. Mrs. Hernandez doesn't know what has happened. She went to lunch at a neighboring farm about a mile away and she hasn't come back yet."

Jacques remains motionless for several seconds, completely tetanized. There hasn't been any violence near his farm for more than 20 years. He rapidly returns to reality and instructs his farmhands to take the body down and into the house, and to lay it out on the large table in the dining room. He asks Farid to go and fetch Mrs. Dumaine and the children without telling them what has happened. He then runs into his own house and opens a chest located in a room adjoining his bedroom, from which he removes two military rifles, two revolvers and some ammunition. He goes into the garage and loads two jerry cans of petrol that he had the good sense to stockpile despite the shortages into the boot of his car.

When Françoise and the children arrive, Jacques makes them get into the car straight away, without any explanation, without allowing them to go and get their things. He asks Françoise to drive. He sits in the front passenger seat, with his guns and pistols at his side. They leave immediately, heading south to the trunk road they need to take to return to Algiers. Jacques tells Françoise not to stop on any account. Their lives depend on it. Françoise is completely terrorized but tries to concentrate on her driving.

They drive along like this for a couple of miles, but they have to slow down when six armed Kabylians on the right-hand side of the road signal to them to stop.

"Françoise, slow down as if you're going to stop, but as soon as you get close to them, put your foot down, even if one of them is in the middle of the road."

Jacques lowers his window and loads his revolver, which he holds in his right hand. He tells the children to lie down on the back seat.

Françoise does exactly what he asked of her. Once she gets within about 20 yards of the group, she heads off to the right, towards the roadside before suddenly slamming her foot down on the accelerator and beeping the horn continuously. The insurgents are surprised. One of them tries to block the path of the car, which hits him with its full force. Another wants to shoot at them. But he doesn't have time because Jacques fires his revolver, which is aimed straight at him, and watches him collapse. Françoise has gotten through. One of their attackers tries to fire a rifle at them, but misses. Françoise, completely panic-stricken, drives at about 55 miles an hour on this tiny country road full of potholes created by the passage of *wadis*. The fugitives eventually make it safe and sound to the trunk road, where they come across three lorry-loads of Senegalese infantrymen, undoubtedly sent as back-up to deal with the rioters.

Françoise is shaking and lets Jacques take the wheel. He explains what happened to his estate manager in coded language, so as not to scare the children. It takes then three hours to get back to the region of Algiers. No-one speaks in the car. The children don't understand what has happened, but the somber and anxious mood of Jacques and Françoise worries them.

On this major road, the atmosphere gradually becomes calmer and Françoise recovers some of her serenity. But, for her, Algeria is finished. No way is she going to stay another year.

In the next few days, they learn that at Setif, during a march to celebrate the German surrender, a police chief shot at an Arab scout leader who was marching with an Algerian flag, killing him without a trial. That was the trigger for the uprising. More than a hundred Europeans have been killed in the region, some of them very brutally. A mayor had his hands cut off. The response isn't slow coming, with soldiers, police, and French settlers launching an atrocious and disproportionate repression. Thousands of Algerians have been brutally killed, mostly without a trial, all because of a march to celebrate the defeat of the Nazis and the end of barbarism!

4

LONDON, UNITED KINGDOM, MAY 7 1945

Someone is ringing the doorbell of the spacious, furnished, three-bedroom apartment that Victoria is renting for the time being in Kensington. That's where she has decided to spend the end of her pregnancy. Its midday on May 7, 1945.

Victoria gets up slowly and opens the door. A young woman, about 25 years old and carrying a suitcase, is all smiles as she enters.

"Hello Peggy", says Victoria, hugging her, "I'm so glad you could come and stay with me for a while. How was the journey? I hope your train wasn't late. I get the impression that you can't really trust the timetable at the moment."

"No problem since Reading. I'm really pleased to come and live with you, you know. Poor thing! You're a widow now and I haven't even seen you since your husband died. What a terrible thing to happen to him. Get out of the grips of the Nazis alive after several years of captivity only to get ill as soon as he gets back to his own country. What a sad destiny! Just long enough to put a bun in the oven, and now you'll have to bring up the child on your own! I haven't stopped thinking about you since I got your letter! How's the pregnancy going? Not too tired I hope?"

"I'm fine. Come on, I'll give you a tour of the flat and show you your room. We can catch up later."

Peggy is a young cousin of Victoria who lives in Reading, in Berkshire. There is an age gap of ten years between them, but they get on like a house on fire. Peggy is single. She had a boyfriend, a young naval officer, but he died two years ago when his submarine was bombarded by the German air force in the Atlantic, just off the Irish coast. While Victoria was at Gaitford, Peggy came to visit her once, at Christmas, in 1944. Victoria recently wrote her a letter, explaining that she was pregnant, and Peggy, who isn't working at the moment, offered to come and help her during the final stages of her pregnancy and the first month or so after the birth. Victoria jumped at the chance. She was wondering how she was going to manage on her own. They both like a good laugh to help them forget their worries and problems.

The apartment was completely refurbished just before the start of the war and is fully furnished. The owners were killed during the Blitz. Their descendants decided to rent out the apartment for a while, and that is how Victoria came to be living there. It's a real godsend because it's very difficult to find somewhere empty to rent in London.

"Wow, what luxury! I wasn't expecting that. Two bathrooms! And all recently done up too! There's only the nursery to decorate. I'm sure I'm going to like it here. I've never had such a lovely room, with my own bathroom. Have you made a fortune or something?"

"Not far off! Even though I don't work, I inherited some money from my parents and from Malcolm, who'd just inherited money from his mother. I'm comfortably off now. We can go wild!" she jokes.

It's immediately obvious to Peggy that her cousin has lost none of her energy or good humor. She admires Victoria's vast bedroom, which also serves as her studio. It is very well lit, with a large easel and canvasses lying on the ground. Some are already finished, whereas others are still underway.

"You know that all the paintings I did at Gaitford were destroyed by the German fighter that crashed into my studio? A real disaster. I cried for hours. But since I've been in London I've really got back into painting again. I'll show you my latest paintings. Still abstract of course. But come to the dining room first. I've made you some lunch."

Effectively, Victoria has dressed the table with a pretty white embroidered tablecloth and her best silverware. Before sitting down, Victoria shows Peggy an impressive radio set.

"It's brand new. Just listen to the sound quality. It's the best one I've ever had."

Victoria switches on the wireless, which takes a little while to warm up. The sound gradually arrives. It's time for the news. They listen to the speaker.

"At 3 a.m. last night, the German troops capitulated. The German general, Alfred Jodl, signed an unconditional surrender, at Reims in France, in the presence of General Eisenhower…"

Victoria and Peggy can hardly believe their ears, even though this surrender has been on the cards for several days. The war has been so long that they had the impression that the hostilities would never end. They are elated by the news. They clap their hands, very moved, and hug each other. For both of them, it means a new hope of a real life, a life in which they can make plans for the future. They are different ages, but both have had their everyday lives turned upside down by the war. Peggy lost her boyfriend and Victoria's husband died.

"Peggy, we're going to celebrate this news properly tonight. We'll try and have a nice little dinner, the two of us. I've got a few bottles of wine and some meat. We just need a dessert to go with it."

During the afternoon, Victoria devotes herself to her passion. She sits on a straight-backed chair to paint, to avoid tiring herself out. She spends time working on a new painting that she began that very morning. The forms and colors bring to mind the seashore, with nuances of blue and gray, possibly inspired by an agitated sea under a sky full of clouds, mostly blotting out the sun. The rest is very abstract. That's what Victoria explains to her cousin, who has some difficulty understanding and appreciating this style of painting.

Peggy spends her time settling in, putting away her things and thinking about what might still be needed for the new baby. She doesn't have any children, but has spent some time over the last few months working with a charity in Reading that helps refuges from London who have left the capital with their families, and often with very young children. This has given her some experience with newborn babies that she plans to put to good use to help her cousin.

Victoria prepares their celebratory meal at the end of the afternoon. She decorates the table with an embroidered white tablecloth that she inherited from her mother-in-law in Gaitford, and a little Union Jack to add a bit of patriotism. Red roses from a bouquet of flowers in her bedroom add the finishing touch to the decor.

For the pre-dinner drinks, Victoria opens a bottle of white wine from the Loire. She says that, exceptionally, her baby must also celebrate the victory, and both women rapidly become very merry. It's Peggy who opens the discussion about what their lives will be like after the war.

"I wonder what I will be doing in a couple of months' time. I'll have to find a job. I'd love to teach, but I don't have the qualifications. I'll have to find myself a husband too, someone ready to have children, and to satisfy me. You know, I had a bit of a taste of that with my boyfriend when he was home on leave. Thank goodness I didn't end up pregnant!"

"I got pregnant when I thought it was no longer possible! I thought I was sterile. That's what the doctors told me. And then a miracle happened", added Victoria with a broad smile on her face. "I was so happy when I found out I was pregnant."

"Your husband comes back after several years of being a prisoner in Germany, almost certainly in terrible conditions, and gets you pregnant. What luck! But please excuse me, it's not very tactful of me to talk to you about that now he is no longer with us. What are you going to do when your baby grows up a bit? Will you try to find a new husband?

"I want to spend my time painting. It's become a real passion. Everything else is still rather vague and complicated."

"Vague I can understand, but complicated? Why complicated?"

Victoria doesn't really want to explain and restricts herself to talking in generalities.

"I find life complicated, what with my art and a child to bring up. I'm not going to be able to stay in this flat for years. It's only a short-term let."

During dinner, the two cousins talk about their family, their parents, their shared memories, their haunts, whilst continuing to sip their white wine. They become increasingly merry and chatty, but they go to bed when the bottle is finished.

Victoria wakes up in the middle of the night and asks herself what she should tell Peggy about her relationship with Phil, the

French airman she met at Gaitford. She has three options: she can tell her everything, pretend that her relationship with Phil didn't start until after her husband had died, or tell her nothing at all. She can't really decide, although she has a clear preference for the second possibility. She eventually falls asleep again, tired out by this final stage of her pregnancy.

The next morning, they eat breakfast together. Peggy leads the conversation and starts talking about Victoria's baby.

"What will you call it, if it's a boy? Malcolm, after his dad? He'll be proud to have a father who escaped from the claws of the Nazis and found his own way back to England. What courage!"

Victoria seems to think for a moment and then, without explanation, she suddenly bursts into tears. Peggy comes closer, to comfort her.

"I'm sorry. I know my stupid questions are making you sad. I'm an idiot. I'll think before I open my big mouth in future. I can see how tactless I am."

"No Peggy, it's not your fault. It's complicated to explain and I'm a bit worried about telling you."

Peggy can sense that her cousin has something important to tell her. She is curious by nature and dying to know more.

"You can tell me about it, if it will make you feel better.'

"I'll tell you everything so long as you promise to keep my secret. Do you promise that you won't tell a soul? You mustn't talk about it to anyone. It's a secret."

Peggy can tell that she has won and overcome her cousin's resistance.

"Cross my heart. I know how to keep a secret. You can trust me."

"I'm sure you'll be horrified by what I have to tell you. Please don't judge me."

Peggy is wondering what on earth her cousin is going to tell her.

"It's not Malcolm's baby."

"What! Malcolm's not the father?"

"No, Malcolm and I couldn't have children. It wasn't for lack of trying before the war. My gynecologist and other doctors told me I was sterile. That depressed me for a while. Then I started concentrating on my painting, which took over an increasingly large part of my life. In any case, when Malcolm came back from Germany he was weak, very ill. He had to be admitted to hospital very quickly. He was coughing up lots of blood. It was horrible. And then, you know? Or maybe you don't? Before the war, we weren't getting on so well any more. Our relationship broke down while we were living in France. We were talking about getting a divorce. He couldn't stand me passing so much time with my friends, the Montparnasse artists, during the evening and the night. We didn't get on anymore."

"Well I never! I had a completely different idea of you two. I'm flabbergasted!"

"We all have our secrets, don't you think? I would never have imagined that you were sleeping with your boyfriend!"

Peggy thinks for a few seconds and a question clearly comes into her head that she can't help but ask Victoria."

"So you had a lover then?"

"Yes."

"And there was I thinking you were living an exemplary life, like a hermit, in Gaitford, looking after your sick mother-in-law all day, when all the time you were living it up, partying and making whoopee in the country. Tell me all about it. I'm dying to know."

"OK, I'll tell you more. I met a French officer at Gaitford, by a river, when I was fishing. He's called Philippe, Phil to his friends. He's 41."

"This was before your husband died?"

"Yes, Malcolm was being held prisoner in Germany."

"I'm sure he must be married?"

"No, he was widowed several years ago. He has two teenage children, a boy and a girl, in Morocco. He's handsome, charming. I didn't even want to resist. He was the one who had scruples, because of Malcolm."

"So what changed his mind? Did you jump on him?" asks Peggy in a fit of giggles.

"He was commanding a group of bombers. It was really dangerous. Someone made him realize that he had very little chance of getting out alive. That disturbed him and he wanted to live life to the full while he could."

"Tell me how things really started between you."

"First of all, we saw each other a few times and we were very well behaved. Then, one day, in August, he took me to a big party at a French airbase under RAF command. There were almost 500 people there. We danced together, we drank and then we went home to my studio, where we made the most of our privacy. We saw each other again afterwards, but then he was wounded and spent several months at a hospital in Rauceby. He's fine now and running the airbase at Gaitford. When I realized I was pregnant, I didn't want to believe it at first. I really thought I was sterile. In fact, it must have been Malcolm who had a problem."

"So did you tell your French boyfriend that you were pregnant?"

"Yes, I did. At first, I wasn't sure that he was particularly pleased about it. Afterwards, he suggested that I could come to Paris, after the war. He is supposed to be coming to see me after the birth. You'll get to meet him."

"So, your future is simple then. You'll go and live in France and marry him. What's vague about that?"

"I'm scared of myself, of my desire for independence. His mother sounds like a right dragon and she lives with him. He already has two children. It's not very easy for me."

"Your baby is going to need a father figure. Perhaps your lover will be a good father if he loves you?"

"Yes, but with the war, his hospitalization, my pregnancy and my move to London, we haven't seen each other very often. We don't know each other all that well. I don't want to lose him, but I don't want to commit myself too soon. My painting is important to me. Basically, I'm living for the moment right now. We'll see about the rest, when the baby is born."

Peggy reveled in these unexpected confidences. Never in a million years would she have imagined that Victoria could have had such an adventurous life, but here she is, with a child supposedly fathered by Colonel Miller, but actually sired by her lover. What an incredible situation! She is happy for her cousin, but she finds her complicated. If she had found herself in the same situation, she would have been so happy to have a handsome French officer who wanted to live with her in her life. Never mind if he had a mother who was a bit bossy. She would just have to make sure that she went to live somewhere else after the wedding!

5

GAITFORD AND RIEVAULX, UNITED KINGDOM, MAY 1945

In the days following the announcement of the German surrender, everyone is in a party mood at Gaitford[3]. A soccer tournament is organized, opposing teams from the RAF bomber bases from around the region. Phil is presiding over the tournament. The Gaitford team makes it through to the final. Two Russian airmen come to watch. They don't speak English and no-one else speaks Russian. But they are likeable and display considerable enthusiasm every time someone scores. The French team from Gaitford wins the final, and Phil has the great honor of presenting them with the cup. The alcohol flows freely during the dinner and the Russians staying overnight at Gaitford are falling-down drunk by the end of the evening. During the week, one party follows another. The Englishwomen organizing these parties and hosting the French airmen aren't very shy and there are those who take advantage.

On Thursday May 17, Phil's superiors inform him that a big French singing star is coming from Paris to sing and dance for the staff. They don't tell him who it is, but they are sure that no-one will be disappointed.

---

[3] *See the end of volume 1 "A French Pilot in Gaitford"*

They have to set up a theater for the show. The best idea is to empty one of the aircraft hangars and prepare a stage, a zone with seats and, at the back, an area in which the rest of the audience will stand. The show will start at 7 p.m. and will last an hour.

Phil announces the news immediately, so that as many people as possible can organize themselves to attend the show and not make alternative arrangements. They have planned for an audience of more than 2000 people. Some people would have liked to have known who was coming and are a bit concerned that it might be an opera singer or a ballet dancer come to perform Swan Lake or the Nutcracker Suite!

The singer is arriving by plane and will land at Gaitford, on Monday, at about 2 p.m. Phil waits for his visitor in the control tower, impatient to find out who has been so good as to come and visit them. A French Air Force DC3 lands, on time, at five past two. Phil sees a woman in military uniform leaving the plane.

Unbelievably, this woman is black. He recognizes her immediately. Yes, it really is her. It's Josephine Baker who will be performing. She's very famous, Josephine Baker, together with her songs and her scanty stage outfits. She has no fears about showing her breasts, or her thighs, barely hidden by her burlesque skirts, like her famous banana tutu. She wiggles her hips in a very provocative manner and everyone knows the tune of her song *"J'ai deux amours"*.

Phil is flattered. As the commander of the base, it is his duty to welcome her personally and to take care of her during her visit. She has come with four suitcases containing her various stage costumes. Smiling, she leaves the plane together with her six-piece band, all of whom are black. Her most famous show, *"La revue nègre"*, wasn't given that name for nothing!

Phil goes to meet her and introduces himself. There is a photographer on hand to immortalize the moment. Phil accompanies

Josephine Baker by car to an improvised dressing room that has been set up for her close to the hangar where the show will take place. They chat for a few minutes. Josephine didn't know that several hundred French airmen had been in England over the last 18 months, fighting under RAF command. Phil takes his leave after introducing her to Captain Vulpillat, who has volunteered to look after her during her stay at Gaitford. There had been more than ten very excited candidates for this high-responsibility post when it became clear who was going to be performing, and Phil had had to draw lots to choose the winner.

At 7 p.m., the hangar is full to bursting and the atmosphere is hot. The spectators clap their hands and call "Josephine! Josephine!" repeatedly. The singer finally arrives, dressed in a long white silk dress with a very low-cut neckline. She knows that most of these men have been a long way away from their wives, fiancées or girlfriends for several months and that this makes them particularly sensitive to her femininity.

She sings a few of her hits and then disappears for a moment to change costume. She returns with even more flesh exposed, in a short skirt and a yellow top with very short sleeves, rings on all her fingers and several brightly colored bracelets on each wrist. Her new outfit is greeted by cries of "Hurrah!" encouraging her to go further. She sings with gusto and gets the audience to join in during the chorus, which, of course, they love. At the end of the show, with her breasts naked and wearing no more than her simple bananas, she performs a demonic dance, moving her hips seductively in a way certain not to leave all these young men cold. She disappears again, this time returning in her air force uniform. It's the end of the show. She has a few moving words for all those who were lost and would not be coming back. Amidst endless cheers, she agrees to an encore and sings "*J'ai deux amours*" again.

Phil goes on stage to congratulate and thank her. Facetiously, she plants a big kiss on his right cheek, leaving a clear imprint of her well outlined, plump, lipstick-covered lips. Everyone claps and Phil keeps this souvenir throughout the entire duration of the cocktail party they hold for his visitor after the show. The airmen drink more than they should, but the party ends in great jollity, without incident.

Josephine departs the next day, leaving the staff at the base to ponder on what they are supposed to do next. The war is over, but no-one is talking about going back to France yet. Phil continues to impose daily training flights on the airmen, which they don't mind now that the Germans have ceased hostilities.

Phil and Victoria speak on the phone once a week, at a fixed time, because she hasn't managed to get a phone line installed in her apartment and has to go to the post office to make a call. Phil is fully aware that Victoria will give birth soon. During their exchanges, he can sense how happy she is with the perspective of becoming a mother. He knows that he would have preferred to have a lover with no children with whom he could have continued his love story. He is frankly none too pleased to find himself a father again, in this rather prickly situation. On top of all that, in this atmosphere of newly restored peace and continuous partying, he is not entirely insensitive to the charms of all these English temptresses who make it clear that they find him very much to their taste.

On Saturday May 26, Phil has agreed to go on a two-day outing with Emma Simons, to Rievaulx in Yorkshire, to visit the ruins of a famous Cistercian abbey. They will have to drive just over 150 miles from Peterborough to get to the abbey. At least four hours on the road. A couple of Emma's friends are coming too, Lucy and David. He is in his fifties and is a history teacher at a school in Peterborough. He has worked on the abbey and its past. Lucy is younger and teaches piano, when she can find some pupils. They are the ones with the car. Emma runs a tearoom in Peterborough, which is where Phil first met her, not long ago. He has since seen her on two consecutive evenings, at balls organized to celebrate the end of the hostilities. She's very funny and makes him laugh a lot. She has just turned forty, and she has short brown hair, green eyes, and looks sporty. She is not married and rumor has it that she isn't too keen on men. Phil has two days' leave. He is delighted to be spending a weekend at this very well-known tourist spot.

They have arranged to meet at 10 a.m. at Emma's place, on Saturday morning. Phil makes his way there by bike and is very punctual. Lucy joins them a quarter of an hour later, at the wheel of her car, an Austin 12. David has had a stomach upset during the night and has decided not to come with them. It's nothing serious, but he was up all night with vomiting and diarrhea. He's feeling better this morning, but he wants some time to recover. Lucy doesn't seem too bothered to find herself without him.

Just the time to load the car, and the three of them set off intrepidly. They get to know each other better in the car. Emma opened her tearoom and bar, Emma's Bar, just before the outbreak of war, from which, paradoxically, she benefited. The 2500 people working at the Gaitford airbase rapidly adopted her establishment as a strategic entertainment center, providing her with a huge male clientele. She had to hire four waitresses and two kitchen staff to help out. Rumor has it that some nights the girls provide the airmen willing to pay for it with home comforts in the small rooms above the tearoom. But Phil has never been sure whether there was any truth in that or whether it was just the fantasies of airmen in want of sex and tenderness. However, they don't talk about any of that.

Lucy and Emma seem to know each other well and pepper their conversation with terms of endearment, such as "darling", "angel" or "sweetheart". When Emma talks to her friend or to Phil, she puts her hand on their arms and gives them a friendly squeeze. Emma visibly needs physical contact with the people she talks to, and

Phil sees that as a sign of warmth. She is always very respectful towards Phil and calls him "Colonel" when she talks to him, even though he told her, right from the start, to call him Phil. In fact, she is very flattered to be going on a weekend trip with a senior officer and she wants him to retain all the attributes bearing witness to his importance. She insisted that Phil come in his uniform, saying that that would undoubtedly make it easier to find hotel rooms for the night.

Lucy drives during the first part of the journey. After an hour and a half, it's Phil's turn to take the wheel. His right hand remains covered by a glove since it was burnt, but he can drive with no problem. The road surface is badly damaged and it's not safe to drive at more than about 40 miles per hour. They have to watch out for the potholes all over the place. At one point, Phil senses a problem with the steering. The car is tending to veer off to the right. He stops at the edge of the road, where he sees that the front right tire is flat, almost certainly a puncture. Fortunately, they have a spare wheel and it only takes Phil about 20 minutes to change the wheel. The three traveling companions can then go on their way again, but they need to find a mechanic to repair the damaged tire and inner tube.

At Doncaster, in southern Yorkshire, they find a mechanic willing to repair the tire on a Saturday. While the repairs are being carried out, they have lunch in an old inn next to St George's Church. They leave towards three in the afternoon, rather merry after a few beers. The culprit responsible for the puncture was a nail. The inner tube had torn, but the mechanic was able to repair it with a simple patch and some special glue. Emma is determined to keep the nail as a souvenir. It will take them almost another three hours to reach the vicinity of Rievaulx. Emma insists that they look for a hotel room close to the Abbey. They ask a local who points them in the direction of Helmsley, which has several hotels and is only a couple of miles from Rievaulx. Effectively, there are four hotels in this town, but the first three are already full. There is going to be a large market there the next day, which has attracted a large number of visitors. At the fourth hotel, the Red Swan, they ask for two rooms, one for Emma and Lucy and the other for Phil. But there is only one room with a double bed available. The manager of the hotel suggests, with a smile on his face, that he could put a fold-up bed in the room. This amuses the ladies, who have a separate little chat on their own. Emma approaches Phil, looking mutinous, and says "Colonel, we don't have a choice. All the hotels around here are full. There is only this room left. We mustn't let it slip through our fingers. If we carry on like this we will all end up sleeping on the floor. Lucy and I will take the big bed and you can sleep on the little one. No problem! Lucy agrees. What about you?"

"I really wouldn't want to disturb you. I'll sleep in the car. It's May. It's not cold anymore."

"Sleep in the car! Aren't you aware that you have two nice women here who will take very good care of you? You don't snore do you Colonel?"

"No, I don't snore. But it would be better for both your reputations. What on earth would people think?"

"But we don't know anyone here. It's the middle of nowhere. Are you scared of us?"

"Well, OK, if you put it like that. I accept your hospitality. It's very nice of you."

Phil finds the situation amusing. If David had come, they would have needed three rooms. Now they are going to manage with just one.

Fortunately, the room is vast and has its own separate bathroom and toilet. There is a double bed and the manager has installed a fold-up bed on the floor.

Dinner time arrives. Emma and Lucy make themselves beautiful while Phil, who has stayed in his uniform, waits for them at the hotel bar. They eventually join him and they all start the evening with a glass of Highland malt whisky.

Already a bit merry, they move to their table, without passing unnoticed. Phil looks handsome in his air force uniform and some of the men nearby envy him for having such attractive companions. The hotel has a single menu, and the portions are not very large. They start with a beetroot salad, which is followed by a mediocre lamb stew. Fortunately, the wine cellar is better provisioned and the dinner is accompanied by a red Burgundy. The atmosphere rapidly becomes joyful, thanks to the good wine. Phil doesn't hesitate to refill the glasses as they empty, and no-one refuses.

The girls are loquacious and mischievous, and they want to find out more about Phil. All they know is that he is a widower with two children that he has left behind in Morocco. Emma is the first to ask him some more personal and direct questions.

"So Colonel, you left Morocco a year and a half ago. Over the last 18 months you must have met some English beauties susceptible to your charm?"

Phil reflects for a moment, on his guard, reticent to divulge anything.

"Yes, in the end. I say in the end because initially we changed location every three months. Then we stayed six months in Scotland before being sent to our final location. Difficult to meet someone under such conditions. But at Gaitford, I met a lovely lady during a fishing expedition."

Phil doesn't want to say any more, but his two companions are waiting impatiently for the next installment. Faced with his silence, Lucy can't help herself and questions him more closely.

"And is this lovely lady still at Gaitford?"

"No, she's moved to London."

"And I suppose you'll be going back to France soon? What a shame! How sad!"

Phil thinks that he has said enough and has no desire to explain that the lovely lady in question is pregnant and about to give birth. He makes a few comments and asks a question to create a diversion.

"No, I think it's better like that. But, as you have seen fit to interrogate me, it's my turn now to pose indiscreet questions. Lucy, you're married, but Emma, you're single. What kind of life do you lead? Do you have some scoundrel in tow?"

Emma bursts out laughing.

"Just the one? Far too few. I like a bit of variety you know!"

Phil can't stop himself from making an ambiguous remark.

"Yes, so I've heard."

Emma doesn't reply, remaining enigmatic but smiling. Lucy, who is a bit tipsy, tells them about her life before her marriage, and her love affair with an enterprising piano teacher before she had even come of age.

During the dinner, a local band sets up to play and the pianist, who is clearly the bandleader, invites the guests to get up and dance to celebrate, once again, victory and the end of the war. Phil successively asks his two friends to dance fast boogie-woogies. The horrors of his war missions are no more than a distant memory. The three of them leave the dining room towards 11 p.m. and start climbing the stairs towards their room, but Phil changes his mind and says "I'll leave you in peace for a while. I'll be back in half an hour to admire your nightshirts. See you later."

"No, stay Phil. We've got a surprise for you. A very amusing game. You'll see", explains Emma.

Phil looks questioningly at Lucy.

"Does Lucy know about it?"

"Yes, don't worry, it's just an amusing party game. I'm sure you'll like it. We're not going to go to sleep straight away, unless you're too tired of course?"

Phil is surprised, but his two friends have piqued his curiosity and he complies willingly.

"OK, whatever you say. I'm dying to know what kind of game you want to play at this late hour!"

When they reach the bedroom, it's Lucy who seems to take command and explains things to Phil.

"We're both members of the British Sun Bathing Society. Have you heard of it?"

"No, never. Is it a swimming club?"

"Not exactly. It's more of a club for naturists. The members of the club like spending time naked in the sunshine when it's hot enough. They also adore swimming nude in the sea or in rivers. It's a sort of return to nature. Nothing perverted about it. Just a quest for moments of complete relaxation and well-being."

Phil was not expecting such an explanation, but as he is very rational, he can't quite make out what it has to do with the party game they were talking about.

"What about your very amusing party game?"

Now it's Emma's turn to speak.

"It's to make getting undressed a bit more exciting. It's a very simple game that we've invented. Everyone throws a dice three times when it's their turn. For each even number you throw, you do nothing. For each odd number, you have to take off an item of clothing. That way, you go directly from being dressed to being totally nude. Would you like to play with us?"

Phil is not particularly prudish. As he's slightly drunk, he even feels like taking his clothes off directly.

"Yes, OK, teach me your game. I'll just keep a glove on my right hand to cover the burns I picked up a few months ago when my plane exploded."

"Colonel, if the glove is the only thing you keep on, no problem!" replies Emma, laughing.

Phil watches Lucy open a wardrobe and take out a sheet.

"It's so we can sit on the floor. It will be cleaner and more comfortable for throwing the dice. Colonel, we've run out of drink. Why don't you go and get us a bottle of red or white wine so we can continue to enjoy the evening?"

Phil returns with a bottle of Bordeaux and three glasses. Emma and Lucy have laid the groundwork for the game in his absence. The lighting has been dimmed and there is a sheet on the floor. He is intrigued by the sound of a bath running in the bathroom. Now they are ready to start playing.

They sit on the floor, each with their dice and a glass of wine. They all throw their dice simultaneously to decide who goes first. Phil gets a six and has to start, followed by Lucy and then Emma. Three times in a row Phil throws an even number, whereas his companions only throw odd numbers and have to remove three items of clothing each. They both take off their shoes and one sock each. Nothing embarrassing for the moment. Then it's Phil's turn to throw a run of odd numbers: 5, 3, 3. Phil takes off his jacket and his shoes, while his friends throw only one odd number each and take off their remaining socks. Emma gets up to turn of the tap in the bathroom and then returns and sits down undisturbed by questions. It's now that the game commences in earnest, as Phil points out in amusement.

"Ladies, I think we're getting to the heart of the matter. Shall we have another drink?"

He fills each glass and the three of them clink their glasses together, looking each other in the eye. Phil throws two odd numbers and takes off his socks. Emma throws a three and slowly, and very lasciviously, takes off her blouse. Phil is slightly disturbed by the sight of the white silk bra of his friend, her plump arms, the start of her cleavage, and a little more when she leans over to retrieve her dice. Lucy also throws an odd number and chooses to take off her skirt. But she has a petticoat on, which keeps her covered temporarily.

Phil now throws a 4, a 5 and a 3, and, to the delight of the ladies, takes off his tie and pants. He prefers to kneel for fear of appearing ridiculous sat on the ground in his boxer shorts. Emma throws a 2, a 6 and a 1. She hesitates briefly, then starts to undo her bra. She delicately passes the straps over her shoulders and then offers it to Phil like a trophy. Phil thanks her while contemplating her ample, very pale-skinned breasts. Phil is excited and his manhood starts to modify the shape of his boxer shorts. His companions notice and smile. Lucy throws two 1s and a 3, leading her friends to applaud. She stands up, takes off her petticoat and then, more audaciously, her panties, which she also gives to Phil. She pauses before continuing and turns slowly, as if she doesn't want to hide anything from her friends and wants them to admire her from various angles. Emma strokes her friend's buttock while she is turning. Phil can't help but admire Lucy's curves, her narrow waist, the dimples at the base of her back and her abundant pubic hair, which is blond like the hair on her head. She also takes off her blouse and entices them to admire her red silk bra.

Once again, they each throw their dice three times in quick succession. Phil throws a 1, a 3 and a 4. His friends shout "Hurrah". He stands up, takes off his shirt, which he gives to Lucy, and then his boxer shorts, which he hands to Emma. Phil is completely naked apart from the glove protecting his hand and has no more clothes to take off. He is rather slim and athletic and his friends compliment him on his physique.

The game is coming to an end and Emma now throws two odd numbers. She has two items of clothing left to take off, her skirt and her panties, and she rapidly removes them whilst standing. Totally naked, she then takes a few steps in the bedroom, like a model presenting outfits from an *haute couture* collection. Cheekily, she approaches Phil, who is seated on the floor, and presses her tummy and pubic hair against the nose and mouth of the colonel, who gently strokes her buttocks. Finally, it's Lucy's turn to throw the dice three times. Two even numbers. The remaining dice gives an odd number, sufficient to get her to take off her bra, which she rapidly removes to reveal a shallow cleavage ending in pointed breasts.

They continue to help themselves to wine, and they laugh while drinking and looking at each other. Emma gets up, takes Lucy and Phil by the hand and leads them to the bathroom.

"As we're not at the seaside, I suggest we take a bath. Look, the bathtub is large enough for two. The water is still hot. You coming Lucy? Shall we start? The colonel can help us if he wants."

Phil lends his arm to Emma, who gets into the water first, and then to Lucy. Lucy doesn't sit facing Emma, instead turning her back to her and affectionately resting her head on her friend's chest. Phil is both a spectator in this strange party game for fans of naturism and a dancer in this three-person minuet. He has had a lot to drink and has lost all his inhibitions. He takes the soap that he sees next to the sink. He has it in mind to help these ladies to wash. He starts by wetting their breasts and cleavage, and then he soaps their breasts and delicately starts to wash them, or rather, to caress them, the soap transforming this operation into a gentle massage that the two friends seem to appreciate very much. Phil doesn't stop there and, plunging his left hand into the water, he seeks out their most intimate places without a word of protest from the ladies, who even spread their legs to make his task easier. Emma straightens up slightly and presses up against her friend. In the water, she guides Phil's hand towards Lucy's pubic hair, and then lower, interlacing her fingers with those of Phil. Lucy is soon in seventh heaven and cannot stop herself from coming. Phil then tries to satiate Emma, by massaging her thighs and lower abdomen. Lucy turns round and, like Emma did for her, she guides Phil's hand until Emma can no longer contain herself and is animated by liberating spasms that leave her satisfied and relaxed.

"Now it's our turn to wash you, Colonel. Two women to take care of you! It's your lucky day!"

Phil gets into the bathtub. They take their time, caressing him gently and soaping him up affectionately. Phil is very excited. The girls take delight in simultaneously placing their hands around his manhood and rubbing vigorously. Phil hasn't had any sex for months and is very tensed up. It doesn't take him long to come.

They then dry each other with the three bath towels laid out for them and go and stretch out on the double bed. They rapidly fall asleep.

Towards six in the morning, Phil wakes up. His companions are still in dreamland, intertwined. Without disturbing them, he gently gets up, without making a noise, and returns to the fold-up bed, where he rapidly goes back to sleep. The three of them wake up towards 7.30 a.m. and prepare to go and eat their breakfast in the hotel dining room, without mentioning the night before. On several occasions they smile at each other in complicity, but without talking about their nocturnal adventures.

Phil doesn't feel guilty as far as Victoria is concerned. He has enjoyed this new experience, which brought him subtle pleasures with two beautiful women. There was no premeditation on his part in what happened. A simple but very agreeable game with his two friends, who seem to know and appreciate each other intimately. What an original way to celebrate the victory of the Allies!

When they are ready, the three friends set off for the Abbey of Rievaulx. They are delighted by the immense ruins that they discover in a sheltered valley surrounded by hills. It's a romantic place covered in flowers. The ground is very green because grass has grown in the middle of the ruined church and the many buildings lend this site a certain grandeur. They are in no mood to be serious and rapidly start playing hide-and-seek, a game that soon has them falling about laughing. After a picnic lunch, they leave for Gaitford in the middle of the afternoon.

Phil is in his office at the air base the following day, May 28, when his secretary puts through a call from London.

"Hello Colonel. My name is Peggy. I'm Victoria Miller's cousin. She gave birth last night. Everything went well and everyone is fine. She asked me to inform you."

"Is it a boy or a girl?"

"Victoria wants to surprise you when you come and visit. She wants to know when you can come and see her."

"I'll arrange to have someone replace me next weekend. Call me again during the week, in the morning, to confirm. And congratulate Victoria for me please!"

Phil doesn't know whether Peggy knows that he is the father of the baby. On the phone, he has behaved more like a friend.

6

FROM TORGAU TO WURZBURG, GERMANY, MAY 1945

On May 7, 1945, Wilhelm Steimer, alias William Clark, decides to stop hiding and become the American journalist whose identity he has taken, and he does so with chutzpah! After crossing the Elbe and changing clothes, he approaches the GIs that he crosses, engages them in conversation and photographs them. No-one questions his new identity. The officers are very busy and are finding it difficult to manage the situation, dealing with all these poor souls in need of food and shelter.

Wilhelm needs more materiel to make a convincing reporter. He has a camera and a number of rolls of unused film, but he also needs some paper, pencils, pens and envelopes. Having explained his situation, he shamelessly asks a non-commissioned officer who seems to be acting as secretary to a higher graded officer if he can obtain some stationery supplies for him. A few minutes later, the officer, who has been suitably impressed, comes back with a block of US Army headed notepaper, two pencils and an eraser. Wilhelm thanks him warmly, photographs him and talks to him, for so long and so charmingly that he gets himself invited to dinner in the tent in which this man takes his meals. He meets other American soldiers who are leaving for Erfurt, a town to the south-east, in the Thuringia, the next morning. It's about 200 km away and precisely in the direction he wants to go. Erfurt isn't far in a truck, but the roads are badly damaged and frequently blocked by military convoys and streams of German prisoners.

He is sitting next to a man called Richard, who is going with them. He will be the highest graded officer in the truck. Wilhelm seizes his opportunity.

"Erfurt! That's exactly where I'm headed! I want to go a bit further on, to Wurzburg, to do a report. The inhabitants must be happy that the hostilities are over, but I've heard that the conditions in the town are awful. I want to understand why. You wouldn't by any chance have enough space for me in your truck? It would be really great if you did!"

"You're in luck. We were full until yesterday, but one of the soldiers who was supposed to be coming with us fell ill and had to be evacuated urgently. So, you can come with us. No problem! We're leaving at 8 o'clock from here. OK?"

"Thanks, that's perfect! I was beginning to wonder what I was going to do. You're a lifesaver. I'll mention you in my article. It's for the Washington Post."

Wilhelm could also do with at least one change of clothes, but he only has ten dollars on him. He will need much more than that just to survive for a few days before finding a job. How is he going to find some money? Wilhelm is not faint-hearted, but he can't see himself stealing a gun and holding up Germans or Americans to extort money from them!

Wilhelm wants to go to Wurzburg because he has put together a plan. He lived in this town for a couple of years when he was a teenager and he went to school there. He can remember his parents' apartment in the middle of town and thinks that he should be able to find some storekeepers that he knew in the past. He is sure that they won't refuse to lend him some money to help out. The difficult part will be temporarily throwing off his disguise as an American journalist and transforming himself into a German non-commissioned officer with no desire to find himself in a prisoner-of-war camp. Wilhelm prefers to look on the bright side and feels that he is up to playing this role.

The next day, the road to Erfurt is long and tiring. More than 12 hours of being tossed around in the back of a truck on potholed roads. Plenty of stops, but not much to eat. In the evening, his friend Richard finds him a place in a dormitory in the barracks at Erfurt. Exhausted, he falls asleep rapidly and sleeps through to the next morning, but he wakes up early and considers the next step in his journey. If he stays in this barracks, as a civilian, he will probably be questioned by officers and required to prove his identity. He thinks it will be safer to leave the place on the pretext of wanting to photograph the damage inflicted on the center of Erfurt by the bombings. With his press armband and camera clearly on display, no-one asks him any questions. His principal problem now is finding someone to take him to Wurzburg without asking any indiscreet questions.

As he passes in front of St. Mary's Cathedral, an idea comes to him. He takes off his press armband, puts his camera into his backpack and enters the church. He kneels on a *prie-dieu*, putting his hands together to pray as if he were consumed by devotion. An old priest comes towards him and speaks to him in German.

"Do you need something my son? I'm ready to listen to you and to help if you want."

"Do you mind if I have a long chat with you Father? Just the two of us?"

"Of course not. Let's go into the vestry."

When they sit down, facing each other, Wilhelm invents a monstrous cock and bull story.

"Father, I'm looking for my parents, who might be at Wurzburg. I haven't heard from them in five months. They are both sick and they need me. I'm their only son. I was in the *Wehrmacht* until the day before yesterday. I managed to cross the Elbe and escape the Russians and now I want to go to Wurzburg to try to find them. If they're still alive, I think I know where to find them. But I mustn't run into any Americans, who will lock me up, even though I know that they treat Germans who weren't in the SS well."

"I'll see what I can do. There aren't many priests in Wurzburg. Many have died! There are two abbots from Erfurt who are supposed to be going there tomorrow in an old car, if they have enough gas. They're a bit younger than me, but not by much. The Americans shouldn't look for any trouble with them. Stay here. I can give you some bread and water. I should know more by lunchtime."

Wilhelm thanks the priest and awaits his return in the vestry. He finds a bible and pretends to read it, to give the right impression. The priest returns after two hours.

"Looks like things are working out for you. My two colleagues are leaving early tomorrow. I told them about you and they are happy to take you with them as a passenger, but you will have to be discreet. You'll have to be in the vestry by 6 o'clock in the morning. Do you have somewhere to sleep here at Erfurt? You can stay here if you don't, and sleep in the armchair. I'm afraid I don't have anything better to offer you. Germany is in a poor state indeed!"

The priest seems to be weighed down by events. He leaves his protégé alone, after giving him some more bread and water. Wilhelm remains shut up in the cathedral, where a few elderly women come to seek comfort in prayer.

The next morning, the two abbots, dressed in cassocks, are punctual in their car, which dates from well before the war. They tell him to get in and lie down on the back seat, and they cover him with a sheet so that only his head is visible.

"If anyone stops us, we'll say that you are sick and that we have to take you to an old uncle who is a doctor in Wurzburg" one of them explains. "Don't say anything much. We'll probably be driving all day."

The road is long and, again, there are repeated stops to let military trucks, armored vehicles and light tanks pass. Like everywhere else, the roads are full of potholes but, fortunately, it hasn't rained recently. The travelers arrive on the outskirts of Wurzburg towards the end of the afternoon, after 10 hours on the road, tired, but without having experienced any real problems. Only the exhaust of the car had played up, starting to come apart, and a GI who was a mechanic in civilian life came to help the two clergymen fix it.

Wilhelm gets out of the car on the outskirts of town and continues his route on foot, with his backpack. He puts his press armband back on and gets out his camera, and, hey presto, he is an American again. He must now track down the people that he knows. From the first few yards, he is struck by the number of damaged or partly destroyed houses. This impression becomes increasingly marked as he gets closer to the center of town. Nevertheless, Wurzburg is not a strategic town, and he can't see why it would have been massively bombed by the British or the Americans. In the town center, Wilhelm is unable to recognize the places he used to hang out fifteen years or so ago. The roofs are carbonized, and walls or entire houses have been demolished. Tons of rubble block the roads, which are devoid of any human presence. They were so pretty those houses, with their timbering! Why attack this historic town so fiercely? Just for revenge?

A GI appears out of nowhere and asks him what he is doing there. In his best American accent, he explains that he is a journalist who wants to take some photos and talk to some of the inhabitants for an article for the Washington Post.

"OK Sir. Good luck! Be careful, it's dangerous. The whole of this part of town has been evacuated. There's no-one left. More houses fall down every day."

"Thank you Sergeant. Can you tell me when the last bombing happened? Do you know?"

"Yeah, two months ago, March 16th. It was the English. They really went at it. Almost 3000 dead in less than an hour. They didn't have any military targets and they just systematically destroyed the old town, quarter by quarter. I heard they did it to undermine the morale of the population to hasten the end of the war."

"Thank you Sergeant. I'll be very careful."

Wilhelm heads towards the very center of town, which has been totally destroyed. His plan is also in ruins. He has no chance of finding anyone he knew before who might be able to help him. It's evening and the sun will set soon. He is likely to find himself alone in a devastated zone with nowhere to go, and his morale is in his boots. A moment later, he sees a man and a woman, probably in their forties, carrying a large shopping bag. They enter a ruined house. Wilhelm approaches them stealthily. He manages to watch them without being seen. The man has come with an iron rod to separate the stones in the ruins. They rummage through the rubble and recuperate objects. The things they find must have belonged to them, unless they are thieves. This gives him a bright idea. Is he feeling lucky?

He looks at the houses around him, or, more precisely, at what is left of them. He decides on a building that is three quarters destroyed, but which must have belonged to rich people if what is left of the façade is anything to go by. Close to the entrance, a staircase has survived, miraculously preserved. He climbs the stairs and opens the first door he comes to on the upper floor. A gutted bedroom. There is no wall at the head of the bed, which is covered by tons of stone, bits of plaster and burnt beams. No ceiling left either. Wilhelm is terrified by the sight of a foot under the bed and another, smaller foot just next to it. The spectacle is particularly horrific because the flesh is half-decomposed and what he can see is more a mixture of bones and tendons than intact feet. Probably a couple that didn't have time to get out and tried to shelter under the bed before part of their house collapsed. They must have perished, crushed by the lumps of stone that piled up in the room.

Wilhelm leaves the room on the verge of vomiting in disgust, but he rapidly changes his mind. He retraces his steps and returns to the chamber of horrors. He gradually removes all the debris that has accumulated on the bed, so that he can get to the two bodies.

For almost an hour, whilst it gets darker and darker, Wilhelm pushes away the rubble and removes the lumps of rock with the help of a lump of wood that he uses as a lever. Half-exhausted, he eventually manages to lift up the bed to reveal the bodies, crushed during the bombing and partially decomposed. Wilhelm manages to overcome his disgust and rummages in their pockets. He feels some hard metallic objects and he pulls out several gold rings, brooches and bracelets, which he hurriedly stuffs into his pocket. His suspicions have been confirmed. When the bombing started, these inhabitants had tried to save their jewelry rather than fleeing immediately.

Wilhelm leaves the house with his pockets full and walks to the edge of town. The abbots who brought him to Wurzburg had indicated the name of the parish that they were going to and he will try to find them for the night.

He has no trouble finding the church because the quarter in which it is located, much further from the center, was not hit by the bombing. He remembers this part of town fairly well, as he used to come here for piano lessons as a teenager. However, when he arrives at the church, the door is locked. He goes to the vestry, which is about 50 yards further on, at the end of a very quiet cul-de-sac. He knocks at the door, and someone opens it. He asks to see the two abbots who arrived today from Erfurt. One of them appears almost immediately.

"Father, I'm back! Could you possibly provide me with shelter for the night? The town center is totally destroyed. My parents must be dead and I don't know where to go. I don't have any money, but I have some jewelry that I got from my parents and would like to sell. If I manage to get some money for it, I'll give you some too. I'm sure you must need some money to take care of all the poor people that you help."

The abbot is not indifferent to this proposal.

"You are generous. You may spend the night here in the vestry. There are some free rooms. Show me the jewelry so that I will be able to describe it if I come across someone with the money to buy it. It's not easy at the moment, but it's not impossible either. There is smuggling and black market trading everywhere and precious objects sell for about a tenth their real value, but at least for that price you get dollars."

Wilhelm takes the jewelry out of his pockets. The abbot is a bit taken aback by the quality of the pieces: two rings with reasonably large diamonds, a necklace decorated with rubies and diamonds and another very heavy gold necklace, together with a bracelet bearing numerous sapphires, and two brooches ornamented with diamonds. He inspects each of the pieces very carefully.

"My father was a jeweler in Berlin and he taught me a thing or two. I think I can safely say that your mother had some very nice jewelry, particularly the diamonds in these rings and brooches. Several carats each and high-quality stones. In peace-time, you could probably get a tidy sum for them, about 25,000 dollars[4] I would think. But as things stand, you'll probably get no more than 2,500!"

"Father, if you find me a buyer, I could leave you 800 dollars of that."

"Oh! Eight hundred dollars! That's a huge sum and it would be really useful to our community. Leave your jewelry with me. It will be easier for me to negotiate a good price for these objects if you are not there. I'll see what I can do tomorrow. For the moment, I'll find you something to eat."

Wilhelm is uncomfortable with the idea of handing over the jewelry, but he can't really see the abbot running off with his loot.

"It's very kind of you to take care of all that. I hope you are a good negotiator!"

The abbot takes the jewelry away, to put it in a safe place. For a quarter of an hour, Wilhelm wonders whether he hasn't been a bit hasty and isn't about to be ripped off. He'll never know how much the abbot really manages to get for the sale of these objects! But he doesn't really have a choice because he can't complete his journey without at least a little money. If he tried to sell the jewelry himself, he might create some serious problems for himself and finish up in prison. The abbot returns with some food and wine, and shows Wilhelm to his room. Wilhelm eats and then, exhausted, rapidly falls asleep.

---

[4] *25,000 dollars in 1945 corresponds to about 375,000 dollars in 2015*

7

GAITFORD AND LONDON, UNITED KINGDOM, MAY 1945

Phil can't wait to see Victoria and her baby, whether it's a boy or a girl. This birth is bound to make his life more complicated, but it's impossible not to be curious. On Tuesday May 27, he asks Captain Jopet, who has been in command of the squadron since Phil's plane exploded, to come and see him. He and Jopet are friends and Jopet is the only person he has told about his affair with the beautiful Victoria Miller. Once ensconced in his office, Phil tells Jopet only half the truth.

"I have a personal favor to ask of you. I would like to go to London this weekend to see my girlfriend Victoria Miller. She's passing through and she phoned me. Could you stand in for me? I'll need you to be at the base from Friday until Sunday night. I know it's a bit long, but there's not much to do now the war's finished."

"I see, you lucky bastard! Still in love then? How fortunate you are! I've only managed a few flings since we've been here. I'm happy to cancel what I had planned and replace you, on one condition: that you tell me all about your weekend and your plans so that I can dream on!"

"Sure. It's very nice of you. I'll pay you back some day."

Phil is happy to have a sort of confidant with whom he can speak about Victoria, even if he only recounts a fraction of his adventures. He has known Captain Jopet for years and is sure that he can count on his discretion.

Phil is impatient for Friday to arrive so that he can meet up with his dear sweetheart and spend two days at her side. However, he is finding it hard to come to terms with being the father of a new child. Things have happened too quickly and the situation is complicated, with Maggy, his mother, who can be difficult, and his other two children, Paul and Claire. As he can't resolve all the problems straight away, he has decided that it would be wise to make the most of the present without worrying too much about the future. For him, the most important thing is to see Victoria, his great wartime love, again. As far as the baby is concerned, what suspense! He doesn't know if he has a new daughter or a new son, and he won't find out for another few days.

After the captain has left the office, Phil's secretary knocks on the door and enters.

"Colonel, a telegram from the Ministry of the Air in Paris has just arrived for you. Here it is."

Phil opens the telegram immediately. He is worried that it might be bad news about his children, but instead, its contents relate directly to him: "Promotion to the grade of Colonel, retroactive since May 1, 1945; Congratulations; Charles Tillon p.p. the Minister of the Air." Phil had been promoted to Lieutenant Colonel when he left for Britain a year and a half ago. His progression has been rapid. Now he is a full colonel! He can hardly believe that he, the son of storekeepers from Bois-Colombes, has been promoted to the rank of colonel at the age of 41! But will he still fly regularly as a pilot now that he has been promoted? Probably not, but he is now within reach of the highest spheres of the air force.

That evening, in the officers' mess, Phil buys everyone a drink to celebrate his new stripe. Everyone congratulates him openly, with no ulterior motives. The firm but courteous manner in which he manages the airbase, and the energy he expended to ensure that several airmen received medals are appreciated by all. During the week, he writes to his mother and children to tell them about his promotion. He is flattered by the honor bestowed on him, but doesn't let it go to his head. He has other things to worry about at the moment, but he is sure that Maggy, who has always paid close attention to his professional progress, will be delighted with the news. So why not make her happy?

Phil takes the London train from Peterborough early in the afternoon of Friday May 30. He looks handsome in his dark blue uniform, adorned with the five stripes he is now entitled to as a colonel, the highest rank below the generals. In his hand, he carries a suitcase containing his civilian clothes, toiletries and two presents, one for Victoria and the other for her new baby. He has spoken again with Peggy, Victoria's cousin, over the phone during the week to confirm his arrival. She asked him not to reserve a hotel room because Mrs. Miller was going to prepare a bed for him in her own apartment.

His train should take three hours to cover the hundred miles between Peterborough and London. Phil passes the time imagining what he will say to Victoria about their relationship and where they should go from here. Phil knows that, now that peace has been re-established in Europe, the airmen at Gaitford will soon have to return to France, but the date for this repatriation has yet to be fixed. His immediate perspectives are different though, as he must return to the military hospital at Rauceby for another operation. The burns on his right hand have not healed properly and Dr MacIndoe, who treated him after his accident, has offered to carry out a skin graft in July, which will see him hospitalized until September. Another three months of doing nothing! It will feel like an eternity, but the doctor has told him that he might have functional and esthetic problems with his hand if he doesn't get it seen to. Phil doesn't want to remain an invalid, so he has agreed. He will be allowed to have visitors, but he won't be able to leave the hospital. If all goes well, he will leave for Paris in October, with a new post, probably at the headquarters of the air force, *Boulevard Victor*, in the 15th *Arrondissement*. He will go back to his apartment on *rue Lecourbe*, with his children, Paul and Claire, and his mother! Not the easiest of situations to deal with!

It's half past five. Victoria is impatient for the arrival of Colonel Destivel. She has asked her cousin to be discreet and to disappear after his arrival, although they will all dine together later. The two cousins have prepared a simple but excellent dinner with roast chicken cooked with herbs as the main course.

Victoria has made herself beautiful, but she is worried about what she has to say to Phil. Should she tell him straight away or have a long chat with him first? Not an easy decision. She'll decide when the moment arrives.

The doorbell rings. Peggy is in a rush to see what the colonel looks like. She hurries to open the door while Victoria waits calmly in the living room. But it's a false alarm: just the janitor bringing them the newspaper. A quarter of an hour later and the doorbell rings again, causing both cousins to jump. Peggy rushes to the door again and this time it is Phil, who has found his way easily around Kensington. Peggy introduces herself, leads him to the living room, and then disappears.

Victoria and Phil are finally together. Phil holds her in his arms for a long time and then they look at each other, smiling, both very moved, without speaking. Victoria rests her head on his shoulder for a moment, with infinite tenderness.

"I've been waiting so long for this moment," she says. "I've been impatient these last few days. How good it feels when you hold me in your arms!"

"Oh my darling! I'm so happy to see you again."

"I was really sorry that you couldn't come to London to be with me for the birth. But never mind, I won't keep you waiting. Let's go straight to the nursery."

Phil follows his beautiful girlfriend into the room on tiptoe. He finds a large room, painted white, in which a teddy bear and a ragdoll are already in evidence. Phil looks around him and is confused.

"I can see two cradles. Which one belongs to my child, so we can get to know each other?"

Victoria looks a bit concerned, but continues to smile.

"Surprise! I had twins. A boy and a girl. I didn't know in advance. The doctor who delivered them noticed once the first baby had come out. Let me introduce you. They're gorgeous."

Victoria begins by picking up her daughter very carefully and showing her off to her father.

"This one is Helen. Helen, I'd like you to meet a charming French colonel. His name is Phil and he's your dad. Look how cute she is! A button nose and fine features. She's already very feminine, with her blond hair."

Helen gives a hint of a smile when her papa takes her into his arms for a moment. Phil is moved. Victoria then takes the baby boy out of his crib and goes through the same presentation ceremony.

"This one is George, like the King. I tried to choose names that are used in both England and France. George has more defined features and he's already very strong. You see, for a woman who couldn't have children, I've done pretty well. A boy and a girl at the same time! But I imagine you must be feeling a bit shell-shocked? You've just doubled your offspring. There are four little Destivels now! That's a big family!"

Victoria has presented the babies in a playful manner, apparently very much at ease, but deep down she is anxious because she isn't sure how Phil will react. He was certainly not expecting to become the father to two little English children at once, Helen and George Miller. As their mother, Victoria is delighted with these two births, but she is scared that it will put their love to the test.

"Come, my love. These little angels will continue their nap. They had a bottle not long ago. We'll come back to see them later. I asked Peggy not to say anything. I preferred to break the news that there were two of them to you myself. You know, I was as surprised as anyone! I can understand that you might need some time to take it all in."

After placing the two babies in their cradles, Victoria approaches Phil and gazes at him, smiling, before placing a delicate kiss on his lips.

"We have so much to say to each other, to get to know each other better. Come on, let's go back to the living room."

Phil remained silent during the presentations, absolutely dumbfounded by the announcement of these two births. He stays silent now, invaded by a flood of contradictory thoughts. Victoria takes his hand and leads him into the living room, where she asks him to sit next to her, so that they can talk.

8

GERMANY AND FRANCE, MAY 1945

In his travels from Torgau to Wurzburg, Wilhelm has already covered almost 250 miles. He has another 370 miles or so to go, to reach his destination and his heart's desire. He has thought about his beloved every day since being forced to leave France for the abominable Russian front and its indescribable horrors. His mind was filled with images of his lover, night and day, when he had the good fortune to be transferred to German Intelligence. More recently, whilst passing through the zone occupied by the Americans after the signing of the armistice, the memory of his lover's softness and tenderness have provoked an irresistible desire in him for them to be reunited, body and soul. It has become imperative to return to the place they met, with the hope of rekindling their love. But with the war, and the three years that have separated them, will that be possible? Wilhelm is prepared to do anything to bring it about.

After leaving his jewelry with the abbot, he had started to have doubts. Was he going to be swindled, robbed? But, in fact, everything has gone exactly as he had hoped. The abbot managed to negotiate the sale of the jewels rapidly, and returned with a thick wad of dollars. Wilhelm thanked him warmly and gave him a third of the money. He now has 2000 dollars[5] in his pocket, pretty much what the

[5] *About 30,000 dollars in 2015*

abbot had predicted. For the moment he is doing fine, provided nobody steals from him. As a precaution, Wilhelm puts several wads of notes in the pockets of his pants and hides the rest at different places in the lining of his jacket. As the jacket is a bit big for him, it isn't really deformed by the presence of the notes.

He must now leave Wurzburg and head towards Heilbronn. About 60 miles to cover. Wilhelm has chosen Heilbronn for his next stop because this town suffered a large number of Allied bombings, including one particularly murderous one in December 1944. All that is good for his cover as a reporter! Apparently, the entire town center was destroyed. Maybe he'll find some more expensive jewelry in the rubble! But this bombing happened six months ago, in December. Anything worth taking would almost certainly have been removed long ago!

Once again, Wilhelm displays no sign of hesitation. He enters the barracks occupied by the Americans at Wurzburg and introduces himself as a reporter for the Washington Post, explaining that he wants to go to Heilbronn to continue reporting on the towns that have been bombed. The gods are with him again and, the next day, he finds himself with a bunch of GIs, in a convoy heading towards Heilbronn. He isn't too keen to engage in conversation with the American soldiers and instead feigns sleep. He pretends to doze, sat at the back of the truck, jolted as the vehicle passes along a road that has been heavily damaged by tanks and bombs. He opens his eyes when the food is being handed out and gladly received what he is offered. His neighbor takes advantage of the opportunity to start a conversation.

"So, man, why does a journalist with the Washington Post want to do a piece on Heilbronn? Why there? What a crazy idea! No-one's ever heard of it in the US!"

"It's an article on the Allied bombings, not on a particular town, but on Germany in general, after our, um..."

Wilhelm was about to say "surrender", but manages to stop himself in time, instead ending his sentence with "victory", and reminding himself that he will have to be more careful.

"Where are you from, man?" continues the GI. "I'm from a little town near Cheyenne in Wyoming. It's a hell of a way from here."

"Washington DC" Wilhelm improvises. "I've always lived there and that's how I managed to get a job with the Washington Post."

Wilhelm doesn't want to answer a battery of questions and the best way to avoid that is to ask some questions himself. He asks his neighbor what life is like in Cheyenne, if Wyoming is pretty and what job he does. The GI is only too delighted to talk about himself and his region, and Wilhelm continues to question him until they reach Heilbronn, without having to deliver any precise information about himself. The truck isn't going into town and Wilhelm gets out a couple of miles further out. The officer sitting next to the driver gives him some advice.

"Watch out you don't get yourself attacked walking on your own. The roads aren't very safe at the moment."

Wilhelm thanks him for the advice and finds himself on a deserted road. He isn't wearing any distinctive signs and can, therefore, pass himself off as an American or a German, depending on whom he meets. However, he is a little concerned. Since the previous day, he has had a nagging pain in his abdomen. It's not very strong, but it isn't going away, and he feels tired.

After walking alone for a few minutes, he sees a bike coming towards him, ridden by an old man who waves to him on passing. Not the most stressful of encounters. He continues on his way, lost in thought. France is not far away now, and that is where he wants to go. He will need to cross the Rhine in secret, and then go on to the *Côte d'Or* region in Burgundy. It's crossing the Rhine that worries him most for the moment. Above all, it is vital to avoid having to cross over a bridge and find himself at a border crossing where they will pick over his forged papers! But rumor has it that all the bridges on the Rhine have been destroyed anyway.

"Good day Sir, could you spare me any money? I have nothing left and four children to feed."

Wilhelm did not hear the approach of this German in rags who was walking behind him. He plunges his hand in his pocket to find some money to get rid of the man. He only has five-dollar notes and clumsily pulls out a wad of notes, at which the beggar's eyes pop out of his head. Wilhelm offers him a note, but the vagabond suddenly becomes menacing, threatening him in German.

"Give me all of it or I'll smash your face in!"

Wilhelm is sporty and trained in bare-hand combat, and he doesn't give in. His adversary tries to punch him, but Wilhelm manages to avoid the blows. However, he then takes a long knife out of the pocket of his raincoat. Wilhelm backs off and looks around for objects that he could use to defend himself. A couple of yards away he sees a blunt rock that he rapidly picks up with his right hand.

"Clear off or you'll regret it!" he cries.

But the other man has no intention of renouncing and instead advances ever closer to Wilhelm, with the knife in his hand. Wilhelm throws the rock, with all his might, in the direction of his aggressor, who is not quick enough to duck and falls down, knocked out cold, in the middle of the road. Wilhelm drags him to the ditch at the side of the road. The vagabond's forehead is bleeding profusely. A few rapid twitches and then he stops moving and remains perfectly still. Wilhelm examines him cautiously and observes that he is no longer breathing and his heart has stopped beating. He hides the body in the ditch, covering it with branches and grass and then, sweating heavily, he continues on his way towards the town, traumatized by this attack. He doesn't know whether the man is really dead, but it doesn't matter anyway. It was self-defense. Fortunately, the road is deserted and no-one saw them. He comes across a few men on foot or on bikes, but none of them try to speak to him. The number of people milling around increases as he gets closer to the center of Heilbronn.

Wilhelm is disconcerted and isn't sure what to do next. The center of Heilbronn, like that of Wurzburg, is a sea of ruins. Where should he go? Should he try to find a priest again? An American barracks? He rapidly gets a grip on himself as he becomes aware of the up-side of the situation. He is lucky. He is still alive! Things could have turned out much worse for him. If the guy who attacked him had managed to stab him a couple of times, he probably wouldn't be here. The problem now is that his gut is increasingly painful and he needs to see a doctor.

All this thinking about doctors has suddenly given him an idea! He questions a GI about where the Americans are stationed in this town.

"Do you know if there are any doctors or surgeons there?" he asks.

"I'm not sure, but I think they transfer the serious cases. It's only a small barracks. Why? Is there something wrong?"

Wilhelm doesn't answer the question, but he thanks the GI for the directions, which he follows: straight ahead to the north, less than half a mile. At the entrance to the camp, he presents himself as an American journalist and asks if he can see a doctor. He is sent to see a military doctor who examines him straight away.

"So, you've had a pain on the right side of the abdomen for about 24 hours, and you've not had your appendix taken out?" asks the doctor.

He meticulously examines Wilhelm, pressing his abdomen on the right, and then the left, and making him lift his right leg several times, which aggravates the pain. When he presses hard on the right side of the abdomen, Wilhelm flinches and grimaces.

"I strongly suspect appendicitis in this case. The problem is that we don't have a surgeon here. I'll transfer you elsewhere, to somewhere where they can operate if necessary. It will be more prudent. We don't want you getting peritonitis. You can do without that! There's an ambulance taking another patient away tomorrow morning. You can go with him. The ambulance will take you to the zone occupied by the French, at Fribourg, where there is a big garrison. We've signed agreements with the French military doctors. There aren't enough doctors around here at the moment. If that's OK with you, I'll write you a letter to give to the doctors at the hospital there. For tonight, we'll find you a bed in a dormitory."

"OK doctor, thank you."

Wilhelm is reassured to be taken in hand, particularly as the voyage to Fribourg in the Breisgau will bring him nearer to France. There, he will even be very close to the Rhine.

At the end of the following morning, he arrives at Fribourg in an ambulance. He is rapidly examined by a French surgeon, who confirms the diagnosis of appendicitis and tells him that he will operate during the day. They talk in a mixture of French and English. Wilhelm has the impression that they are taking good care of him, but there is something that troubles him on deeper reflection. What will happen to his clothes, in which he has stashed all his money, really large amounts of cash? If everything is stolen, it will be back to square one. He was unbelievably lucky to come across some expensive jewelry, a real hoard! He won't get a second chance, that's for sure!

He calls for the supervisor of the surgical department to which he has been admitted and explains his concerns.

"I have a problem. I'm an American journalist, in Germany to report on several towns bombed by the Allies. I have to have an operation. I really don't want my things to be stolen while I'm unconscious. There's my camera, which is expensive, used and unused rolls of film and the cash my newspaper gave me to help me to survive for a month in this country."

"I understand," she replies. "Give me your things and I will put them in a safe place."

She places the patient's personal effects in a cardboard box, which she then seals with adhesive tape. Wilhelm feels reassured and ready for his operation. He is entitled to a blood test and, one hour later, he is taken to the operating theater on a stretcher.

At the end of the afternoon, feeling queasy and having thrown up several times, he gradually comes round. The surgeon arrives.

"You did, indeed, have appendicitis and we were right not to wait. But it was a bit odd when you came round. You didn't want to speak English anymore and you were speaking German instead. Your accent was perfect by the way. Where did you learn to speak German?"

Wilhelm is sufficiently alert to sense the danger and replies, without hesitation "At high school in Washington. My parents paid for a German tutor who worked on my accent. That's why my newspaper chose me for this article on Germany."

The surgeon is visibly convinced by this response and leaves his patient in peace. Wilhelm makes good progress and, after seven days of rest, Wilhelm tells his surgeon that he feels great and wants to leave the hospital. The doctor agrees but tells him to come back in a few days so that he can check that everything is healing properly and take out the remaining stitches. Wilhelm has no intention of staying very long in Fribourg, but he promises to return for his consultation. His clothes are returned to him and, relieved, he finds the cash that he had stashed in the pockets of his pants and he can feel two wads of notes hidden in the lining of his jacket.

At Fribourg, Wilhelm is close to the Rhine and to France. All he has to do now is cross the river incognito and head towards Dijon, the penultimate stage in his journey. During his time in hospital, he was able to consult a map of the region, which he has kept, and he has decided to try to cross the Rhine just north of Neuf-Brisach.

His route will now first take him to the small town of Gottenheim, and he will then head east. He decides to buy a bicycle and offers a good price to a German he meets walking along and pushing a bicycle that seems to be in good condition. Enthralled by the dollar bills that Wilhelm dangles under his nose, he doesn't hesitate, no doubt concluding that he can easily buy another one at a much lower price.

After buying enough food for two days, Wilhelm mounts his bicycle towards six in the evening, with his backpack firmly on his back. He pedals to Gottenheim, and then to Ihringen. A steeper, more winding road takes him to Breisach, which he skirts around to the north. A bit tired, he reaches the Rhine towards 8.30 in the evening.

Wilhelm walks along the river. Obviously, there are no bridges still standing. They have all been bombed. The only way to reach the French side is to find a boat. The road is deserted. It's a wooded site, surrounded by very leafy hills. After walking for about

20 minutes, Wilhelm spots a boat that has been dragged up onto the bank. It doesn't look new, but it seems to be in working order.

He waits until night has almost fallen before dragging the boat down to the river. He has found a rope to keep it still, tied to a tree, once it is in the water. That will be essential, to ensure that his means of transport stays put until he is ready to move. The two oars should enable him to navigate towards the other bank without being dragged away by the current. This preparation should enable him to recover his force for crossing the river.

Towards 11 p.m., Wilhelm begins to execute his plan. He manages to put his bicycle in the boat, which doesn't seem to be taking on water. That was his principal concern. He rows as hard as he can and gradually gets nearer to the French side. He reaches the bank about half a mile downstream.

Wilhelm is euphoric. In his complicated journey to France, the most difficult part, in his mind, was crossing the Rhine, and he has done it! What joy! Now he needs to get to Dijon, as a prelude to the reunion he is preparing. He has some money and a means of transport. The rest of the voyage should not be too complicated, provided he is discreet and manages to hide his German origins.

Wilhelm is exhausted, so, before getting back on his bike, he rests for a while to build up his strength. He sits on the grass and makes himself comfortable. He is starving hungry and eats some of the victuals from his backpack. Concentrating on his frugal meal, he doesn't hear the man approaching him from behind, who, like a panther, jumps on him and knocks him out with a violent blow.

9

OXFORD, UNITED KINGDOM, JUNE 1945

John Luxley is not in high spirits when he gets up on Friday June 22. He has been back at the University of Oxford for a week. He has managed to return to the Mathematics Department, where he worked before the war. His occupations as a heavy bomber pilot and then as a mathematician at the Bomber Command research center, and his accident have sorely tested him. He has returned to his research on probability, but the war has disturbed him. His wounds have not entirely healed and he still walks with a cane, although he can feel that his state of health is improving daily and that he will soon be able to walk unaided.

He often catches himself thinking about Edith, the wife of the vicar with whom he lodged at Richmart in Buckinghamshire, a short bike ride from Bomber Command. His relations with Edith were unconventional, to say the least. A woman at least 15 years his senior, but very beautiful! He would love to be able to snuggle up to her this morning. That would make him feel safe and, perhaps, chase away the melancholy that his dogged him since the armistice. Disappointed by his return to Oxford, he dreams of discovering other horizons, meeting new people and, above all, finding a noble cause to defend, some kind of ideal. Two days ago, he wrote to Princeton University in the States to apply for a post as a lecturer and researcher for two years, to give him a change of scenery for a while. It's a university with a good reputation, with a number of eminent scientists, like Albert Einstein and Kurt Godel, on its staff. He will have to wait a month or two for the reply.

John has a couple of days of freedom during the coming weekend and doesn't want to stay put or go and visit his parents. He decides to take the train back to Richmart, to wander around a bit and maybe go and see the vicar, to say hello and see how they are getting on. He left the family about a year ago and he would like to know what life has in store for them, now that the war is over. He won't be sorry to see Edith again either!

On Saturday, after an uneventful train ride, he arrives at Richmart in the early afternoon. The town is calm. It hasn't been bombed and nothing seems to have changed. He goes into the pub he used to frequent. Then he goes to the vicar's house and rings the doorbell, but no-one answers. John rings again several times, but with no response. A neighbor leaving her house and pushing a bicycle approaches him.

"If you're looking for the vicar or his wife, you'll probably find them at the church. They often go there on Saturdays to prepare the service for the next day."

John knows the way and walks there, with the help of his cane. When he arrives, he gently pushes the door open slightly, and espies Edith, arranging some flowers in a vase so as to make the place look a bit less austere. A beautiful summer flower bouquet in which John recognizes the white arum lilies that she grows in her garden. With pleasure, he contemplates this woman, who appears so virtuous at first sight, in this house of God. John gently pushes the door open wider and enters the church without a sound. Only when he is close to his former landlady does he speak.

"Hello Edith! What a beautiful bouquet of arum lilies!"

"Oh! What a surprise! It's John, our John from last year! I didn't hear you coming! How wonderful to see you again!"

Edith puts down her scissors, takes off her gardening gloves and gives John a big hug, like a mother reunited with her grown-up son after a long period of absence. She notices that he has a walking cane in his hand.

"You have to use a cane to help you walk? Were you injured? Not too badly I hope?"

"I nearly died in a V1 explosion near London! I was in hospital for several months, but I'm improving all the time now."

"Oh! Poor John! You can tell me all about it. I'm so sorry. In any case, it's very nice of you to come and see us. Robert has gone to see a sick parishioner, but he will be back soon."

"What about your daughter, how is she?"

"Margaret has gone to spend the weekend with her uncle so that she can spend some time with a cousin that she is very close to. She should be back tomorrow night."

Robert arrives at this point, astonished and happy, in equal measure, to see his former lodger again. He and his wife offer to put John up during the weekend, an offer he accepts without hesitation.

Edith and John return to the house together, as the vicar still needs about an hour or so to finish preparing his Sunday service. John tells Edith about his accident, his injuries, his long stay in hospital, and his laborious recovery. Edith has continued her peaceful life as a vicar's wife and says nothing about their previous relations.

John finds his room exactly as he left it. Without wasting time, Edith goes to find him some sheets and a blanket. They make the bed together, both disturbed to find themselves alone in this large house next to a mattress dressed in a creaseless white sheet, its beautiful smooth surface inviting them to indecency!

"I'm home! Hello! Are you there? Where are you?"

It's the voice of the vicar, who has finished preparing his service earlier than planned. The sound of his voice brings them back down to earth with a crash.

"John, do you mind finishing your bed on your own? I'll go and make us a cup of tea." Edith leaves John on his own, conscious that the waves of warmth that invaded her lower abdomen a couple of minutes ago could yet lead her into the arms of her young former lover. She would have neither the desire nor the strength to resist!

John had studied Edith carefully while she bent over in front of him whilst they were tucking in the sheets. Her ample bodice had offered a glimpse of her generous breasts, which he had so liked to squeeze and caress a few months ago. He too was ready to act when the vicar had arrived.

During tea, John talks to the vicar. Ever courteous, he asks about the topic for the next day's sermon.

"I'm going to give a speech that touches on politics tomorrow! We need to rebuild our country. In England, there are rich people, but there are also very poor people. It is vital, now more than even, to share. I've gone over some texts from the New Testament touching on this topic. Beatitudes and passages about the work of the apostles. Jesus was clearly always on the side of the poor and extolled the virtues of sharing. I'm going to give my parishioners something to think about on this subject. It would be wonderful to create a society in which everyone was willing to share. There would be no more poor people. Don't you think that would be a great cause to fight for?"

"You're a real communist Reverend!" adds John, laughing.

"Maybe! The communists aren't all bad you know! Their principal flaw is their opposition to religion, but morally speaking, there isn't much between us."

John is amused to discover this progressive side to his host, a man he had previously seen as essentially focused on religious practice. He doesn't like communists as embodied essentially by the Russians, but he recognizes that they were valiant allies during the terrible conflict that has just ceased in Europe. It's the start of a political awakening in John. Absorbed in his mathematics before the war, he had been insensitive to the proselytism of some of his colleagues in Oxford who had tried to win him over. John now has a desire to think more deeply about the English social system and what could emerge as the new world order.

John's day at Richmart continues with some reading. He has brought a book by H.G. Wells, Ono-Bungay, with him and plunges into it while his hosts are occupied. The description by the author of new arms based on radioactivity worries him, although he knows that it is only science fiction. If there were fewer inequalities between people and peoples, perhaps there would be fewer wars, or maybe even no more wars at all? There would then be no need to race towards the development of new, increasingly terrifying arms, he reasons, whilst reading.

Edith has prepared an excellent dinner and the vicar has opened some bottles of home-made ale given to him by one of his parishioners, to accompany the meal. They have much to talk about. The reconstruction of their country, the political future of Churchill, John's plans to go to Princeton and the medical studies that Margaret, the daughter of the house, would like to start when she finishes high school. John feels at home in this family and he tells them so.

After dinner, John insists on helping to clear the table despite his residual mobility problems. He dispenses with his cane momentarily to free up both his hands so that he can be more effective. Once in the kitchen, he places the glasses he was carrying next to the sink. There is water on the tiles and he almost slips on the wet floor. Instinctively, he catches hold of Edith around the waist, to stop himself falling down.

"Excuse me, Edith. I nearly fell! How lucky that you were there! I wouldn't want to break my leg again!"

Edith looks at him without saying anything, an affectionate smile on her face. John can remember when his landlady smiled at him like that before, a few months ago! Tonight, he would very much like her to come to his room, as she did in the past. But that was when the vicar was in hospital! He can't imagine that Edith will be able to leave the marital bed tonight to come to his room at the top of the house.

Later, when he goes up to bed, John cannot resist the temptation of leaving his door ajar. His conversation with the vicar was very interesting and he intends to go and listen to the sermon tomorrow morning. The social aspects of the vicar's speech have made him realize that he has never really thought enough about politics. With his passion for the sciences, he has never manifested the slightest interest before in the possible ways in which societies could be organized. He has now decided to fill in the gaps in his thinking that have been revealed.

The day has been tiring and John soon drifts off to sleep. In the middle of the night, he wakes up to the sound of footsteps on the stairs leading to his bedroom, followed by a gentle scratching at the door.

"Come in Edith" he whispers, "I've been waiting for you!"

The door opens slowly and, in the shadows, a voice says "I'm glad you're awake John. I've come up because there is a window banging and it's making a noise. It's stopping us from sleeping. Don't get up. I'll do it."

The vicar closes the offending window.

"Goodnight John. Sweet dreams!"

10

GAITFORD AND LONDON, UNITED KINGDOM, JULY 1945

Tuesday July 3, 1945: Phil has organized a leaving party at the Gaitford air base. His superiors have agreed to let him return to Rauceby Hospital so that Dr. MacIndoe, the talented surgeon from New Zealand who looked after him during his first stay there, can operate on his right hand. But how tedious to have to spend the entire summer in hospital now that the hostilities are over! Another three months before he can go back to France!

Phil has invited the closest of his French colleagues, the two group leaders, the four squadron leaders and the British officers responsible for logistics on the ground, together with the female staff members with whom he works. Everyone is sorry to see him go. The base at Gaitford is like a large family that is beginning to fall apart, even though the date for the return of the French airmen to France has not yet been set, almost seven weeks after the German surrender. Harmony reigns among these people of different nationalities, and there have been few altercations, apart from those between young recruits that had drunk too much whisky and were interested in the same WAAFs[6]!

---

[6] *Members of the Women's Auxiliary Air Force*

Tonight, the chef has pulled out all the stops, and the menu is superb:

Mixed starters
Crayfish in Mornay sauce
Roast chicken
Cheese
Iced raspberries

<u>*Wines*</u>
Sauternes 1934
Calon Ségur 1912
Champagne 1921

Phil wonders how the chef has managed to get hold of such old wines. The Saint Estèphe, Calon Ségur, dates from 1912. It is 33 years old and has lost nothing of its superb qualities, delighting those guests with some knowledge of French wines. Phil calls for the chef to ask him where he got this vintage wine from, but the chef contents himself by smiling and saying "Honor where honor is due." Phil will never know his secret. At the end of the meal, a card does the rounds and everyone writes a message, particularly the ladies:

- With the best of my heart,
- To Colonel Destivel, looking forward to being your future "chauffeuse" in Paris,
- Let's hope it's as much fun as it has been at Gaitford when you get to be Air Attaché in London,
- For the record, I've never come across as many RAF people as happy and proud to serve under an officer of a different nationality. Thank you!
- To Colonel Destivel, whose overriding calm in the most perilous of situations has always inspired us.

The next day, it's time to go. Phil has organized two days in London with Victoria before he has to be at the hospital for his operation. Before being driven to the station, Phil has a final walk around the base, through the principal buildings, the control tower, the officers' mess, the aircraft hangars and the munitions stores. He is overcome by emotion several times. He is haunted by the faces of some of those who died, each one seeming younger than the one before. In his head, he says a long goodbye to his crew, the six comrades killed during his accident! His eyes fill with tears. These months spent at Gaitford have been the most intense and surprising of his life. There were all those bombing runs, but also his encounter with Victoria, his lover, the woman he adores so much, who has given him two children that he did not expect to have!

Phil was effectively dumbfounded to find that he was the father of not one, but two babies. It has taken him a while to get used to the idea. But after spending two days with Victoria, his discomfort was overcome by her sweetness, beauty and humor. He told himself that he would work out how to manage the situation later, after his return to France in October.

In the train taking him to London, Phil has some time to think. He lists the problems that he will need to solve when he comes out of hospital in three or four months. Where to live? France probably, but why not London? Maybe he could get himself nominated as a military attaché? Will Maggy, his mother, continue to live with him and help him raise Paul and Claire? And Victoria? Will he ask her to marry him so that his children can take his name and cease to be Millers? In that case, it would be easiest if Maggy reclaimed her independence and went to live elsewhere. But how would Maggy react to such a change? He couldn't possibly leave his mother in distress if she took it badly! Phil doesn't dare imagine his mother's reaction when he tells her that he's coming back from England with a wife and two babies in his luggage! Paul and Claire would get used to the situation quickly, but Maggy? With her dammed character! The situation is not going to be easy to manage.

Victoria is waiting impatiently for her Phil. But she is also worried because she knows that he is going to have another operation, and she is concerned about his health. Phil's plane accident has traumatized her. She really hadn't expected it. She tries to break the spell by envisaging the worst that could happen. During Phil's visit, Peggy, her cousin, will give the twins their bottles at night. That way, Victoria can devote herself entirely to Phil. Today, she has chosen her best summer dress, in light cotton, fitted close to the body and covered in red and pink flowers. She has almost lost her pregnancy weight and returned to her old shape. She started painting again a week ago and has just finished a figurative work depicting her two babies lying on cushions and smiling.

Phil rings the doorbell at about 6 p.m. with a bunch of red peonies in his hand.

"Wow, you look lovely in that dress! These flowers are for you. Look, they even match what you are wearing."

She also finds him very handsome, in civilian clothes this time, with light toile pants and a sky-blue shirt. She throws herself into his arms and embraces him.

"I'm so glad you're here. Ever since your accident, I'm scared stiff of losing you."

The twins are asleep and Victoria takes Phil to her room to show him her new painting. He finds the composition charming and he tells her so. She serves him some tea and scones in the living room and explains that Peggy will be looking after the twins overnight.

"Tonight we can go out. I've reserved a restaurant. I'm paying. It's not far from here. We can even walk there."

The rest of the afternoon flies by. Phil thinks that the twins have changed a lot since his first visit. He takes them in his arms and thinks about when Paul and Claire were babies. Phil finds his life strange, taking many unexpected turns, some of which have been tragic, whereas others have been so sweet and exulting. Victoria has the impression that he is interested in the babies now and that he has made considerable progress since he saw then for the first time a month ago.

Towards 7.30 in the evening, they go out, leaving the children with Peggy. The sky is clear and this start of July is warm in London. Victoria has reserved a table for two in a restaurant with a terrace. It's warm enough to eat outside. Victoria is very relaxed and happy to go out, even though she loves looking after her babies. She and Phil became lovers almost a year ago and now they have two children, although they have hardly seen each other these last few months. They can count their meetings on the fingers of one hand. But now they will be able to live their dream.

They start with drinks before dinner, with a white wine from Meursault. They look at each other, amazed to be face-to-face at last, with some time to themselves. They talk a lot, mixing French and English, but they avoid talking about their future.

At the end of the meal, Victoria takes Phil's hand in hers, caressing it and squeezing it, and then places a sensual kiss on it whilst contemplating him with a naughty glance. Phil is unsettled. Victoria pays the bill despite Phil's protests. On the way home, they stop several times, happy to be able to hold each other, but impatient to return to their love nest.

When they arrive at the apartment, all is calm. No crying from the twins and Peggy, discreet as ever, is in her room. They rapidly find their way to Victoria's soft bed, with its fluffy perfumed sheets, a small piece of paradise that will hold them for the entire night.

They are happy to rediscover one another's bodies, to caress each other, prolonging the pleasure for as long as possible. Their lips murmur words of love that delight and excite them. Once the flames of passion have died down, Victoria and Phil fall asleep with their bodies entwined, waking early in the morning, both astonished and charmed to find themselves still embracing.

Peggy looks after the twins again on Sunday, and Victoria and Phil spend the morning lying on the grass in Hyde Park. At lunchtime, they go to a pub to have a beer and eat some good sandwiches made with white bread, grilled chicken and mustard.

Phil has to leave for Rauceby Hospital on Monday morning. He tackles the subject of their future on Sunday night, after a dinner prepared by Victoria.

"I feel so good with you, my darling. I don't want to lose you. Do you feel the same? What do you think should happen when I come out of hospital? Do you want to stay in London?"

"I don't want to lose you either. It took me long enough to find you, you know! I think the best thing would be for me to move to Paris. But I need to think about it. I'll write to you and tell you more when you are at Rauceby."

They both have heavy hearts on Monday morning when the time comes to say goodbye. Ever since they met, their lives have been full of separations, which they are both finding harder and harder to bear.

11

MORLEAU IN BURGUNDY, FRANCE, JULY 1945

On July 1, at about 6 a.m., Françoise Dumaine arrives at Chagny station, accompanied by her three children, Agnes, Michel and Romain.

As the widow of an air force officer who died in action two years earlier, she was given first priority for places on the Atlantide, a ship specially chartered for the repatriation of French families stranded in North Africa due to the war. The crossing to Marseilles was pleasant, with very little swell, and entertainment in the evenings, including a ball after the first dinner. The captain had even asked her to dance two consecutive dances and murmured some gallant compliments about her appearance in her ear.

Françoise has had only one idea in mind since the violence they had witnessed at Bougie on May 8: leaving Algeria as soon as possible, to get back to her house in France. At 31, she feels full of energy and ready to rebuild her life.

This evening, after a train journey that has taken all day, she arrives in Burgundy tired, but joyful. A couple of miles in a taxi and she will be home, in the village of Morleau. Her grandfather bought this house in the 1920s, for holidays in the country. Françoise had left it in a rush five years earlier when the Germans had arrived. She had first fled to her cousins in Pau, and then to Algeria, to be with her husband.

Three weeks ago, she wrote to the mayor of the village to tell him that she was coming home, and to Marie Gerbot, the woman who, for the last ten years, has looked after the house when it was empty. A very good woman, Marie! She lives very close to Françoise's house, only about a hundred yards away, making it easy to keep an eye out. She has a set of keys and does the housework regularly. Françoise lost her own keys during the exodus, but she will go to Marie and ask for hers.

In the taxi that takes her home, Françoise finds the evening light magical. The sun is nowhere near set yet, but its golden oblique rays lend a richer color to the fields of wheat, which is ripe and ready for harvest. The omnipresent rows of grapevines on the route to Morleau from the slopes of Beaune testify to this region being, above all, a wine-producing region. The villages of Montrachet are close by.

The taxi soon arrives at Morleau. The driver turns left onto *rue de la Colline* and takes them to Marie Gerbot's house.

"Wait for me with the kids for a minute. I'll just go and get the keys to the house."

Françoise gets out of the taxi and rings the bell several times. No-one comes to the door. It's as if Marie isn't there! The gate is locked and the shutters are closed. Maybe she is in her kitchen garden behind the house? Françoise rapidly walks round the house, but there is no-one there! She goes and rings at a neighbor's house. She hears footsteps and the door opens.

"Oh, Mrs. Dumaine! What a surprise! Everyone in the village was wondering what had become of you. We haven't seen you since the start of the war!"

"I'll tell you all about it some time, but I've just arrived from Marseilles with my children and I'm in a hurry. I'm looking for Marie Gerbot. She looks after the house for us and she has my key. But no-one is answering."

"You're looking for Marie? Haven't you heard what happened to her? It's really sad! She died a year ago, when a munitions train exploded on the railway track."

This news hits Françoise hard, because she was very fond of her housekeeper. Marie dead! Because of the war! Why her? And now, how is she going to get into her house? The neighbor understands her distress and tries to reassure her.

"It shouldn't be very hard to get into your house. Go and have a look!"

Françoise is in a state of shock when she leaves the neighbor. She goes back to the taxi and asks the driver to take her to her house. He stops about 10 yards away from the railings and takes the suitcases out of the trunk. Françoise thanks him and pays. She waits until he has gone and then goes up to the railings with the children. The gate isn't locked. She pushes it, impatient to see her home again. She stares for a moment at this beautiful house built in the time of Louis XV, with its elegantly curved staircase and wrought iron balustrades and its form, so typical of Burgundy: the first floor with all the principal rooms, and a second floor under the eaves with windows and a bulls-eye. On the right side of the house, a tower added at the start of the 20th century and in keeping with the original building, making it look like a little chateau. She is surprised to see that the shutters are open. On closer inspection, she is very annoyed to find that several windows are broken. She has the surprising impression of the sound of voices coming from inside. She walks up to the front door and taps hard with the knocker. She hears footsteps. The door opens and a strapping great man of about forty or so, unshaven, not particularly clean, and smelling of wine asks her roughly "What is it? What do you want?"

"I want to come in. This is my house. What are you doing in my house? Who are you?"

"So this is your house is it? That's a good one! This is our house. Clear off! Go and see the mayor. He'll explain it to you."

He closes the door and Françoise hears it being double-locked. Completely stunned, she sits on the steps of the house, exhausted, and begins to cry. Her children, by her side, do not understand. They have often seen their mother sobbing but, since the German surrender, her tears have dried up. Agnes approaches her mother affectionately and says "Don't cry, Mom! What's the matter? Who was that man?"

Françoise forces herself to stop sobbing.

"I don't know. The house is occupied. We'll have to go and see the mayor but it's getting a bit late. Come on, we'll walk to the town hall anyway."

Romain starts asking for something to eat in his baby language and makes it clear that he is too tired to walk. Françoise is at a loss to know what to do. Her thoughts overwhelm her. They must hurry up and go find the mayor. But Romain is too small to be left on his own. He will have to be carried. And then there are the three suitcases. They can hardly leave them outside in the road, but they can't carry them either as they are too heavy, and she daren't leave them in the courtyard in front of the house for fear that one of these screwballs will steal them!

"You're Mrs. Dumaine, aren't you? I saw you arrive. I'm Georges Guérin. You probably don't know me, but I remember you from before the war. I'm living in the house next door at the moment. You can come to my house with your children. There is enough space. You can go and see the mayor then, or tomorrow. Come on, I'll show you my house."

Françoise looks at the man wide-eyed. This man says that he is her neighbor, so it's not really strange that he is willing to come to her aid. His wife must be at home. Why not go and have a look?

"Yes, I'm afraid I don't remember having met you before. So you're my neighbor? Delighted to meet you. There was no-one in your house before the war. Thank you so much for offering to put us up. We've just got back from Algeria. I'll tell you what happened to us if you like."

Mr. Guérin takes two suitcases and says that he will come back for the third. He then opens the gate leading to his house.

"It's an old farm. Down below, there was a stable and a barn with room for several cows. I had it converted into living space before the war, but the house remained uninhabited until the liberation of this region. I've been living upstairs since last October, but it's only temporary. You can stay on the ground floor with your children. There is a dining room, a living room, three bedrooms, and, of course, a kitchen and a bathroom. You're more than welcome until your house is emptied of its occupants."

He shows Françoise around the house.

"Sit down at the table in the dining room. I'll get you something to eat."

Georges Guérin goes upstairs and returns with some tea and fruit juice, together with some bread, chocolate and a few slices of cake on a tray.

"Mr. Guérin, you're our savior! The kids are starving and so am I."

Georges is wearing a wedding ring, and Françoise says "You must introduce us to your wife. I hope that we won't be in her way?"

"Unfortunately, I'm living alone at the moment. Those Nazi bastards sent my wife to a camp, at Ravensbruck, close to Berlin. A concentration camp for women. It was liberated by the Russians at the end of April, but I still have no news of my wife!"

"Oh! I'm so sorry. But why did they arrest her and not you?"

"I was in the Resistance, and we blew up a train. I must have been denounced. The gestapo came right to my little factory near here and they burnt it down. That was a year ago. My wife went to see the damage, but I wasn't there, and they took her hostage. I've been desperately waiting for her return ever since. But, I have little hope of ever seeing her alive again."

While the children and Françoise are eating, Georges tells her that he founded a factory that made cookers that sold well in the region, as well as those of Lacanche.

"We used to make our own cast iron pieces, because we had the machine tools to do it. Our cookers had an automatic cleaning system that worked really well, which I invented myself. I'm a mechanical engineer by training."

Effectively, Françoise has heard of this little factory several houses away from hers, set up in a building resembling an ordinary house that didn't spoil the view. Several memories come flooding back at the mention of these premises.

"I remember now. You used to have a superb sports car. A Bugatti wasn't it? My husband liked fancy cars too. He told me about it."

"Yes, that's right. Before the war I was mad about sports cars. I even entered a few races. No problem with the mechanical side.

When I needed new parts, I used to make them myself with our machine tools."

Françoise is happy to see that her neighbor isn't just anybody, but an ingenious industrialist who is probably rich too. She thinks he must be about fifty. He is still in pretty good shape, with very dark hair and eyebrows, an impressive appearance. She can sense that this man is a fighter. Hardly surprising that he was active in the Resistance.

Françoise rapidly tells him her story, the hurried departure from her holiday home in June 1940 when the Germans arrived, her escape, and then North Africa, the birth of her youngest in July 1943 and the death of her husband, a pilot, a matter of days later. She then asks Georges if he knows who is living in her house.

"Your house is lovely, but it's vast too" he answers, "A real little chateau. When the *Wehrmacht* asked the mayor for somewhere to billet about 40 soldiers in 1942, he had to act rapidly. Twenty-five were billeted directly with people from the village, but there were about 15 left. Your house couldn't stay empty and it was occupied by non-commissioned officers and soldiers. They didn't stay long, maybe a couple of months."

"Germans in my house! How horrible! I didn't know. I hope they didn't do any damage?"

"Hang on a minute, I'm not finished yet! In February 1944, the mayor was ordered to house about forty French refugees. The Germans had evacuated all the coastal towns in the north of France to perfect their defenses against a possible Allied landing. Several of these refugees were put in your house. Some are still there because their own houses in the villages they came from were completely destroyed. The one who opened the door to you is a bit of a half-wit and thinks he's going to be living there for ages. But I'm sure the mayor will find another solution. I don't think there's much damage, just a bit of cleaning up to do."

Things are becoming clearer to Françoise now. She will go and see the mayor the next morning. In the meantime, she puts the contents of the suitcases into the cupboards in Georges' house, and makes the children some dinner with food supplied by her host. After dinner, everyone goes straight to bed. Françoise, absolutely drained, falls asleep immediately.

The next morning, she gets ready quickly and goes to the town hall, leaving her children in the house, with Agnes in charge. The town hall is about three hundred yards from her house, along the national 74 road. The mayor's new secretary, who wasn't there before the war, says that the mayor is at home this morning. Françoise knows the mayor well. He is called Henri Joly, and they were both born in 1913. They're as good as friends! He is a vintner, but also a poet in his spare time, and he wields the French language with elegance. They enjoy chatting together about everything and nothing when they meet in the village. The thought of seeing him again warms Françoise's heart, to such an extent that she almost forgets that her house is occupied. She walks to his house, at the other end of the village, and finds him ready to leave for work in his vineyard. Henri is astonished to see her.

"Oh! What have we here? What a surprise! Françoise has come to see me! I haven't heard from you in five years. All I know is that your husband died in 1943. I thought of you when I heard the news. Poor thing left on your own with two children! What can I do for you my dear?"

"Didn't you get my letter from Algeria saying that I was coming back? I sent it about a month back and I was surprised you didn't reply."

"I didn't get it, but, you know, I'm not mayor of Morleau anymore. I left office on May 14th, with immense relief after all these hard years of occupation. The new mayor is called Roger Dubois. He works for the SNCF at Chagny. That's why I didn't get your letter. When did you get back?"

"Last night. My boat from Algiers landed in the morning and the four of us took the train from Marseilles. Yes, there are four of us now. My youngest is called Romain and he's nearly two. I arrived exhausted to find my house occupied by refugees who slammed the door in my face. To top it all, I lost my keys while we were away and I just found out that Marie Gerbot, who used to look after the house for us, is dead. It's awful! Fortunately, my new neighbor has taken us in and explained the situation. But I want my house back. It's my house. It isn't the Soviet Union here yet, as far as I know!"

In his heart of hearts, Henri is glad that he is no longer mayor and will not have to deal with this tricky situation.

"Go and see the new mayor. He lives about a hundred yards away. I'll show you the way. Pop round and see me whenever you like. We've got a lot of catching up to do."

Françoise walks towards the new mayor's house, while her friend Henri goes into his own house to speak to his parents, who live under his roof.

"I've just seen Françoise Dumaine. She arrived from Algiers with her children yesterday and didn't know there were refugees living in her house. Her neighbor, Georges Guérin, has offered to put her up temporarily. I didn't want to worry her. I didn't say anything about him, but someone should tell her to be careful!"

Françoise rapidly reaches the mayor's house and is happy to find that he is at home. She explains who she is and asks him to evict the occupants of her house straight away, so that she can move back in, because she intends to live at Morleau all year round with her children. After hearing her out, the mayor looks concerned as he replies.

"I understand your disarray, Mrs. Dumaine. We have a council meeting this evening and I will speak about your problem in the hope of finding a rapid solution. But I can't just evict them today. When they arrived in the village, it was the previous mayor who put them in your house, with the agreement of the council of course. They are not in your house illegally. We will have to find them another house. Stay at Mr. Guérin's house for the moment. I will come round at 10 o'clock tomorrow morning to let you know what we decide."

Françoise leaves disappointed, but she can see that she will have to be patient. France isn't back to normal yet. The armistice was signed less than two months ago. In the afternoon, she walks around the village with her children. There is no running water at Morleau yet. The inhabitants get their water from communal wells. There are four such wells for the three hundred inhabitants. Some collect rainwater from their guttering and store it in tanks. They then have pumps to drive the water into the kitchen. That is the case in Françoise's house, provided nothing is damaged.

Life is not simple in the village. Once they have boiled their linen, the women go to the communal wash house on the road to Chassagne. No-one has a modern bathroom. To take a bath, they have to heat the water and use small tubs or baths made of zinc. The bedrooms are often equipped with special furniture, containing a basin, so that the inhabitants can wash. A jug is used to fill the basin with water. Not having running water makes life more difficult for the inhabitants, but it also makes for more exchanges between them, during their meetings at the wells and the wash house. These meetings provide them with an opportunity to discuss things and to gossip about the people and the village. The news of the return of

Françoise and her children has thus spread like wildfire, and many people come up to greet her during her walk.

The next morning, the mayor is punctual when he comes to tell her the news.

"We've found a solution to rehouse the refugees. We are going to requisition an unoccupied house near the level crossing. But you will have to wait another week. We will have to organize a few sanitary elements to make the house habitable. Once the refugees have left your house, the council will take care of the cleaning and we will make a list of possible damage with a bailiff so that you can demand war damages. It's the third of July today. You should be able to move back into your house towards the 10th and certainly before the national holiday on the 14th. That's the best we can do."

Françoise has no real choice and she thanks the mayor. In the next few days, she takes care of what she can organize already. She goes to see the teacher and gets her two eldest children enrolled in the local school for the start of the school year in October. For Romain, who is only two, she looks for someone to look after him at home every morning and, when necessary, in the afternoon. She finds a woman called Yvonne Guérinot, who has a three-year-old daughter herself, lives in the same street and is only too pleased with the prospect of earning some extra cash.

In the meantime, Georges Guérin is taking great care of Françoise and the children. Every morning, he comes to see Françoise to ask if everything is OK and whether she needs anything in particular. He says that he feels like a father to her and kisses her on each cheek the first time that he sees her during the day. She finds him pleasant and funny, but she is astonished by one thing. On the several occasions that she has spoken about staying with her neighbor to the inhabitants of Morleau, she has felt a certain embarrassment on the part of those she has spoken too. Once, a woman said "Ah! You're staying with Georges Guérin, the one that had problems after the death of his first wife!" But she was unable to find out anything more.

The refugees leave Françoise's house during the morning of July 11, and Françoise visits the house with the mayor in the afternoon. There is no major damage, just a few broken panes of glass that have been replaced temporarily with sheets of cardboard, some broken glasses and plates and two ripped mattresses. Other than that, everything is dirty and there is a lot of cleaning to do. She insists on doing the cleaning herself. She spends the whole day of July 12, and the morning of the following day, throwing out garbage and cleaning the floors and furniture.

Her neighbor invites her to dinner at his house on the evening of July 13. He says it will be a simple affair and that he has invited his mother, an old lady who is apparently very funny, to whom he would like to introduce her. Françoise has planned to move into her house during the morning on July 14, the first Bastille Day holiday since the end of the war in May. She will have just the contents of her three suitcases to transport. The rest of her luggage should arrive at any time.

Despite her tiredness, Françoise spends a little time getting ready for dinner. Fortunately, it's summer and the weather is fine and hot. She makes up her eyes discreetly with some kohl she bought in Algeria, outlines her lips with some lipstick and puts on a light, short-sleeved dress, leaving open the first two buttons of its white bodice. She doesn't put any stockings on, and wears red high-heeled shoes that match her lips. Leaving the younger children in Agnes' charge, she ascends the external staircase leading to the residence of her neighbor on the first floor and rings his doorbell.

It is eight o'clock. When Georges opens the door, she observes that he has also gone to some effort, with his light brown toile suit, a long-sleeved shirt with a white pocket handkerchief and well-polished shoes. Georges asks her to make herself comfortable in the living room and offers her a whisky. She doesn't often drink, but she remembers having appreciated this beverage on the two or three times in her life that she has tried it. Her first mouthful makes her grimace, eliciting a smile from her host. Françoise rapidly begins to feel more relaxed and she asks Georges a few direct questions that have been bugging her concerning his first wife.

"Georges, I believe that you were married once and that your wife died?"

"Have the villagers been telling you about my first wife?"

Françoise is discomforted by this question as direct as her own and isn't sure how to respond at first, but she eventually decides to tell the truth.

"A woman did, indeed, tell me that you had some problems after her death, but she didn't say any more. What kind of problems?"

"It's perfectly simple and I'll tell you bluntly. There are those who have accused me of killing my wife. No less than that, and do you know why? Because I decided to get married again shortly afterwards and was daft enough to say so."

"What do you mean by 'shortly afterwards'?"

"Oh, rapidly, in the week after her death, in 1943. A few months later, they dug up her body and carried out an autopsy. They didn't find anything of course. My wife wasn't sick and she was asphyxiated by the exhaust fumes from a poorly burning wood stove."

Françoise tells herself that he seems honest enough but that he must have had a mistress for a long time to announce his remarriage so rapidly! She can't see how she can find out any more without appearing tactless.

"We can eat now, if you want" adds Georges.

In the dining room, the table is laid for two.

"Isn't your mother eating with us?"

"No, she's not very well."

"Are you afraid of me?" he adds.

This last question is punctuated by a strange laugh that does not bode well to Françoise.

Outside the house, someone quietly opens the gate leading to Georges Guerin's house. He walks towards a small lean-to on the right, under which it is dark. He sits on a chair and waits.

12

LONDON, UNITED KINGDOM, JULY 1945

The doorbell of Victoria's apartment rings at 7 p.m. on July 12. Peggy opens the door to a voluble man, of medium height in his mid-forties. He is unshaven and a bit hairy, and he asks, in poor English, "Is this house of Victoria Miller? I am Serge Andropov, old friend from Paris. Tell her I wish speak with her."

Peggy leaves Serge on the landing and goes to inform Victoria of his visit. Victoria can hardly believe her ears.

"Serge Andropov, here! What a surprise! Yes, he's a friend from Paris. Show him into the living room. I'll just run a comb through my hair and I'll be there."

Serge enters the apartment and looks around, astonished, at the luxurious rooms he passes through. When Victoria arrives he speaks to her in French, a language in which he is much more comfortable.

"Hello ducky," he says, "I haven't seen you in over five years! But it looks like you have made your fortune in the meantime. This is one opulent apartment. And you're more beautiful than ever my darling. The years haven't marked you at all! I got your letter but I didn't reply as I was coming to London anyway."

"I'm so glad to see you, Serge. You haven't changed a bit! Still living a bohemian life?"

"Always! Especially since the liberation of Paris. The town's coming to life again. There is an incredible ambiance at the moment. You can dance every night in the clubs, to jazz music by Sydney Bechet, Lionel Hampton and loads of others. It's fabulous. Everyone is out to have a good time. *Saint-Germain-des-Prés* is the new hotspot. How about you? Are you still painting?"

Victoria and Serge have five years of catching up to do. Victoria invites him to stay for dinner. Peggy doesn't want to disturb them and eats her meal in the kitchen. Victoria tells Serge about the austere years spent with her mother-in-law in Gaitford, the destruction of her paintings by a German fighter that crashed into her studio, her husband who was a prisoner but managed to escape only to die shortly after his return, and, to complete the tale, the birth of her twins. She says nothing about meeting Phil.

Serge tells her that he left Paris for the *Côte d'Azur*. He assumed a false identity to hide his Jewish origins and worked in the fields. He began painting again almost a year ago.

Victoria is most interested in talking about painting with Serge. They first met among the group of painters in Montparnasse.

"I'm still into abstract art. Are there still a lot of abstract painters in Paris or was it just a fashion that passed with the war?"

"Of course there are still painters active in the field of abstract art in Paris. I'm sure that you've even met some of them. Do you remember Poliakoff, Staël and Masson? Did you ever meet them?

"Yes, I got on really well with Poliakoff and I met many other abstract painters in the galleries. But I've forgotten most of their names. Just talking about it makes me want to return to France."

"Yes, great idea! Come and live in Paris! You can come and live with me darling! We'll paint beautiful paintings and make love all the time! Do you remember the night we spent together? I loved stroking your body, your soft skin. You showed a bit of character darling!"

"Shut up Serge. You're embarrassing me! I'd had too much to drink and I didn't tell my husband I would be staying out all night. He was very worried and furious when I got home the next morning. But, you know, I don't regret it. We had a good time. It was a bit of a discovery for me in my very conventional life. I'm free now and I don't want to lose my freedom. Do you think you could find me an apartment to rent in Paris? I'll come with my cousin Peggy if she agrees. She'll help me to look after the twins and she'll learn French. It could be useful to her later."

"How many bedrooms do you want, and in what neighborhood?"

"Three bedrooms and a room I can use as a studio, plus a living room of course. A well-lit apartment at the top of the building. Somewhere where I can paint in comfort. I've got a fair amount of money. Inherited. It shouldn't be a problem paying the rent. I'm not sure where though. A lively neighborhood. You were talking about *Saint-Germain-des-Prés*, or maybe close to the *Jardin du Luxembourg*? That's quite close to *Saint-Germain*. What do you think?"

"Near the *Jardin du Luxembourg*. That's a good idea. You could take your little cherubs for walks there. There are some very nice buildings surrounding the gardens."

At the end of the evening, when they say goodbye, Victoria asks him to keep her informed for the apartment. Her decision is as good as made. She will go and live in Paris. Peggy agrees to come with her. Serge adores Victoria and says he will find her an apartment to rent. She will send him enough money to pay three months' rent in advance. Victoria can already see herself as a Parisian by September, ready to devote a large proportion of time to her art.

Victoria has trouble falling asleep when she goes to bed. Images of her future life in Paris spontaneously pop into her head. Phil coming to see her on some evenings, her first exhibition in a gallery, dining with her painter friends, her twins at a French high school, her walks in the *Jardin du Luxembourg…*

13

FROM CASABLANCA TO PARIS, JULY 1945

Maggy has finally got what she wanted for so many months: her repatriation to France with the children, on a French Navy ship. She hasn't stopped for the last two weeks, sorting out all the things that had accumulated in her house in Meknes over the last four years. They will leave from the port of Casablanca on July 6, and the crossing will take several days.

Excerpt from the diary of Claire Destivel

Friday July 6, 1945

They were supposed to come and get us at about eight in the morning. For once, we were actually ready on time. But we still hadn't left by half past eleven. It's enough to put you off being on time for the rest of your life! We boarded the boat at about 12 o'clock. We're really lucky as we have a cabin, whereas most people are sleeping in dormitories, and that is really annoying!

I had no regrets as I saw the Moroccan coast getting further and further away, and I am firmly resolved never to set foot there again. I wished a final silent goodbye to my friends from Meknes and then we were off on our way to France. Once we got into open waters I had to go and lie down because I was seasick as a result of all the rolling, pitching and tossing. On top of that, my bed is close to the machines, so I have to listen to a perpetual mechanical lullaby. Maggy is holding up well and has gone to dinner. We're on a military hospital ship and they use bugles for everything. There's no point moaning or resisting. Five minutes late in the dining room and they won't serve you. It's a bit much!

It's the second time in her life that Maggy has made a long boat journey. The sea is rough, the boat pitches and tosses, and a lot of the passengers are ill. But Maggy is fine, very excited to be returning home. It is 7 p.m., time to go to dinner. Maggy is really hungry and not suffering from as much as a hint of nausea. The children have sea sickness and have stayed in their cabin, like most of the other passengers. Maggy goes down to the dining room, where she sees a military man with lots of stripes, almost certainly the captain of the ship. He is helping a very elegant elderly lady in a black dress decorated with a gold brooch to her seat, on his right. The lady is wearing a black hat, which remains on her head throughout the meal. There are still a large number of unoccupied places and a waiter indicates to Maggy that she can sit where she likes. Maggy is intrigued by this old lady, and she chooses a place not too far away, so that she can observe her. However, she is too curious to stay still very long and she soon gets up to go and question the waiter.

"Excuse me, could you please tell me who the old lady in black is?"

"Of course! Didn't you recognize her? It's the Maréchale Lyautey. She often comes to Morocco and she travels on French Navy ships. It's the third time I've seen her. She's in great form for her age!"

Maggy is gobsmacked! The Maréchale. A woman with a strong personality, so rumor has it. Maggy has heard about her but has never met her. And here they are on the same boat, in the same dining room!

What an opportunity! A story to tell her family when she gets back to France. She knows that Mrs. Lyautey is still very active and is involved in lots of charitable works in Morocco, despite being more than 80 years old. She absolutely must meet her, talk to her. That would really impress her listeners! And it could help boost Phil's career. Maggy literally devours her dinner. She's not adverse to the wine they offer her either. After the dessert, she remains at table, scrutinizing the Maréchale to determine when she will get up to go back to her cabin. That's it, the time has come. The Maréchale is folding her napkin! Maggy leaves her chair and walks over to Mrs. Lyautey perfectly naturally, just as she is getting up. She holds out her hand and says, respectfully, "Maréchale Lyautey, I am honored to make your acquaintance. Please allow me to present myself. I am Marguerite Destivel, the wife of Colonel Philippe Destivel, who spent several years in Morocco before becoming the commander of the air base at Gaitford in England. I stayed behind in Meknes to look after the children."

Maggy, no doubt due to the jitters provoked by this encounter, has got it wrong and introduced herself as Colonel Destivel's wife rather than his mother. The Maréchale is surprised and somewhat sardonically says "Delighted to meet you. If I'm not mistaken, your husband is a colonel in the air force. So, you've caught yourself a young husband my dear lady. Congratulations!"

Maggy realizes her error, blushes and corrects herself.

"No, I'm so sorry. I meant to say that I'm Colonel Destivel's mother, not his wife. My son is a widower and I am a widow. Given his responsibilities, he needed someone to look after his two children during the war."

"That makes more sense! You've been very lucky to have had the chance to spend several years in Morocco. You're not too sad to be leaving such a marvelous country I hope?"

Maggy is not the slightest bit sad to be leaving a land where they eat only chicken and mutton and are boiling hot half the time, but she knows that it is better to keep that to herself.

"Yes, Maréchale, it's heartbreaking, but I don't have a choice. I hope to come back soon."

Their first conversation ends there. Maggy regrets her error, which has made her appear a bit ridiculous. She hopes that no-one else overheard. She can't wait to talk to the Maréchale again.

Early on Saturday morning, a sailor knocks on the door of Paul and Claire's cabin. He introduces himself as Pierre, and tells them that he is going to clean their cabin, which they must leave for about 20 minutes. They are still in their nightclothes. They hurry to get ready, but have too little time to stuff everything back into their suitcase. They then go off to breakfast. When they return, all the clothes that they had left in a heap on the floor have, as if by magic, been folded and placed on their beds. Everything is spick and span. Their maid in Meknes never did that much for them. During the day, Claire runs into Pierre, the sailor who cleaned their cabin.

"Thank you for cleaning up our cabin so well" she says, politely.

"It's nothing Miss. That's what I'm here for. You write very well you know. You left a notebook open on your desk. A diary I suppose. I read a few lines, without turning the page, mind. It was very well written. How old are you?"

Claire is furious and feels that her intimacy, her inner world, has been violated by a stranger.

"But a diary is personal!' she thunders, incandescent with anger. "You had no right to read so much as a single line. Don't you ever do that again! Do I make myself clear? Otherwise I'll go straight to the captain!"

With that, she marches off in a huff. Never again will she leave her diary open when she is out of the room. What a lout Pierre is, even if he is quite cute!

Excerpts from the diary of Claire Destivel:

Saturday July 7, 1945

We can see Gibraltar and we are following the French coast, with the Cordillera in the background. The mountains descend directly into the sea and are very craggy, with deep gorges forming pointed headlands and bays. The scenery is magnificent, like all the coasts around Spain. Life on board is monotonous, with no distractions, obviously, as it's a military ship. We make do with walking round the bridge a hundred times whilst contemplating the coasts slowly passing by. We tear around the boat, which has five levels, not counting the hold. The food's not bad. We all eat together at the same table. It's amazing how much gossip there is.

In the evening, the sailors do what they can to amuse themselves. Their favorite pastime is playing leap-frog. A ball is organized for later, and Claire espies Pierre, the sailor who dared to read her journal, there. She walks towards the dancefloor and Pierre comes over to her and apologizes. She says that she forgives him but that he mustn't do it again. He asks her to dance a waltz with him and holds her close throughout the dance. Claire savors the moment.

Excerpt from the diary of Claire Destivel

Sunday July 8, 1945

The chaplain said mass on board today. The nurses and some of the officers sang very well. I was a bit distracted. We were crammed in like sardines, but it was good to hear mass in the middle of the sea.

All day today, we are following the coast of the Balearic Islands. We can see rocks just under the blue waves. Tonight, there was another ball. I was lost in my thoughts, transported to an unreal world, with the ship slicing through the sea, the music, the mountains tinged with purple light on the right and a horizon lost in shadow to the left. It was so romantic! Pierre was there. He took me to a dark corner on the bridge and kissed me with his tongue. It was the first time I'd ever been kissed like that and I liked it. I don't want this journey to end.

On Monday July 9, 1945, the ship is in the open sea. The passengers are excited because the captain has told everyone that France should come into view towards nine o'clock. But it's foggy and they have to wait until midday, close to Toulon harbor, before they finally catch a glimpse of the mother country. What emotion after six years of exile! But the port is in a terrible state. The jetty, the fort, the quays, all destroyed. There are ships underwater, with only their funnels and some debris visible. The passengers must remain on the ship until the afternoon of the following day.

Claire continues to write in her diary:

I saw Pierre again and he took me to his cabin. We lay down next to each other for a while. How confused I felt when he caressed me! Unfortunately, there was a noise. We left the cabin quickly and said goodbye.

Tuesday July 10, and it's only after seven long hours of waiting that the passengers can finally disembark. Their bags are carried by German prisoners. Maggy, Paul and Claire take their places in the beaten-up buses that will take them to Toulon station. With some difficulty, Paul finds three places together in the last carriage of the train. They pass through Bandol and La Ciotat, and they find the Cote d'Azur magnificent. They arrive at Marseilles towards 11 o'clock in the evening. They receive a warm welcome, with the Marseillaise resounding in the station, and a distribution of tea and cookies. The train then continues its journey, arriving in Lyons at 7 a.m. the following day. The passengers are served breakfast, and then they continue on their way, through Dijon and Sens, eventually arriving in Paris at six in the evening.

Claire records her impressions of the apartment on *rue Lecourbe* in her diary.

We arrived home at about eight in the evening, filthy and revolting. I'm sure anyone who saw us would have taken us for garbage collectors. How lamentable! I've never been so dirty in my life. I'm so tired I can't even face thinking. Still, I felt a pang of regret coming back to this town where I was so happy before.

On July 12, Paul and Claire get up joyfully to go and see their grandparents in Asnières. The grandparents have not been warned that they are coming, so the reunion is bound to be emotional. The two children lose their way a bit in the Metro, but finally arrive at their grandparents' home towards the end of the morning. Their grandparents are stupefied and barely recognize them because they have changed so much over the last six years. Their cousin Philippe, a firm favorite with Claire, is there too. He now has a pince-nez and a moustache and looks like an important gentleman. They all have lunch together, in a very congenial atmosphere.

On July 13, Paul and Claire decide that they want to go and see the Bastille Day parade the next day. They manage to convince Maggy to let them go alone, without adult supervision.

Saturday July 14

We arranged to meet my cousin Philippe at Saint-Lazare Station at seven in the morning to go and see the parade. Everyone in the family said that there would be a huge crowd and we would be crushed to bits, lucky if we didn't need an ambulance. When we got to the heart of the action, there were already five or six rows of people lining the sidewalk. We looked pitifully at each other and then we walked rapidly up the Champs-Elysees. We finally managed to find ourselves a place on a windowsill. Climbing up, we could see really well. Obviously, you had to have good balance, it wasn't easy, and we waited patiently for 10 o'clock. There was plenty to see. People arrived with stepladders, double and triple ladders, little stools. Some came with ice cream, others climbed up on awnings, trees or bus stops. We saw some fighting, some people who had funny turns, everything really. We could see the parade really well, even the big cheeses, de Gaulle, de Lattre de Tassigny and Leclerc, and the whole thing lasted three hours.

Over the next few days, Maggy spends a lot of time cleaning everything in the apartment on *rue Lecourbe* and doing the shopping with Paul and Claire. But not all of her activities are physical. She also thinks a lot about her future and she is incensed that she cannot speak with her son, who has been admitted to hospital again in England. It's yet more uncertainty. He doesn't know where he will be sent next. Maggy doesn't want to leave the Parisian region now that she has finally managed to return and she will take it really badly if she has to go back to Algeria or to one of the other colonies. But she will just have to grin and bear not knowing for the moment.

14

"I did the cooking, so please be indulgent!"

So begins the dinner to which Françoise has been invited by Georges Guérin. She has been feeling uncomfortable since she learned that some of the other villagers suspect Georges of having murdered his first wife. She has never been in a situation like this before. A husband murdering his wife! You come across things like that in whodunnits and in Greek tragedies, but not in real life! Georges senses her discomfort and tries to soothe her.

"So, is this the first time you've eaten alone with a murderer?" he asks. "No, I'm only joking. I was actually very shocked by the whole thing. The people in the village have stayed friendly enough but I can imagine the gossip about Georges Guérin when my back is turned! Especially seeing as my business was doing very well before the war and a lot of people were jealous! I don't know whether I will stay here long. Things would have been much simpler if the doctor who carried out the autopsy on my wife had been able to conclude that she died of carbon monoxide poisoning. It's not easy for me at the moment you know, what with the death of my first wife, the fire at the factory, and my second wife in a concentration camp, probably dead as well!"

Françoise is moved by Georges' speech, which is simple and straightforward in both content and delivery.

"Yes, I understand entirely. It can't be easy, and there is nothing worse than uncertainty."

The rest of the meal is much more agreeable. Georges talks about literature, the pre-war authors that he likes, but he shocks his guest's sensibilities when he vaunts the merits of Robert Brasillach, a man executed by firing squad during the purge a few months previously.

"But you, a member of the Resistance, how can you mourn the loss of this man, a fascist collaborator and anti-Semitic to boot!"

"It's more complicated than that. He was a great writer. I don't agree with all his ideas, but he didn't kill anyone. He was killed for what he wrote! He was condemned to death after a trial lasting only a couple of hours, with a rushed deliberation! That doesn't make France look very good. Lots of very well-known writers and artists, like Paul Valéry, Colette and Jean Cocteau, members of the Academy who weren't on his side asked Gaulle to pardon him, but the commies wanted his scalp and they won the day."

This conversation stimulates Françoise's interest in Georges' political opinions and what he did during the war.

"Did you join the Resistance at the start of the war?"

"Up until the start of the war, I was a supporter of the PPF, the *Parti Populaire Français*. After that, I became disenchanted with the way the party was going, its antisemitism and its enthusiastic collaboration with the Germans. But it took me a while to distance myself from them. I joined the Resistance in the middle of 1943 and I carried out dangerous missions right from the start. I became an expert in the production and handling of explosives. I already knew a bit about that sort of thing before the war. I had a friend who taught me stuff. He worked in the marble quarries at Chassagne."

"Didn't your involvement with the PPF cause you problems during the purge?"

"Yes, especially seeing as I got on very well with the Germans at the start of the occupation. I met some very nice soldiers in the ranks of the *Wehrmacht*. Fortunately, when the time came to defend myself, several Resistance members who had seen me in action testified in my favor. Right now, I can't wait for all this talk of the war to stop. I want to set up a new factory, but I'm not sure what I want it to produce yet. I've got a few ideas for new cookers or heating stoves, or even new parts for cars. I'm waiting for my war damages, and then I will bounce back."

Georges answers Françoise's direct questions with sincerity and she forms a rather positive opinion of him.

When they say goodnight, Georges says "It's Bastille Day tomorrow. There's a ball at Morleau to celebrate. Would you like to go?"

"Yes, of course, I'd entirely forgotten! It would be a good idea to put in an appearance, now that I'm living in the village all the time. I mustn't be seen to be keeping my distance from the other inhabitants!"

"OK, I'll see you tomorrow then Françoise. I look forward to asking you to dance and holding you in my arms!"

He says these last words with a grin, and they amuse Françoise, who finds her host rather handsome. Françoise reflects on her unusual neighbor as she goes to bed. Tired, she rapidly falls asleep. Georges, for his part, finds his neighbor pretty, intelligent and elegant, in both her appearance and the way she expresses herself. He would like to know more about her and would very much like to visit her house, the external appearance of which has already won him over, with its impressive steps and facade.

Georges clears the table and goes to his bedroom. He has just started to undress when scratching noises at the door to his apartment attract his attention. He listens carefully. It sounds like someone knocking gently to get someone to open the door for them without drawing too much attention to themselves. He rapidly puts on a silk dressing gown to go and see what's going on. Just in case he needs to defend himself, he takes a revolver from the drawer of the bedside table, loads it, and puts it in one of his pockets. Georges is brave and has seen other brave men too. He slowly opens the door a little and peers out.

"Georges, let me in. I want to talk to you," whispers a silhouette in the moonlight, with a marked accent.

Georges doesn't recognize the person in the half-light and takes out his revolver.

"Who are you? I don't know you. Come in, but watch out! I'm armed and I won't hesitate to shoot!"

Georges walks behind the bearded individual. He switches on the light to find out who it is.

"Georges, don't you recognize me? I didn't have a beard three years ago. Don't you remember?"

His voice and his accent are familiar to Georges, enabling him to identify his visitor rapidly. It's the beard that threw him initially.

"Wilhelm! Well I never! You're alive and you've come back! You've kept your word! It's incredible. I was convinced that you'd died on the Russian Front! Here, have a chair. Are you hungry or thirsty? Let me get you something. Tell me all about it. Well I never!"

Georges gets out two glasses, a bottle of white wine from Blagny, some ham and parsley terrine and the leftovers of the damson tart that he served Françoise. They begin by clinking their glasses, looking each other straight in the eye. Wilhelm rapidly tells Georges what has happened to him over the last three years, describing in detail his journey across Germany, his flight from the Russian army, crossing the Elbe, his disguise as a journalist, crossing the Rhine and then France.

"When I got to the French side of the Rhine, someone I hadn't seen came and knocked me out to rob me. I was unconscious for several hours. When I woke up, all the money from my pockets had been stolen. Luckily, I'd hidden two wads of notes in the lining of my raincoat and they were still there. I went to Dijon to get some false American identity papers. You remember, my father is German, but my mother was born in the United States. Unfortunately, even though I was willing to pay a high price, I couldn't find anyone who could produce the documents I wanted. I hid for a while up in the hills above Pommard. I couldn't find anyone for my papers at Beaune either. I wanted to come and see you earlier, with everything already sorted out, or nearly so, but I couldn't. I was impatient to find you. I kept asking myself if you were still living in this village. What memories! Did you get into any trouble when the German troops had to leave France?"

"A bit, but it all got sorted out. I could see that the wind had changed direction. I joined the Resistance in 1943. Thank goodness! I became an expert in explosives. I blew up railway lines, goods trains, electricity lines. I'm almost a hero to some! But someone denounced me, and the Gestapo blew up my factory in reprisal. I hid."

Georges and Wilhelm then talk about how they met when Wilhelm was staying with the other officers in the house next-door, Françoise Dumaine's house.

"I'm so happy to see you! Where are you staying at the moment?"

"Nowhere. In the woods up on the hills. I've still got some money left, but I'm scared that someone will find out that I'm German. I don't want to end up in prison."

"Stay here then. There is a free apartment on the ground floor and I can help you with your papers. I still have friends!"

They continue to talk for a few minutes. Georges watches Wilhelm yawn several times. He switches off the light, takes him by the hand and leads him to an unoccupied bedroom.

"You can sleep here tonight. I'll put some water in the jug."

His German friend has a quick wash and then throws himself onto the bed and falls asleep almost immediately.

The next day, Françoise and her children are ready early. Their house has been freed of its occupants and they can now move in. For the moment, they have only three suitcases to carry over the few yards between the two houses. Several trunks, which have been loaded onto another boat, should be delivered soon. Towards nine in the morning, Françoise knocks on Georges' door, but no-one answers. She soon gives up but scribbles a warm thank-you note, ending with "See you at the ball tonight." She passes the message under the door.

By midday, Françoise is well installed in her house. The beds are made. The clothes have been put away. She has found enough crockery in the cupboards to lay the table and the four of them eat their first post-war lunch in this house, which is rather large for them. The water pump in the kitchen is working, supplying the house with rainwater from the tank.

They then go for a walk around the large garden behind the house. Several of the young apple trees seem to be leaning. Apparently, the Germans used to tie their horses to them. The grass is tall and needs cutting with a scythe. They discover lots of fruit on the trees in the orchard: golden apricots that will soon be ripe, peaches with red highlights, firm pippin apples and very juicy pears. The children love them.

Françoise wants to modernize the furniture and decoration of the house. She has started to list the things she needs to buy and plans to go to the notary in Chagny to withdraw some money as soon as she can. It was with this man, Mr. Buisson, that she placed the money she inherited from her parents seven years previously. She has had no information about her riches since then. She can't wait to see how her investment has fared!

During the afternoon, she goes for a walk in the village and greets several people she meets. Her children become acquainted with other boys and girls from Morleau who, like them, will be going to the village school at the end of the summer. They have a lot of fun playing skittles and bowls, games of which have been set up for the national holiday. Agnes and Michel try to climb up a greasy pole, without success. Françoise takes them to the *Café Préteau* for a snack and some lemonade. It is there that a dancefloor has been installed for the ball in the evening. The first Bastille Day ball since the armistice!

Everywhere is decked out in red, white and blue. The café has been decorated with lots of small French flags and a long red, white and blue garland. Françoise is soberly dressed in a close-fitting light gray dress. She has a fine chain around her neck, and discreet eye make-up.

She arrives at the ball just before 8 p.m. The dancefloor is already crowded. The men are wearing suits and ties, probably the same ones they wore for their weddings. Several are wearing berets or hats. There are also women dancing together, as often happens in the country. Not all of them are emaciated from lack of food. Some of them seem to have no necks, in their Sunday-best dresses. Everyone is smiling and there is a feeling that the circumstances are unique.

The mayor comes over to ask Françoise how her move back into the house went. He then asks her to dance to "the Blue Danube", which the accordionist interprets with brio. Her friend Henri Joly, the former mayor, then comes over and brings her a glass of white wine. It's the first time that they have both been at a ball together. Before the war, Françoise and her husband never attended the ball. The social gap between them and the people of Morleau, a village she only came to for her vacation, was much too great!

Henri and Françoise sit down at a table so that they can talk more easily. Henri brings her up to date with news about the village, concerning the elections that took place in April and May. She tells him a bit about her life in Algeria, a country that no-one else in the village has ever been to. After a few minutes of conversation, Henri broaches the subject of Georges Guérin.

"How was your stay at Georges' place? He's a funny man, you know. Very intelligent. Initially a collaborator and then a member of the Resistance. How did you find him?"

"I found out that there are people who think he killed his first wife. He didn't dodge the issue when we were talking. He really helped us out by putting us up until the house was ready. I don't think he's a murderer. Was there a trial?"

"Yes! They found him not guilty. The analyses didn't show anything after they dug up the body. No proof, just suspicions."

"As for his role as a collaborator, I don't think he was the only one at the start of the war. He told me that he was very active in the Resistance afterwards. Is that true?"

"Yes, absolutely. He turned out to be very gifted at manipulating explosives! He blew up German communication lines and freight trains on their way to the Boche. Afterwards, he was almost certainly denounced and he had the Gestapo on his back."

"Were things tense here in Morleau during the German occupation of the village?"

"No, not really, up until 1943 anyway. Most of the German soldiers were courteous. What was hard and created tensions was the requisitions, the periodic obligation to provide them with the produce of our lands, potatoes, wheat, even wine and horses. It was the same in all the villages. As the mayor, I stayed on good terms with the guys from the *Wehrmacht*. The odd glass of white wine here and there, and they agreed to decrease the quotas they had imposed. It was fine until they introduced compulsory work service. Things went downhill from there and some of the young men from the village had to leave or went into hiding."

Françoise occasionally looks around to see if there is any sign of Georges Guérin.

"Does Georges Guérin generally come to the balls in the village? He said he would dance with me."

"Yes, usually. But he never stays long. He comes for a chat really. I've never seen him waltz! But maybe I'm wrong. Come on, why don't we dance?"

After several polkas and waltzes, the two friends return to their seats. Françoise asks Henri a few questions of a more personal nature.

"So, you're still single at 32? Don't you want to get married?"

"I'd love to, yes! Just a question of finding Miss Right!"

Françoise is astounded that her friend has never married. He is handsome, tall and strong, but also charming and cultivated, and he writes poetry.

Towards 10 o'clock, Françoise decides to go home. She leaves the ball, disappointed that her neighbor has stood her up, but hoping that nothing bad has happened to him.

15

RAUCEBY, UNITED KINGDOM, AUGUST 1945

A club, a heart, two non-trump cards. There are four of them in the same room, passing most of every afternoon playing bridge. Three young English officers needing surgery to deal with the consequences of burns, and one older and higher ranked officer, Colonel Destivel, who is champing at the bit and can't wait to leave the hospital. Only one of the men has the use of his right hand to write, and he is acting as the scribe for his friends when they want to send letters.

It's been almost a month since Phil had his skin graft. Dr. MacIndoe, who treated him after his accident in September 1944, has taken some skin from Phil's thigh and sewn it onto the back of his right hand. The operation went well and the surgeon has promised him superb esthetic and functional results. But Phil must be patient. He won't know until the end of August how things have actually turned out. His discharge from hospital is scheduled for the end of September.

For the moment, his right hand and his thigh are wrapped in thick bandages. In three days' time, these bandages should be replaced by thinner ones so that he can begin his rehabilitation.

Phil thinks about Victoria a lot and writes to her once a week. Her letters bring him words of love that move him. Each time, he reads and rereads them, again and again. Most are written in French because Victoria wants to get back into the habit of using this language that she will have to speak daily if she moves to Paris. She tells him what she has been up to, nicely describing her new paintings and how the babies are progressing.

Phil also takes care of his older children by correspondence. Paul and Claire have returned from Morocco and he is trying to organize their new life in Paris. He regularly sends Maggy instructions: - Sign Paul up for Buffon and Claire for Victor Duruy, two good high schools close to home, for the return to school in October,

- Buy some clothes, because it's much cooler and wetter in Normandy, where they will spend the end of August with their grandparents, than in Morocco in high summer,

- Sign the children up for the scouts and girl guides, to make sure that they have regular, cheap activities when they go back to school.

At the end of the morning, the nurses have to give Phil a bath. For that, they need to remove his bandages carefully. The process is less painful than during the first few weeks after the graft, but the sight of the uncovered wounds is still just as difficult to bear. The smell of ether, which he has never gotten used to, makes him feel sick.

When Phil looks at his hand and his thigh today, he shares his thoughts with the nurse.

"Just one thousand-pound bomb, stuck in the hold, exploded about 10 yards away from me when my plane was landing. It killed the other six crew members immediately! I survived because my seat was shielded. I was really lucky to make it out alive, but it's taking so long to heal! Four months in hospital the first time and probably three this time! Seven months for my burns to heal properly. It's frightful! I daren't even think about the damage our planes inflicted on the human populations when there were a thousand bombers with the same target. Lucky for us, the French mostly had military targets, but a lot of German towns were bombed by other RAF groups."

The surgeon comes to look at the grafted zone and is satisfied. The healing is going well. No sign of any infection! Phil goes back to his bed and lies down for a while. Jim, one of his roommates, returns to the room in a state of excitation.

"Come quickly and listen to the radio! The BBC is on in the rest room. There's some amazing news!"

All four men rush to listen to the radio.

"Early this morning, the Americans destroyed the town of Hiroshima in Japan with a terrifying new weapon: a nuclear bomb. A single bomb, dropped from a plane, destroyed most of this large town, killing more than a hundred thousand people in a matter of seconds. The Americans hope that the Japanese, discouraged and under the threat of a second atomic bomb, will surrender immediately, bringing an end to this conflict that continues to claim many victims daily in this region of the Pacific."

The three English airmen all took part in the destructive bombing of German towns, without precise strategic objectives. They had obeyed orders, but they felt guilty after these missions, even if the Boche were perfectly happy to bomb the center of London and other English towns with their planes and their famous V1 and V2 flying bombs. But this is on a completely different scale. The images that pass through their minds today are incredible. They can imagine themselves at the controls of the bomber dropping, for the first time in human history, such a small bomb capable of doing the work of a thousand four-motor heavy bombers in just a few seconds! The youngest of the airmen is shaken.

"Just think of it, Jim, you press the button to open the bomb hatch, and a couple of seconds later there are tens of thousands of people dead, burnt, carbonized, suffocated, fatally wounded! The entire population of a town! During our missions over Germany there was a whole fleet of us, five hundred or a thousand bombers. We had precise objectives, the bases launching V1s, the factories of the Ruhr. Now you only need one plane to do the work, with one bomb that destroys everything, without the precision of a strategic target. It's horrible! I'm resigning from the air force as soon as I get out of here. I can't stand that, it's apocalyptic!"

"But what if you kill fewer people in the end with a bomb like that? If the enemy gives in straight away, whereas the war would carry on for much longer with conventional means, with many more victims. At the end of the day, it saves lives."

"Perhaps, but these atomic bombs will be developed further. Countries with scientists will make loads of them. The whole planet will end up exploding in a huge firework display. The grand finale! Just imagine Hitler or some other mad dictator with a weapon like that. Good job the Germans weren't fast enough to get there first! No, I don't want anything to do with it. I'm going to protest with the pacifists! I'm through with the military!"

Phil is also thrown by the news and doesn't know what to think.

"It's too early to decide! We'll have to wait and see whether Japan surrenders."

But Japan doesn't want to surrender. On August 9, the Americans drop a second bomb on Nagasaki. Thousands more deaths in the blink of an eye! On August 17, Emperor Hirohito orders his troops to lay down their arms, the prelude to the end of the Second World War. The airmen hospitalized at Rauceby celebrate the news with dignity. Those authorized to drink a little alcohol make the most of the opportunity. The era of reconstruction can really begin now.

Phil hasn't heard from Victoria recently and is worried. He is finding it hard to concentrate on his games of bridge. His roommates find him morose. They end up asking him what's up, but he prefers not to say.

When Dr. MacIndoe next comes to see him, on August 20, it's the surgeon who is worried. Phil has a fever. An infection is developing and becoming painful on the back of Phil's right hand. The doctor prescribes penicillin again. Phil complains of a headache the next day and has trouble swallowing his food. The muscles of his right arm are contracting and it's very painful. He can't move his face. On August 24, he is transferred to the infectious diseases department. He is alone in a room in which silence reigns. The diagnosis is redoubtable. No-one knows how it happened, but Colonel Destivel has contracted tetanus.

16

MORLEAU IN BURGUNDY, FRANCE, AUGUST 1945

Georges, Françoise's neighbor, stood her up on July 14. He didn't turn up to the village ball despite agreeing to meet her there. She has had no news of him for a month. He hasn't been seen in Morleau. His house is silent. Letters are piling up in his mailbox. The postman regularly knocks at the door, but no-one answers. It's strange though. Françoise speaks about it with her friend Henri, the former mayor, who provides her with some extra information.

"You know, I think I might have seen him on the night of the ball, at the wheel of his car with a passenger in the front. Just before you arrived. The car was heading south towards Chagny or Chalon-sur-Saone. But I'm not sure about that. It's not unusual for him to go away anyhow. I'm sure he'll be back soon. Do you miss him?"

"I thought he was nice. You know, I'm starting to get bored here. It's depressing to think that I might have to stay in Morleau all year. What's more, I saw the notary yesterday. I'd placed all my money with him, and it hasn't brought in much. He used my cash to buy shares in companies that were badly hit by the war. I haven't got much left. I'll have to live on my war-widow's pension until the stock market goes up again, if it ever does! With three kids to bring up, I'm going to find it a bit hard to make ends meet! I'll have to find a job, but I can't imagine what for the moment. I don't know how to do anything, other than being a mother!"

"You should remarry instead! Find yourself a rich vintner from Puligny or Chassagne. Wine sales will soon go up again and Montrachet wines are very prestigious!"

"But I'm not for sale! I know you're only joking, and I would love to marry someone rich, but not for his money! How about you? When are you planning to get married?"

"I'll let you into a little secret. I recently met a girl called Emilie. She's the daughter of a vintner from Puligny. I really like her and we're thinking about getting engaged soon."

This news is no great source of delight to Françoise, who appreciates the fact that her friend Henri is single. Becoming a widow has brought her closer to him. They have a lot in common. They are the same age, neither has any attachment and they live in the same village. She is worried that he won't pay any attention to her anymore if he is in love with a young woman that he hopes to marry.

Another event is also making Françoise sad: the repatriation of her husband's body, from Algeria, on August 13, a Monday. The ceremony is very sober and she is there with her children for his burial in Morleau cemetery. Agnes, who adored her father, is in tears. This new burial takes Françoise back two years, to when she lived through the drama of being widowed, just a fortnight after giving birth. The period that followed had been horrible. She had been glad to leave Algeria, but now she finds that her life as a widow was simpler and happier there. She's finding it hard to get used to living in Morleau, where she feels isolated.

On August 15, the village church is packed full of people for the Assumption service, even though not all the inhabitants are religious. Some prefer to go to the café while their wives, who are more devoted, go to sing at the service. And then there are the communists, increasingly numerous in these parts. A number of the inhabitants are not vintners. Instead, they work in the tile factory at Chagny or in the flourmills on the Saone plain. These people are openly anti-religious. But this religious festival is, together with Easter, amongst those attracting the largest numbers of people.

Françoise arrives at the mass five minutes before the start of the service. She sits with her children, in the second row, on the right. The inhabitants of the village have their own places in church. It's not official, but has been confirmed by years of practice. During the sermon, Françoise finds it hard to concentrate and her mind wanders. She doesn't really listen to the priest's speech and starts wondering who she will meet on leaving the church, because, at the end of the mass, the parishioners greet each other, often staying to chat for a good quarter of an hour.

She remains lost in her thoughts until the communion. Her two sons are finding the time long and begin to make a noise. She glares at them and then tells them off. After the last *"ite missa est"*, rather than returning directly to the vestry, the priest comes over to her to offer her some words of comfort after the burial of her husband. She is touched by his attention to her, but the priest is very talkative and she is worried that she will not get to see the people she was hoping to talk to outside the church. The conversation finally comes to an end and she can, at last, leave the church. How disappointing! There is no-one left! The route home takes Françoise and her children past the cemetery.

"Come on, let's go and say a little prayer over your father's grave."

Françoise takes advantage of the moment to talk to them about their father, saying that he is in heaven watching over them. As they leave the cemetery, they hear a voice.

"Hello Françoise. How are you? And how are the kids?"

"Oh! Georges! You vanished! I'm so glad to see you again."

"Yes, I'm sorry. I had to go to Paris in a hurry for business. It wasn't planned. I got a telegram. I didn't have time to let you know. I'm sorry. I got the official confirmation of the death of my wife at Ravensbruck in March. I was expecting it, but that isn't quite the same thing as being sure."

Françoise offers her condolences and kisses him on both cheeks. They walk back to their homes together.

"Come to lunch with us next Saturday, if you're free," suggests Françoise as they say goodbye. "I'll show you my house. I'd like your opinion about a few changes I want to make."

"Yes, OK. I'd like that. I'll come. But don't make too much effort for the lunch, I'm no ogre! I'll bring some red wine."

Saturday soon arrives. It's still very difficult to get hold of food. Françoise has managed to lay hands on a chicken and some potatoes. She gathers some fruit from the garden to make a fruit salad. Some slices of salami cooked with garlic will do for the starter. One of the inhabitants of the village gives her some soft cheese and some sour cream.

It is a beautiful hot summer's day in Morleau. Françoise is dressed lightly, but smartly, in a white blouse and a gray skirt. A Berber necklace encrusted with red and yellow stones that she brought back from Algeria lies at her throat. Some lipstick, also somewhat carmine in color. A high bun on her head. Very simple, but very elegant too.

Georges is on time and rings his neighbor's doorbell at 12.30 precisely. He is also simply dressed. He is slim and his blue shirt suits him. He has shaved off his moustache and looks younger than before. Not a day over 45! The children have promised to behave and the two eldest will eat at table with them, although they are not allowed to talk. Romain, the youngest, is having a nap. Agnes, who is 12, has made a point of wearing her prettiest dress.

During lunch, they talk a lot about the reconstruction of France, and the forthcoming parliamentary elections, which will take place in two months' time. These will be the first national elections since the German surrender. Women and military personnel have the right to vote. Françoise has never voted before. She no longer has a husband to tell her what to do, and she is determined to make up her own mind.

After the meal, Françoise shows Georges around her house, which seems to interest him a great deal! He suggests improvements to some of the rooms as if he would shortly be living there himself. Upstairs, she shows him all the bedrooms, including her own, which looks out in two directions, over the Saone plain to the south and towards the hills and the quarries of Chassagne to the north.

"I'm sure you must be very comfortable in this large well-lit bedroom." says Georges.

"The room is lovely, but a bit lonely," she replies with a sigh.

Georges smiles sympathetically. The visit ends with the office-cum-library installed in the tower at the corner of the building.

"I'd love to have an office like this!" enthuses Georges.

They are alone and Georges continues "Maybe we should think about being lonely together? I could be a father figure for your children. We've both been widowed. I'm older than you, but perhaps not too old? Do you think there's any hope for me?"

Françoise can hardly believe what she has just heard, particularly as she finds Georges rather charming, even if he is almost

20 years older than she is. But she knows that she shouldn't throw herself into the arms of someone she doesn't know very well, particularly when his past has been a bit sulfurous. But she gives him an encouraging response anyway.

"Let's get to know each other better. We'll see where that leads us."

Georges then takes his leave, cheekily, suggesting that they take a trip to Verdun on the Doubs with the children in three days' time. If the weather is up to it, they can swim in the Saone.

Back at home, Georges daydreams about the future. He can already see himself as a chatelain, living in Françoise's house. He finds her very beautiful and elegant. He has a few secrets to hide, of course, but they shouldn't be too hard to keep under wraps. On Françoise's side, Georges' discreet and respectful advances have opened up a whole new perspective, making her see Morleau differently.

They leave by car, with a picnic, for Verdun on the appointed day. Just under 20 miles, rapidly covered by George's Peugeot 202. Everyone sings in the car. The children love bathing in the river. The seaside was very pleasant in Algeria, with the warm sea. At Verdun, where the Doubs flows into the Saone, a little beach has been created. The more audacious can slide into the water at speed, in a wheeled cart that runs down a vertiginous wooden slide. Agnes and Michel are not scared and hurtle down the slide several times. Françoise and Georges put on their bathing suits in one of the little wooden cabins reserved for bathers. They study each other discreetly, analyzing their respective forms out of the corner of an eye. They each find the other attractive. Georges is muscular, almost athletic. Françoise has harmonious curves. Her black one-piece swimsuit, which is wet after a first swim in the river, sticks to her skin and reveals the form of a bust that is still firm, the nipples visible under the material. Georges cannot help but say "You suggested that we get to know each other better. I think we're headed in the right direction! Your swimsuit is perfect for you. You look lovely!"

Françoise doesn't reply, but smiles, thinking at the same time that Georges isn't bad either, in his navy blue swimming trunks. After lunch, the children play together while the adults sunbathe. They must wait at least two hours after eating before they are allowed to go back into the water, to make sure that they digest properly. Towards five in the afternoon, they all go into the water one last time before heading off to a cake shop in Verdun for a treat.

Two days later, Georges invites Françoise and her children on a hike to *la Roche Dumay*. They leave from Morleau, about three miles from their destination. Romain stays in the village with a neighbor, as he is still too young for such an outing. They pass through Puligny and they climb to the hamlet of Blagny. Their route then takes them towards Gamay. They veer off to the right to climb to a cavern carved into the hill. Georges has some food in his backpack. On the way, he plays hide-and-seek with Agnes and her brother in the vineyards they cross. Françoise is glad to see the children happy and enjoying themselves with this man who seems so at ease with them.

Georges tells Françoise that he stayed hidden close to the cavern for several weeks at the end of the war, with a reserve of explosives that the Germans had never found. He even tells her a secret.

"I still have a hiding place near here. I've hidden lots of money there. And gold! But don't tell anyone!"

When they go their separate ways, Georges hugs Françoise and kisses her gently on the cheek, murmuring "I'm very lucky to have met you." Françoise is charmed and wonders where all this will lead.

The next morning, Françoise has a problem. The pump that supplies her kitchen with water isn't working. No water in the house. What a catastrophe! She doesn't know what to do and decides to go and ask her neighbor Georges for help, as he seems to be very good at solving technical problems. The door of the house is ajar and she enters without knocking. There is no-one in the large living room, but she can hear voices from Georges' bedroom and music from a turntable. She heads towards the bedroom, where she hears a voice saying "Georges, I'm so happy to have found you again. It's as if all those horrible years that separated us never happened."

Curious, Françoise advances to the door, which is half-closed. She sees two men lying on a large bed. She rapidly recognizes Georges, who is entirely naked. At his side is a younger man, also naked, with his face hidden by the sheets. She can hardly believe her eyes when they kiss each other full on the mouth, clasping each other, with certain details of their anatomy leaving her in no doubt as to their mutual excitation. Horrified, Françoise rapidly runs away, very ill at ease. The conclusion is clear: Georges may have been married twice, but he also likes men. She has met a charming neighbor who has all but proposed to her but who likes to go to bed with men. It's incredible! What a disappointment! And who is the man behaving so tenderly with him?

She returns home in consternation, not knowing whether her neighbor became aware of her presence when she stifled a cry of stupefaction.

17

PARIS, FRANCE, SEPTEMBER 1945

Victoria has taken a great leap in the dark. She has decided to rent an apartment in Paris, where she now intends to live. She has just moved in, with the twins and Peggy, her cousin, who will continue to look after the children. Her friend Serge has kept his word. He has found her an apartment to rent just opposite the *Jardin du Luxembourg*.

Victoria hasn't received any letters from Phil recently because she stayed in a hotel for a few days when she arrived at the end of August, and she didn't have time to send him her temporary address. This morning, she writes a letter to surprise him with news of her move.

My darling Phil,
I have some important news for you. I have moved! The road in which I am now living carries the name of one of the most famous airmen in French history. I'm now living at 14 bis rue Guynemer. That's right, I'm in Paris! In the 6ᵗʰ arrondissement! Serge, an old Russian friend of mine found me an apartment to rent on the 5ᵗʰ floor of a beautiful building. I think you would describe it as "Hausmannian". The view over the Jardin du Luxembourg is superb. I also have a large room in the eaves, on the 6ᵗʰ floor. It's very bright and luminous, and I will use it as my studio for painting. Peggy came with me and will carry on helping with the twins, who are doing well and send a big sloppy kiss to Colonel Destivel.

Now, all we need is you. I can't wait to see you again, in the beautiful capital of your country...

Victoria would have liked to have seen Phil's face when he read the letter. But, of course, that isn't possible. He seems to her to be very much in love and he expresses a strong desire to find a solution so that they can continue their love story, which, from the start, has been greatly perturbed by the war.

However, a few major unknowns are making the situation more complicated. When he leaves Rauceby Hospital, Phil will return to France. But, where will he be sent next? Having been married to Colonel Miller, Victoria is well placed to know that officers can be sent to the four corners of the earth, particularly by great colonial powers such as Britain and France. Maybe she was a bit hasty to leave London? A decision of the heart rather than the head.

Fortunately, Victoria's life in Paris is very busy. She has little time to dwell on the uncertainties of her future. Her friend Serge is always around and helps her to renew her links with the milieu of abstract painting, which has become more active since the end of the war. She has been invited to the private viewing of an exhibition at the Jean-Louis Gallery, *avenue de Messine*, in three days' time. Paintings by several artists of various ages will be displayed. She is hoping to recognize some of the painters, and to meet Jean-Louis Raqué, the owner of the gallery.

On the day of the viewing, Serge picks her up at the apartment and accompanies her. He knows lots of artists and has promised Victoria that he will introduce her to people who might be able to help her. The viewing has attracted a large crowd. The champagne is flowing freely and people are talking in front of the paintings. Victoria notices several paintings that she really likes, including one in particular by Poliakoff, a painter that she knew in Paris before the war. They had chatted for hours about abstract art.

Poliakoff had given her some very useful advice that she had followed at the time when creating her own works.

"Nicolai, come over here! This is Victoria, a good friend of mine. She's a British artist who has just arrived in Paris. She couldn't stand being separated from me any longer! I absolutely adore her! Victoria, this is Baron Nicolai Vladimirovitch Staël von Holstein[7]. Have you seen his painting over there? A bit dark maybe, but fantastic nevertheless."

Nicolai comes over to say hello to Victoria, who asks him to tell her about his painting. She really likes this artist, in his thirties and very handsome, even more so than his paintings! They chat together for half an hour. She gives him her address and asks him to come and see her when he has time. She would be delighted to show him the paintings she has been working on recently.

Serge also introduces her to the owner of the gallery, Jean-Louis, a very serious man in his fifties, or perhaps a bit older, with a flattop. He spontaneously asks Victoria for her address in Paris. He would like to see what she does, as he is looking for new talent to display in an exhibition that he is organizing for November. Victoria asks him to come and see her whenever he wants, but preferably at lunchtime.

Serge asks Victoria to go to dinner in Montparnasse with him and a few Russian painters and their companions. She is delighted to accept.

"You're wonderful for introducing me to so many people Serge. They are all so jolly. It's just like Paris before the war. I'm sure I won't regret moving here."

"You'll see. I heard a few comments at the gallery. Lots of people found you very attractive. You're going to be very busy now

[7] *The painter Nicolas de Staël.*

that you're a widow and free! I'm going to get very jealous when they start buzzing round you!"

When she walks home after dining with the artists, Victoria is in a euphoric mood. Thanks to her friend Serge, she is already in contact with the director of a gallery that displays the creations of unconventional painters. Her cousin Peggy is still up when she opens the door to her apartment. They start chatting about their respective days. Victoria tells Peggy about her new contacts with great enthusiasm.

"I think that Jean-Louis, the director of the gallery I went to this afternoon, is going to come here one of these days to see my work. Just think about what might happen if he likes one of my paintings! He said he could put one of my paintings in his next exhibition in November. That would be fantastic! I'm going to have to work flat out to have enough paintings to show him."

Peggy has some information of her own to divulge and tells Victoria that, when she went to the *Jardin du Luxembourg* with the twins that afternoon, a young man sat down next to her on the bench and started talking to her.

"He was really nice. A Breton who spoke English really well. We had a long chat and we are going to continue our conversation next week, on the same bench. I'll find out more about him, if he turns up."

Two days after the private viewing, at four in the afternoon, Victoria is in her studio, in her painting clothes and wearing a large white apron already covered in paint stains. She is coloring in some pretty geometric forms that she has drawn on the canvas in charcoal. While Peggy is out taking the babies for a walk in the *Jardin du Luxembourg*, she hears the doorbell ring. On opening the door, she recognizes Jean-Louis Raqué.

"Come in Jean-Louis. Sorry I look such a mess. I was working in my studio. Follow me and I will show you my paintings."

Victoria has six paintings to show him. She explains herself by telling him about some of what has happened to her, including the destruction of her paintings at Gaitford by a German fighter that crashed into her studio, and coming to Paris with her children.

"Ah! You have children, so you are married. I thought you were single."

"I'm a widow. My husband died a few months ago, when I was pregnant. I had the twins after he died. My cousin came to Paris with me and she looks after the babies a lot. It's thanks to her that I can carry on painting."

Jean-Louis stops in front of one of the paintings, an abstract composition completed the day before, combining elongated, regular forms in soft shades of green and gray. The overall effect is very harmonious.

"Can I take this one away with me? I love it. If it's OK with you, I'd like to display it in the November exhibition. We'll have to talk about the sale price and I will need some biographical information about you. The story about the destruction of your paintings by a German plane is very moving. We mustn't leave that out. But, just one question: do you have enough money to live on and enough time to paint?"

"Yes, I'm well-off financially and I can spend about half my time painting. And, you know, I really want to make up for lost time."

Jean-Louis hurries off, the painting under his arm, leaving Victoria completely stunned. One of her paintings is going to be displayed alongside those of the great abstract painters, so soon after her arrival in Paris! A well-known gallery owner who trusts her. How wonderful! She must tell Phil about that straight away. She writes to him immediately, explaining what has just happened.

18

RAUCEBY, UNITED KINGDOM, SEPTEMBER 1945

Phil begins to emerge from his torpor to discover, with some astonishment, his hospital room and his bandages. He hasn't had any pain for the last few days. The doctors have been decreasing the dose of sedatives administered to him over the last three weeks. They were afraid that they were going to lose him, but, fortunately, the tetanus remained restricted to his limbs. His respiratory muscles were not affected. With some difficulty, he asks the nurse looking after him what day it is.

"It's the 12th of September," she explains, "You've been here for three weeks. I see you're feeling a bit brighter this morning. You had tetanus, but you're going to get better. You've had a lucky escape! And the skin graft is fine too. Look, you've only got a light bandage and the part of your thigh they used for the graft has completely healed."

Phil makes a great effort to think straight and asks if he has had any post while he has been here. The nurse leaves the room and comes back with two letters.

"Colonel, we informed your family that you had a few health problems that made it impossible for you to write, but we didn't tell them that you had contracted tetanus."

Phil is feeling too weak to open his letters and read them himself so he asks the nurse to do it for him. But the letters are written in French and the nurse has such difficulty reading them that Phil finds it hard to understand what they say. The first letter is from Maggy. Everything seems to be fine in Paris and the children will be going back to school soon.

When he sees that the second letter is from Victoria, his face lights up. However, the nurse reads French so badly that he doesn't understand a word. He ends up asking for the letter and manages to read it on his own. He is extremely happy to learn that she has taken the plunge and moved to Paris. He can't help but find the current situation stupid: him, a Frenchman in the middle of England, confined to a hospital room, and her, his darling, in Paris waiting for him with the twins!

Phil's physical condition rapidly improves and he is able to start the rehabilitation exercises for his hand. His surgeon has given him a foam ball that he has to knead all day. At the end of the third week in September, they take off the last bandages. The grafted zone has healed well and his hand looks almost normal. He can hardly believe it.

One day, a visitor is announced and he has the surprise of seeing John Luxley appear before him.

"Hello Phil! I had trouble finding you again. I called the base at Gaitford to ask for your address and here I am! Oh! Your hand looks perfect. They really know how to look after burns here. I'm so happy for you. I suppose you'll be going back to France soon?"

"Yes, at the end of next week I hope. Seven months in hospital in all during my two stays at Rauceby. You wouldn't believe how long that feels. On top of that, I managed to get tetanus. I was lucky to survive. I've only just recovered. But now I'm going to be able to return to my children and friends, and a normal life. It's nice of you to come and see me. So how are you? I see you're not using a cane anymore."

"My fractures have completely healed. A few scars, but I'm basically OK. I've gone back to work at Oxford University, but I'm finding it hard to settle for the minute. I applied for a post at Princeton in the United States, but that particular dream is over. They just turned me down. I'm looking into other possibilities elsewhere at the moment."

Phil and John carry on talking about the end of the war and the atomic bomb. Both had been part of the armada of bombers that had left to attack Germany, each with their own weapons, contributing to the success of the operation. Both are struck by the dramatic shift in warfare marked by the destruction of Hiroshima.

"At a push, just one plane, one pilot and one bomb would be enough to win a war now. The supremacy of the Americans is overwhelming while they are the only ones with nuclear technology. But what will happen when another country gets hold of this type of bomb? I imagine the Russian scientists are working round the clock to get there. The pressures on them must be enormous."

Phil is as perplexed as John in the face of this new reality. Phil has become the medical team's favorite patient and, as such, he easily obtains permission to invite John to lunch in his room. The nurse even finds them a bottle of red wine to accompany the meal.

Phil hasn't drunk any alcohol for several weeks and the sedatives enhance its effects. Phil rapidly loses his inhibitions and talks more openly to John than he might otherwise have done.

"Do you know, John, you turned my life upside-down the day we met. Do you remember? You showed me mathematically, by a simple probability calculation, that I had less than a one in two chance of getting out alive!"

"That was on the day we first met, the day the V1 got me! My memories of that day are very vague. How did I turn your life upside-down? It seems to me that it was more a case of me being turned upside-down that day, blown to bits even!"

"No, let me explain. I met a lovely English woman, the wife of a colonel, but her husband was in a prisoner-of-war camp in Germany. We were attracted to each other, but I thought it would be really bad to seduce the wife of an Allied officer, and one imprisoned in Germany to boot. I absolutely refused to do that. And then, thanks to your calculations, I was persuaded that I wasn't going to get out alive and I changed my mind. I decided to live life to the full in the days I had left."

"And that really changed your life?"

"Yes, it really did. We fell in love, me and this woman. Her husband escaped from Germany, but he died shortly afterwards. We saw each other again then."

"And?"

"I'll tell you the rest another day, if we see each other again."

John is tactful and doesn't try to find out more, even though he is dying to know if Phil is still seeing his beautiful conquest.

"But, John, you should tell me a bit more about yourself if we're going to get personal."

"Oh, I've got interested in politics lately. I think our social system is very unfair. I want to work towards greater equality between citizens. At Oxford, one of my mathematician friends takes me to meetings. It's all very interesting. I'm reading a book by Karl Marx to try to improve my knowledge. Some of it is much more difficult to understand than mathematics! This war has brought us closer to the Russians, who were impressive allies and fighters."

They carry on talking until the middle of the afternoon. As John is about to leave, Phil gives him his address in Paris so that he can write to him, if he has time.

Phil's last few days at Rauceby pass very quickly. He leaves the hospital at the end of September. A Halifax from the Gaitford base takes him back to Paris. He is relieved to have got through this trial successfully and is happy with his new hand. He has had no esthetic or functional problems due to his burns and he is now ready for his new life.

19

MARSEILLES AND THE COTE D'AZUR, FRANCE, SEPTEMBER 1945

"Wilhelm, put all your things in this suitcase. We're leaving in an hour. Surprise!"

"We're leaving? But why? We're fine here!"

Georges Guérin is desperate in Morleau! He heard a cry in his house, and the footsteps of someone leaving. Someone must have entered his house and seen them together, in bed, enjoying themselves. But Georges was unable to identify the intruder who discovered them. If it was his neighbor, Françoise, whom he would like to marry, it's a catastrophe! All his plans are in tatters. She'll probably talk about them and incite indignation. If it was another of the inhabitants of Morleau, the news will be around the village in no time and that will be the start of mockery and jeers, and even insults! Georges doesn't have much time to think. Best to get away from there with Wilhelm! Then he'll think about what to do.

Georges thinks it is most likely that the intruder was Françoise. He needs to shut her up so that she doesn't say anything to anyone about what she might have seen. Georges takes a sheet of writing paper and a pencil.

Dear Françoise,

Unforeseen events have forced me to leave Morleau in a hurry. I have learnt that some old acquaintances familiar with my actions in the Resistance have it in for me and are trying to find me. Don't talk about our friendship or plans, or of me either, to anyone, because they might attack you and your children. I'll send you a more detailed letter later, with an address, so that we can write to each other. I hope you understand the meaning of this letter.

Yours affectionately,

Georges

Georges discreetly places this ambiguous letter in his neighbor's mailbox, without being seen.

An hour later, Georges and Wilhelm are in the car heading towards the South of France. Georges explains to his companion that he thinks it would be better to leave Morleau for a while, as he is worried that the French Police are after him and he does not want to be interrogated about his activities with the PPF during the early years of the war.

They arrive at Lyons during the evening. They sleep in separate rooms at the hotel and leave early in the morning. Georges promises his friend that he won't be disappointed tonight, when they arrive at their destination. He says that they will stay for a while on the Cote d'Azur, without indicating exactly where they are going, and says that they are going to have a good time. Wilhelm doesn't know this part of France, but he has heard a lot about it. It will be like an unplanned vacation for him and his sweetheart.

They speak little and initially travel a long distance on the national trunk road. They then travel along smaller roads that Georges seems to know well. He has no need to consult a map or to ask his way. Wilhelm dozes in the early afternoon, after their picnic, lulled by the purring of the motor. Georges lets him nap for almost an hour and then gently wakes him.

"Wake up sleepyhead! We're nearly there. I must absolutely start calling you William, and you will have to get used to it. The best thing would be for us to speak English. Don't forget that you are American. No-one must suspect your real nationality. You'll remember that won't you?"

"OK Boss!" replies his friend, with a broad grin on his face.

Another quarter of an hour in the car. Close to a village, Georges turns off onto a dirt road on the left. There are lots of stone pines and a few sparse villas, visibly uninhabited. The sky is bright blue and it's agreeably warm. They can hear the sound of cicadas in the gardens. George stops in front of a gate and gets out of the car, with a set of keys in his hand. He opens the gate without difficulty. He drives the car through the gateway and parks it in a place where it cannot be seen from the road. The two men then follow a sinuous pathway that gradually narrows and leads to a small bungalow that is not visible from the road.

"Surprise! Welcome to my house in the South of France! I bought it two years before the war. Not many people come here, but we're near a town called Cassis. It's a marvelous place, you'll see. We're only a couple of hundred yards from the Mediterranean. The coast is beautiful. I haven't been here since the middle of '42, more than three years ago! The garden's completely overgrown. Come on! Let's see what kind of state the house is in!"

The lock has not been forced. What a miracle! The exuberant vegetation in the unmaintained garden must have discouraged uninvited guests. The interior of the house is very simple. Whitewashed walls, a kitchen, one bedroom and a small room with a sofa bed and two bicycles. There is a shower outside that they can use to cool off. Once the water and electricity have been switched back on, there is running water and the lights come on. In the cupboards, Georges finds the crockery that he had left there, together with sheets and covers for the beds.

They rapidly clean the place up. Georges scrubs the kitchen and William sweeps the floors. Together, they make the beds. They are both delighted to find themselves in such splendid isolation from the rest of the world.

"Come on, let's go for a walk around the house. There are some lovely paths not far away."

Their progress northwards is slow, because the path has not been maintained. They have to skirt around the brambles that have developed. Georges has picked up a stick, which he uses to push the branches out of their way.

"Look where we are. It's cultivated here. Vines. They make some good wine in Cassis. Red and white. The hills are so beautiful. We'll stay out of the way though, because the grapes will be harvested soon and there are lots of people in the vines at the moment."

William admires the surrounding hills, all of which have been planted with vines. They make a litter on the ground from the tall dry grass, and they lie on it, side by side, holding hands. William says to Georges "I'm not sorry to have taken so many risks to find you. It's good to be here together, the two of us."

They stay like that for a good hour, talking to each other tenderly and reciting poems quietly in German and French. They also make plans for the following days.

"Tomorrow morning, we'll go to the village. I'll show you the seashore and the port. There must be restaurants open. Another day, we'll go and see the *calanques*. You'll see, it's incredibly beautiful."

The evening is warm. After a good dinner eaten on covers laid down in a corner of the garden that they had cleared, they rapidly move to the bedroom, away from prying eyes, where they manifest their mutual attraction.

At the end of the following morning, Georges and William walk to the village together. There are lots of people in the street, lots of work going on. The laborers are bare-chested and are removing rubble, undoubtedly generated by the war.

"The port is at the end of this road. The view is wonderful. And we can buy some fish."

Georges likes to go to the port via this dark road, which is suddenly illuminated as it reaches the sea. The war already seems a long way behind him. He is happy to show his young, very handsome friend around the Cote d'Azur.

When they arrive at the end of the road, Georges can hardly believe his eyes. There are two large ships, lying on their sides at the entrance to the port, casting a desolate atmosphere over this dear place.

"Excuse me," he asks a passerby, "do you know when those two boats sank?"

"The boats? The big one is the Sampiero Corso. It's a recent boat, more than a hundred yards long. It was taking passengers to Corsica. The other one, the smaller one, is the President Dal Piaz. The Germans didn't have enough boats, so they requisitioned them and incorporated them into their fleet. They were torpedoed in June '44, on the 22nd if I remember rightly."

"Torpedoed or sabotaged? Why would the Germans destroy boats that were useful to them?"

"No, it was an Allied submarine that torpedoed them before the Provencal landings, to weaken the German fleet. It was entirely justifiable, but now the boats are spoiling the view here and they get in the fishermen's way."

Georges is disappointed. It will probably take months to restore the beautiful pre-war appearance of this port.

The next day, Georges and William go as far as Marseilles. They aren't there to visit the town, but to visit Giorgio, one of Georges' contacts, who should be able to make a false American passport for William. Giorgio runs the *Café de la Victoire*, which has recently opened close to the opera house. Georges and Giorgio got to know each other and helped out in the PPF, when relations were at their best with the Germans. Like Georges, Giorgio chose to join the Resistance in 1943. He now has contacts with some of the staff at the American Consulate. The request made by Georges and William does not strike him as odd. They just have to pay, and the asking price is not anodyne. Dollars and gold pieces are accepted, even encouraged, but not French money. Giorgio takes William to his cellar, where he takes several photographs of him. These photos will be used to make the passport, which should be ready in a week. He seems to be used to this type of transaction. At the end of the meeting, Georges hands him an envelope full of notes. The meeting has taken half an hour.

In the following days, Georges shows his friend the treasures of the Cote d'Azur. They go for long walks along the coastal paths. They often bathe in the water, swim and then read and sunbathe on the sand for hours, without being disturbed. They visit towns and spend several days in Nice. They stay at the Benedictine monastery at Cimiez, where Georges has the chutzpah to seek out a monk he knew just before the war. William loves this town and wants to stay here for as long as possible. They also discover Entrevaux, a town located further inland, in the *Alpes de Haute Provence*, that they reach by train from Nice. They climb small peaks, returning exhausted and sleeping like cherubs. They wonder what the future has in store for them, but they both know that they need to put their questions aside for the moment, so that they can enjoy the present without worrying about tomorrow. You don't live through many periods like this in the course of a life!

On the way back, they pass through Marseilles again, to see Giorgio and recuperate the American passport for William Robins, a journalist by profession. Several false stamps attest to the use of this document since 1944. Giorgio assures them that it will be impossible to identify it as a fake.

Back at Cassis, they leave early one morning to go walking in the *calanques*. After an hour or so, they go down onto a deserted beach that is very difficult to get to due to the low concrete walls built by the Germans to make landings along this coast more difficult. But these minor fortifications do not impede their passage on foot, as they were above all designed to prevent motorized vehicles from progressing too rapidly.

The beach is deserted, and they take great pleasure in swimming naked in the warm water and then drying each other off away from prying eyes. However, their intimacy is disturbed by a group of eight men, who arrive on the beach armed with picks and shovels. They also strip off and dive into the waves. They are very exuberant and they shout loudly and make lots of noise. William listens.

"Do you hear that Georges? It's strange but those workmen are speaking German!"

"That's hardly surprising. They're prisoners of war. There are loads of them in France. Some of them were caught in Italy or Germany by the Allies and then sent to France. It looks like they're being employed here to destroy the fortifications built on Nazi orders."

"Would you like to go and say hello?" he adds sarcastically.

"Shut up! It's odd for me to see them working here while I am on vacation."

"They're not unhappy. They're better off here than in Germany. I think they are even paid a basic wage. They have to go back to their lodgings at night, but they are pretty much free during the day. They have to do the jobs they have been given, but there is no-one watching over them."

"I'd rather we left now, if you don't mind."

They get up, get dressed and climb up the slope towards the walls. On the way, they have to pass by the prisoners at work. A stone rolls under William's shoe and he trips and falls over. He can't help but swear and a loud cry emanates from his mouth.

"*Cheise*[8]!"

William has expressed himself in German and the whole group looks around, astonished. One of the prisoners stares at William for a long time, taking in the details of his appearance.

"It's Wilhelm!" he declares in German, as he approaches. "How incredible to see you here! I can see it's you even with the beard. What are you doing here? How come you're free?"

William looks at him, startled, and then pulls himself together and replies in English.

"Sorry, I don't understand what you are saying."

---

[8] *Shit*

But the German answers him, in bad English "Perhaps, but we know each other before, loved each other even. In Stalingrad, you remember I think? That you cannot forget. I know the scar on your neck. And you swear in German."

William does, indeed, have a scar, from a burn, circular and about an inch and a half across, on his neck. He keeps walking, climbs over the wall and joins Georges, who has heard nothing of the conversation. They continue their walk in the *calanques*. William is reluctant to tell Georges about what happened with the German prisoners, but he eventually steels his nerve to explain.

"Did you hear what happened back there? One of the German prisoners recognized me! What a surprising coincidence. We were friends in Stalingrad. I told him in English that I didn't understand German, but I didn't fool him. He remembered the scar on my neck!"

Georges reflects for a few seconds and his face gradually darkens.

"But that's disastrous! We can't stay in Cassis. We must leave. We should even separate. If the French police identify you, I'll end up in prison for a long time, and you too!"

They end their walk and Georges decides to close up the house and leave. As they depart, he hands his friend some money and curtly says "Here's some money. We will go to Marseilles station and you will buy a ticket for Paris. We have to go our separate ways. I'm sorry! But it's every man for himself now!"

William understands that it's the end of their idyll and remains silent. Georges stops close to the station.

"We had a good time but it's over now. Don't ever talk about this to anyone. Good luck!"

William is left dumbfounded and alone on the sidewalk, suitcase in hand, as he watches Georges hurtle off at speed. He hasn't left an address or any means of correspondence. William is in no hurry to enter the station and instead sits down on a bench. He understands that his friend has dropped him like a hot potato after he has taken so many risks and covered so many miles to find him in France. An incomprehensible breakup as they were so happy together on the Cote d'Azur. Georges must really have some skeletons in his closet to have been so afraid of being found in the company of a German carrying fake American identity papers.

William meditates for a long time on his bench. After an hour or so, he decides to stay in Marseilles for a while and finds a room in a discreet hotel close to the café where they went to see Giorgio to get his forged papers.

Meanwhile, Georges drives very fast on the narrow roads heading due north towards Lyons. He isn't sorry to have dumped William, even though the last two weeks have been fun. William was handsome and nice, but it's nevertheless the fault of that damned German that his matrimonial plans are likely to go awry. He decides to return to Morleau, to talk to Françoise. Maybe she didn't see him in bed with William after all? He has to be sure before giving up on her.

It is not until the last moment that George sees the horse-drawn cart blocking the road just after a bend. He turns the steering wheel hard to the right to avoid it and crashes at full speed into a plane tree along the edge of the road. His forehead smashes violently into the windscreen and he dies instantly!

20

PARIS, FRANCE, OCTOBER 1945

The Halifax bringing Colonel Destivel back to France lands at Villacoublay aerodrome towards 4 p.m. Suitcase in hand, Phil descends the steps of the mobile staircase brought out to the plane. It's a bit chilly in the Parisian region at the start of October this year. He puts on his air force raincoat. He looks better dressed this way, with his cap decorated with gold stripes.

The formalities are rapidly completed. A chauffeur-driven car is waiting for him, to take him wherever he wants to go in Paris. Two days of freedom before his meeting with the Air Force Chief of Defense Staff.

"Take me to the 15ᵗʰ *arrondissement*, the start of *rue Lecourbe*, near the Metro line that runs above ground. Do you know the way?"

"Yes Sir, no problem."

Phil hasn't told anyone exactly when he will be coming back and will surprise Maggy and the children when he knocks on the door of their apartment in less than an hour's time. At last, he will be able to lead a normal life, after the last two years spent in England. Or, more realistically, an almost normal life! Victoria's face floats into his mind and makes him realize that he has some way to go before he can have a harmonious life including Paul and Claire, together with the two twins, who don't even carry his name, Victoria, whom he loves, and his mother, who is bound to try to put a spanner in the works if she can. Things will be made even more difficult by the fact that he has got used to making his own decisions concerning his private life over the last two years. He is in a hurry to see Victoria again, his beautiful and affectionate girlfriend who surprised him by moving to Paris. He feels that he cannot live without her. Why not go and see her straight away?

"I've changed my mind. Take me to *rue Guynemer* next to the *Jardin du Luxembourg*. I'll go to *rue Lecourbe* later."

"Yes Sir."

When he arrives, Phil walks around the gardens for a while, contemplating the building in which his girlfriend lives. He thinks he can see lights on the fifth floor, but he isn't sure that the windows are those of Victoria's apartment. He decides to enter the building. The entrance is well decorated, with several columns in pink marble. After checking with the *concierge* that Mrs. Miller lives on the fifth floor, he takes the elevator and rings the doorbell, very moved by the situation. Peggy opens the door and recognizes him straight away.

"Oh Colonel! What a nice surprise! My cousin was worried because she hadn't heard from you. She will be reassured to see you. But she isn't here at the moment. She went out with one of her friends about an hour ago, to stretch her legs. The twins are starting to get hungry and I have to go and prepare their bottles. Victoria and her friend should be back soon. Would you like to wait for them in the living room?"

Phil is disappointed. No, he doesn't want to wait for them in the living room. He wants to wait for her, and her alone.

"Who is this friend anyway? Victoria has just arrived in Paris and she already has friends who don't work and come to see her in the middle of the afternoon?"

Phil is rather put out but he joins Peggy in the children's bedroom. Helen and George have changed a lot since he last saw them in London. They are almost five months old. He gives Helen her bottle while Peggy takes care of George. The little doll smiles at Colonel Destivel all the time and seems to be fascinated by his gold stripes. Phil hears the sound of the front door opening and the voice of Victoria.

"We're going up to the studio" she calls to Peggy without opening the door. "See you later."

Phil signals to Peggy that she should not say anything about his presence. He wants to surprise Victoria when she is alone. Time is dragging, even though he is occupied by the end of feeding time. He has taken George in his arms. He's strong, a bit chubby! Maybe a future airman. About a quarter of an hour later, they hear voices again.

"Goodbye Jean-Louis. Thanks again for taking this painting for your exhibition. I'm very flattered."

"You really are very charming. I would like to invite you to dinner. Would you like that? We could go to a restaurant close to the *Champs Elysees*. How about next Saturday?"

Victoria is astonished by the attention paid to her by the gallery director. She doesn't know anything about his private life. He hasn't said anything about a wife. But this man who appreciates her paintings is offering her the chance of a lifetime as a painter.

"Yes, next Saturday will be fine" she replies without hesitation.

After accompanying her friend to the elevator, Victoria returns to the children's room, where she discovers Phil, with George on his knees.

"My God! Phil! You're here! You've come back! What a surprise! I was worried that I hadn't heard from you, even though I knew that I might not get your letters because of the move."

Phil passes little George to Peggy and comes to embrace Victoria tenderly. He holds her close to him for a long while, whispering in her ear.

"No more separation, it's over! I want you with me all the time. This last month has been too hard my darling!"

Phil tells her about the end of his stay at Rauceby, and the health problems that almost killed him. He proudly shows her his right hand, with almost no scarring after the graft. Victoria shows him around her new apartment and he admires the balcony, which looks out over the *Jardin du Luxembourg*. As in London, she has three large bedrooms, including one for Peggy.

"Come and have a look at my studio. It's an absolute godsend!"

The studio is accessible via a small interior staircase. Several maids' rooms have been knocked into one and the attic space recuperated to create a beautiful luminous space that also looks out on the gardens. Victoria has set up her easel and paints there. She has also set up a relaxation area, with a coffee table, a sofa and two poufs. There is also a portable gas stove so that she can heat up a snack.

"It's great working here."

Victoria tells him enthusiastically how she met Jean-Louis, the gallery owner, with whom she has just been for a walk around the gardens and who is going to display two of her paintings in an exhibition next month. She, an unknown artist, will have paintings hanging next to those of famous artists like Kandinsky!

She then prepares him tea, accompanied by some scones that Peggy made earlier. Inevitably, they find themselves seated side-by-side on the sofa, their bodies touching, which excites Phil, whose lips seek out those of Victoria. A long slow kiss, Phil's hand caressing the breasts of his beloved, and their tongues meet. Phil wants to go further.

"Would you like me to undress you? Is anyone likely to come up?"

"I would like that very much, but it's not a good time for me. I'm sorry. Are you disappointed?"

Phil is disappointed, but he understands. He raises the question of the rest of the evening.

"I haven't told my family about coming back to Paris. Do you think I could stay here tonight? Can we spend the whole evening together?"

"Tonight I'm going to a dinner with some artists. There will be painters and sculptors there. It would be very difficult for me to cancel as I'm bringing the main course. It's not far from here. If you'd told me earlier that you were coming I would have wriggled my way out of it."

Phil understands but is sad anyway. He feels that he has messed up his return to Paris. His girlfriend has rapidly organized a whole new life from which he is excluded. He will soon rediscover the constraints linked to his family, the presence of his mother, who will undoubtedly be very inquisitive, and his older children, to whom he will have to dedicate at least some of his time.

It's half past six. He has no choice and he decides that it is time to go home, to *rue Lecourbe.*

"Come back and see me soon. If you come on the off-chance, you're more likely to find me at lunchtime. I look after the children in the morning and Peggy takes over in the afternoon. Go and see your older children. They'll be so happy to see their dad at last!"

They say a tender goodbye as Phil leaves.

Rue Lecourbe is not far away, only about a mile. Phil wanders down *rue de Vaugirard* in a dream, suitcase in hand. He regrets going straight to Victoria's apartment. He thinks about his life, which is clearly going to be complicated, in Paris, or elsewhere, as he doesn't even know where he is next likely to be posted. Fortunately, as he nears his home, the thought of seeing his children again fills him with joy, and he speeds up. When he arrives, rather than taking the elevator, he takes the stairs, almost at a run, to his landing. It's been ten months since he left his children in Meknes, Morocco, after coming to see them on his release from Rauceby Hospital.

"Hi! It's me!" cries Phil as he opens the door to his apartment with his keys.

It's Claire, his daughter, who arrives first, followed by her brother Paul, and Maggy, who cries out joyfully "Oh Phil! What a surprise! You're back from England. We were worried about your health, but you look like you're in great shape. Are you staying for good now? Not leaving us again? And how's your hand? Show us the hand they operated on."

Phil's hand is inspected, palpated from all angles and admired by his two children, who have nothing but praise for English surgeons. They have the impression that their father has been repaired and renovated, a bit like a car coming back from mechanic after its dents have been bashed out following an accident.

Phil contemplates his children. They have grown. Paul really looks like a man now, with his muscular shoulders strengthened by swimming and stubble, visible even after shaving, coloring his cheeks and his chin. Claire is now a pretty blue-eyed brunette, with regular features, short hair, and a figure that is almost womanly.

It's soon time for dinner. Phil is bombarded with questions about his final months at Gaitford, the mood after the German surrender and his time in hospital. Paul and Claire then tell him about their vacations in the *Vendee* and in the mountains. Occasionally, Phil drifts off into his own thoughts and is only half listening. He feels uncomfortable when he thinks about Victoria and his other two children that Paul and Claire know nothing about.

Maggy is sweeter than usual and doesn't exasperate her son, other than by high-handedly presenting him, at bedtime, with a list of things that urgently need doing in the apartment that she had written for him a few weeks earlier. Phil feels like he has been placed in manacles. Over the last two years, he has got used to not having any constraints.

Despite his tiredness, Phil has trouble going to sleep as he is troubled by his return home. But the next two days, Saturday and Sunday, enable him to find his place again with his children, who are delighted to have him back.

On Monday morning, he has a meeting at the Ministry with General Valin, the Air Force Chief of Staff, one of the first airmen to have joined the Free French Forces of General de Gaulle in 1940. Phil has already met him several times, at Gaitford and London. He is only six years older than Phil and is already in charge of French aviation, which is becoming increasingly important.

The general asks him about his health and his operation, and says that he looks in good physical shape. He then raises the subject of the parliamentary elections scheduled for October 21.

"Do you realize Destivel that we, career military personnel, are going to be allowed to vote and to elect our members of parliament, and our wives can vote too! It's vital for the future that military personnel have a political conscience and do not just execute the orders of the powers that be. Maybe there would have been opposition to the Vichy regime if we had been allowed to vote before the war. But there you go, enough of that for now. Let's talk about you. You've gained a great deal of experience at the head of a bomber group and then in command of a heavy bomber base with 2500 staff. What you learned in England will be useful to aviation in France even in peacetime."

"Yes Sir. One of the first things I noticed when I arrived in England in '43 was the very high degree of organization at the air bases. It took me by surprise. Lots of ground staff with clearly defined functions. The same for the airmen, a whole set of logistics. Everyone knows what he is supposed to do, and when. In France, the flying staff are well trained, but we're generally less rigorous. We don't stick to the defined procedures. Do you see what I mean?"

"Absolutely, even if I haven't flow for a few years, I've heard about accidents that could have been avoided in North Africa. For your next posting, do you have any preferences?"

Phil is taken by surprise. He wasn't expecting to be asked that question. He doesn't know where there might be a post free and, in the past, he has always been sent wherever his superiors saw fit, whether he liked it or not.

"I don't know Sir. Do you have any suggestions?"

"Yes, we were thinking of you for the post of commander of the base at Oran. The political situation in Algeria is a bit tricky at the moment and the Minister and I would like to strengthen the French presence by developing this base that the Americans have been using a lot recently."

Phil doesn't need long to decide. Going to Algeria would be a total cataclysm for his personal life. He can't see himself asking Victoria to follow him and he would probably be separated from his children again.

"Sir, I've already spent several years abroad, in Morocco and then in England. I would like to stay in France now, preferably in Paris. I'm a widower and I have two children that I haven't seen for two years, so the prospect of going to Oran really doesn't tempt me at all!"

"I can see that you're not enthusiastic about my suggestion, but think about it anyway. It would be a very good career move. I'll see you again next week."

Phil doesn't say anything to Maggy and his children about the outcome of this interview. As far as he is concerned, it's a no-brainer. He doesn't want to go to Oran. But will he be able to oppose the will of his superiors? For the moment, he has a week off before having to go back to work. He has every intention of making the most of it. The children are at school in the morning and afternoon, and that leaves him lots of free time.

During the first day of his vacation, he lunches at home with Maggy, who doesn't seem to be getting any older despite the passage of time and her having recently reached the grand old age of 72. This provides him with an opportunity to sound her out about whether she has any plans for the coming years.

"Mom, thanks again for looking after the kids so well for me during the war. I don't know what I would have done without you. But they're getting big now and they're almost independent. They'll be finishing high school soon. What are you going to do with all the extra free time you will have? Do you have any plans?"

"More free time! You must be joking! Who do you think is going to do the housework, the shopping, the cooking and the washing here? Until you marry again I can't see me having much free time."

Phil realizes that, unfortunately, she's right. He floats the idea of hiring a maid or a cleaning lady.

"A maid! Could you afford it? Have you figured out what that would cost? Plus it's wasted money! Get married first! Then we'll see. You're 41. You need a wife, younger than you, but not too young. Someone with a bit of experience of life, someone classy who will know how to act as the wife of a colonel, a woman you could have more children with. You're a colonel. What's the rank after that? Captain?"

"No Mom, I've already been a captain. You still haven't got the military ranks clear in your head. After colonel, its brigadier general."

"Oh my God! General! You're going to be a general! I have to live long enough to see that. My son, a general!"

"Calm down Mom. If it happens at all, it won't be for a while. I've only just been promoted to colonel."

Maggy has no hesitation imagining the future ideal wife for her son. She has already thought it all out. She isn't wrong to ask him whether he has done his sums. He hasn't. He realizes that over the last two years, he's lost touch with reality. While he was in England, at Gaitford, he didn't have to worry about the logistics of everyday life. He was fed, had his laundry done and was driven around completely free of charge. Now he will need to buy a car and spend money on vacations and on clothes for everyone. He doesn't have any savings. His late wife's illness cost him a fortune. The war has completely disorganized everything. There are the twins too and it's only right that he should give Victoria some money for them. He should talk about that with her the next time that they see each other.

The next day, Phil lunches rapidly with his mother, using the excuse of a meeting with a colleague to leave in a hurry, without even drinking a cup of coffee. Phil leaves in civilian dress, much to Maggy's astonishment.

"You're meeting a colleague and you're not going in uniform?"

Phil immediately recognizes the inquisitor in his mother and can't help but sigh.

"My colleague also has a few days off. We're supposed to be meeting in the *Jardin du Luxembourg*."

Maggy doesn't seem convinced by her son's explanation, and he finds it infernal having to explain himself to his mother.

Phil walks with a light step. He rapidly arrives at *rue Guynemer* and goes up to the fifth floor, where he rings his girlfriend's doorbell. Peggy opens the door and sends him up to Victoria's studio, where she is currently painting.

"Oh Phil! I'm so glad you've come to see me!"

"I have a few days off. I was really impatient to see you again. It didn't work out the way it was supposed to last time! I was worried you wouldn't be here today. Do you have some free time?"

"Yes, as long as you want. This painting can wait. Would you like some coffee? I'd love one myself. After that we'll go and see the twins."

Sitting on the couch, they chat, each with a cup in hand. But Phil says nothing about his interview with General Valin, who suggested sending him to take command of the air base in Oran. Victoria tells him about her paintings, the friends from before the war that she has met up with in Paris, dinners and night clubs in *Saint Germain-des-Prés,* trumpeters, saxophonists and jazz singers, some black and others white, that seem to be forever passing through.

Phil is rapidly disturbed by the physical presence of his girlfriend and experiences a strong desire to kiss her. Their lips meet and their fingers delicately unbutton, unfasten and open their clothes, allowing them to feel the warmth of their skin, to stroke each other gently and to transmit the most beautiful of pleasures.

They remain silent for a moment, happy and peaceful. After dressing again, they go for a walk in the *Jardin du Luxembourg,* under the trees, with their leaves already turned to gold by the fall. Phil tells Victoria that he will soon know where he is to be sent next.

21

MARSEILLES, CASSIS AND MORLEAU, FRANCE,
OCTOBER 1945

William remains in Marseilles for several days. He is dejected and stays in his hotel room most of the time. Oscillating between sadness and anger, he still can't believe that Georges dropped him so suddenly. He can't leave it there. He needs to see Georges at least once more, to talk things through. It's impossible to discover love, to dream about someone for years afterwards and to cross hundreds of miles to be with him, confronting numerous dangers along the way, only to spend a few marvelous days together and then to be separated again, for no apparent reason, in a matter of minutes. He doesn't know where Georges is, but it seems most likely that he will have returned to his house in the *Cote d'Or* in Burgundy. William decides to leave Marseilles and to take the train to Morleau. It's a long way, but at least there is a direct train to Chagny.

During the journey, he spends a lot of time thinking about Georges and what he wants to say to him. Maybe he misjudged him, deceived by his apparent charm? Maybe Georges just wanted to seduce a younger man and have a good time? If that is all it was, what a disappointment!

He arrives at Chagny in the middle of the afternoon and walks the remaining mile and a half to Morleau, suitcase in hand. A pistol that he bought on the black market in Marseilles is hidden in his suitcase, wrapped in a shirt. William's anger grows as he nears Georges' house, and, when he finally arrives, he bangs violently on the door. He knocks several times, but nobody answers. William was convinced that he would find Georges at home and is now completely disconcerted.

He realizes that his behavior is absurd. Georges may have gone out for a walk, or even further afield, and he has no way of knowing where. Defeated, he collapses and sits down in front of the door, sobbing. He doesn't hear the man climbing the external staircase leading to the front door where he is seated.

"I'm sorry to intrude, I saw you from the road. Were you a friend of Georges?"

Dumbfounded, William looks up into the face of a man in his fifties. He pulls himself together and says, in French, with a strong American accent, "I'm looking for Georges Guérin. Do you know if he is in Morleau at the moment?"

"I'm the mayor of the village. I'm very sorry, but I have some bad news for you. Mr. Guérin died in a car accident in the South of France, at about seven in the evening, four days ago."

"What? Georges in a car accident! I don't believe it! How awful! I thought I would find him here. What exactly happened?"

"He crashed into a tree along a road in the South of France. That's all I know. Are you family? We've been trying to get hold of his relatives to organize the funeral. Mr. Guérin had been the owner of this house for several years, but no-one knows if he has family living close by."

"No, I'm a friend. An American journalist. I don't know his family."

"That's a pity. Do come and see me at the town hall if you remember anything important about Mr. Guérin. I'm afraid I must go now. I have work to do."

Françoise arrives just as the mayor is leaving. Seeing how upset the man outside Georges' door is, she wants to be nice to him, but she also wants to know more about him!

"Would you like to come over to my house for a cup of tea? I live next-door. We can talk about Georges. I've only just learned about his death too."

"Yes, thank you. I'd appreciate that. This news is most distressing."

While Françoise prepares the tea, William sits in the living room, with his head in his hands, and cries. Georges' accident happened at about seven in the evening, four days ago. That means that he must have died just after they separated. William will never know the truth about how Georges felt about him. He isn't angry with his friend anymore, just sad about his death.

Françoise returns to the living room with two cups of tea and a pressing need to know more about William.

"Had you known Georges long?"

"Yes, a few years."

"He was a nice man. I arrived in Morleau recently with a lot of problems to sort out. He was very helpful."

"I'm sure that everyone must have liked him."

"Not everyone. There were rumors about him in the village."

William's thoughts turn immediately to his friend's homosexuality.

"Rumors?"

"Yes, he was suspected of killing his first wife. Not exactly commonplace. But they found no proof."

"What! Georges was married?"

Françoise observes the American's face darken and rapidly become hateful.

"Married? Yes, of course. Twice even! But his second wife was sent to Ravensbruck by the Nazis. He was looking to remarry."

William is knocked sideways by this news. Georges had never told him that he was interested in women too. He feels like someone has just hit him over the head with a hammer.

"Was für ein Bastard[9]!"

William could not help but swear in German. As he lowered his voice, Françoise saw that he was furious, but didn't hear what he said. William asks if Georges had any children.

"No, no children. He told me he didn't have any close family. He was an only son. Both his parents are dead. So there can't be any direct heir to his estate."

"That's a shame. Georges seemed to have lots of money. He told me that again recently. What will happen to everything now?"

"I know that he had a hiding place near here during the war. He told me himself, but I don't know if he left anything in it after the armistice."

"Do you know where this hiding place is exactly?"

---

[9] *What a bastard!*

"I know roughly where, but I don't have enough information to locate it precisely."

Françoise reflects for a moment. She thinks that this is the man who was in bed with Georges when she discovered that he was homosexual, *in flagrante delicto*. She had been struck by the change in his expression when she had explained that Georges had been married twice. If her guess is right, then they have something in common. They had both begun to detest Georges following a fortuitous discovery about certain aspects of his life. She wants to know more. Maybe they could team up and work together?

"Do you have anywhere to sleep tonight?"

"No, Georges had invited me to stay with him for a few days. I'll go find a hotel room in Chagny."

"If it helps, you can stay here, at least for one night. My house is large. I'm a widow and I live here with my three children, but there are several spare rooms. I can put you up for a while if you like?"

William doesn't want to be on his own tonight and he willingly accepts this invitation. He isn't very talkative during dinner. Françoise can see that he has been badly shaken up by the death of his friend. She wonders who he is really and decides to wait until the next day to question him further.

The next morning, when the two older children have gone to school and they are alone, Françoise raises the subject of George's hiding place again.

"Do you know where Georges' hiding place is?"

"He spoke to me about it, but he didn't give me enough information to find it. I have a few bits of precise information, but only part of the picture."

Françoise has a hunch and shamelessly takes the initiative.

"What a pity! If there is any money there it's likely to remain buried for years, maybe even centuries! Perhaps we should tell each other what we know? If we manage to find his treasure we can split it between us. There's no rightful heir anyway. What do you think?"

"You're very direct. Do you have money problems?"

"Yes I do and I have my children to bring up. It's not very easy for me at the moment."

"I understand. My life is pretty complicated too and I also need money."

"But if we do find the hiding place, how can I be sure that you won't run off with everything? You're stronger than me and I hardly know you! Tell me something about yourself that you wouldn't like anyone else to know."

William realizes that she won't say anything about what she knows unless he divulges some important piece of information about himself.

"OK. I'll tell you something that you have to keep to yourself. Do you promise that you won't tell?"

"Yes, I promise."

Françoise thinks that William is about to tell her that he is homosexual.

"I'm only half-American. My mom was American, but my dad was German. I don't know if my parents are still alive. They were at Dresden when the town was bombed. I have false papers. Georges got them for me in Marseilles. I spent the last few years in the *Wehrmacht*. I got to know Georges when our army was occupying Morleau. At the time, he did a lot of business with the Germans. We occupied your house in 1942. After that, I was sent to the Russian Front. At the end of the war, I deserted and returned here."

"To find Georges?"

"Yes, exactly."

Françoise might have been shocked. In truth, she is a little, but she rapidly represses the little puffs of indignation that gnaw at her.

"That's good. You've told me a real secret. I think I can trust you. Shall we tell each other what we know about the hiding place? I know that it's located on a hill about a mile and a half from here, close to a cave. What do you know?"

"Georges explained that, from a starting point that I don't know, you have to take two hundred paces to the north and then a hundred to the east. That takes you to a clump of wild box trees, and the hiding place is in the middle of that clump. The trouble is, he didn't tell me where the starting point from which you start counting your paces was."

"Between the two of us, we may be able to manage. Tomorrow morning, we can go to the hill and start searching. How does that sound?"

The next day, whilst Françoise's eldest two children are at school and the youngest is with a neighbor, the two of them set off on bikes with a pick, a spade and a large bag. Françoise takes William to *la Roche Dumay*. The road initially climbs upwards towards Blagny, in the middle of the vines, and then descends again towards Gamay. At the point at which the road starts to descend again, they leave their bikes at the side of the road and climb the hill to the cave. Françoise thinks that the cave could be the starting point that will lead them to Georges' hiding place. She has taken a compass with her so that she can determine clearly which way is north and which way east.

Together, they walk two hundred paces towards the north. It's not easy because the slope is steep. The hundred paces towards the east are easier because the path no longer climbs. At the end of the allotted number of paces, they look around them in search of the clump of box trees, but they can see nothing resembling the type of vegetation they are looking for. They walk all the way around their destination, but there is no clump of box trees! Vexed, they end up returning to Morleau empty-handed.

The next morning, Françoise notices that William has not woken up and has continued to sleep after the children have left for school. Towards 11 a.m., she knocks on his door. No reply. She enters the room. William is not in his bed! His things aren't there! She's afraid that she has been duped and she goes to the shed, where she finds that one of the bikes is missing. The little bastard has gone without her to continue looking! The information he gave her was probably false. There's not much chance of William coming back to see her if he finds something. How could she be so naïve? She has been duped.

Françoise is in a bad mood all day and swears that she will get her own back. She won't hesitate to send the bastard to prison if she gets the chance! Towards nine in the evening she hears a knock at the door. She opens the door and, stupefied, sees William, a broad grin on his face.

"It wasn't easy but I've found Georges' hiding place. I had second thoughts about what Georges had told me during the night and I told myself that we needed to try four hundred paces north and two hundred paces east. It took me a while. I must have tried at least twenty times but it worked! It's a real Ali Baba's cavern!"

22

PARIS, FRANCE, END OF OCTOBER AND START OF NOVEMBER 1945

It's Saturday October 20, and Colonel Destivel is somewhat perplexed. The first parliamentary elections since the end of the war will take place tomorrow. Phil is going to vote for the first time in his life. Military personnel only recently won the right to vote, in August 1945, after women! They can vote, but they cannot join a political party. Phil has thought long and hard and, like many members of the Resistance, his affinities lie with the Popular Republican Movement (the MRP). He can't see himself voting for the socialists or the communists. These elections are doubly important, because, in addition to electing their members of parliament, the citizens of the country are being asked to approve the preparation of a new constitution to be debated by the new assembly.

Paul and Claire accompany their father and Maggy to the polling station, which is close to their home in the 15th *arrondissement* of Paris. They have been very interested in current affairs since their return from Morocco and they want to see first-hand what happens during an election. Paul takes a photo of his father placing his ballot paper in the ballot box. Maggy is happy too, because it's also the first time she has been allowed to vote in a national election. With hindsight, she doesn't understand why women have had to wait so long to obtain this right, particularly as, with her basically authoritarian nature, she finds it hard to tolerate her opinions not been taken into account! Paul also takes a photo of Maggy, immortalizing his grandmother in the process of slipping her vote for the MRP into the ballot box.

Phil hopes that the political climate will become more clement. The French are highly divided. At the start of the week, the former *President du Conseil* Pierre Laval was shot, a few days after Joseph Darnand, the head of the militia. The communists are likely to have a majority in parliament. They were very active in the Resistance during the second half of the war and will undoubtedly reap the rewards of this commitment. Effectively, it is the communists that win, but the MRP, a new party supported by General de Gaulle doesn't do so badly, obtaining 150 seats against the 159 of the communists.

On Tuesday, Colonel Destivel has another meeting with the Air Force Chief of Staff, General Valin. He's a bit nervous, because he really doesn't want to be sent to the back of beyond! After a few pleasantries, General Valin gets straight to the point.

"My dear Destivel, we've had a good think about this and we believe that you would be particularly useful to the air force if you were sent abroad."

At the sound of these words, Phil's head begins to spin and he is very anxious to find out what is coming next. What are they going to suggest? Tahiti? New Caledonia? Vietnam? All a long way away. He might just as well say adieu to Victoria straight away, unless he resigns and rapidly finds a civilian post!

"Yes, we have air bases all over the place, but they aren't necessarily very well organized or equipped. All that needs looking at again and, with the experience that you have acquired in England, you should see things with a fresh eye."

"But where will I be based, Sir? Far away?"

"No, no, don't worry! We want you to be our overseas air base inspector. A very good position. You will be based in Paris, but you will have to travel from time to time for the inspections. Not a bad job in peacetime! No routine and a few voyages. So how do you like our proposal?"

"Very well, in principle, Sir. It sounds like a very interesting post to me. Thank you very much."

Phil leaves the Ministry with a smile on his face. He has immediately understood the advantages of such a post for him on a personal level, the most important thing for him being to remain in Paris.

When he tells Maggy and his children about his new job, they are delighted. Paul and Claire were aware that their father was going to have a new post and were worried that they would be separated from him again or would have to move to the provinces or abroad. Phil doesn't say much about the voyages he will have to make. Everything in good time!

In the following days, he takes possession of his new office at the Ministry of the Air, Boulevard Victor, not far from his home. What a change after all these years of war!

He rapidly tells Victoria his news, passing by her apartment on the off-chance at lunchtime during the week. Victoria has just got up and prepares Phil an English breakfast, with tea, sausages, baked beans, toast and marmalade. Phil admires her fresh-faced beauty, and the intense expression of her eyes. He tells her about his new post.

"That's it! I know what my new post is going to be. I'll be staying in Paris, although I'll have to travel elsewhere occasionally. We can carry on seeing each other, and it should even be easier than before. I have a few ideas about how to make some time for us."

Victoria is delighted with the news. After finishing their meal, Phil leads his lover, who is still in her dressing gown, to her studio upstairs. She is wearing very little and Colonel Destivel has no trouble caressing her breasts, which are easily accessible under her nightdress. What a pleasure it is for him to rediscover the softness and the warmth of her skin. But he doesn't have much time and has to return to work. Just before leaving, Phil makes a suggestion.

"In a couple of weeks, I have to go to Algeria for an inspection. On my way back, I could come and stay with you for two days, if you would like that. I won't say anything to my mother and my children and they will believe that I'm still on the other side of the Mediterranean. Would you like that?"

"Oh yes! What a good idea! We'll be like a real couple for two days!"

Phil has to return to the Ministry, but not without spending a few minutes with the twins first.

The Blida airbase, just outside Algiers, has been chosen for the first inspection. Phil hasn't been given much time to prepare for this mission and he therefore has to work flat out during the days leading up to his departure. He needs to obtain information about the flight and ground staff, the planes available, their maintenance, spare parts and day-to-day organization at the base. But he also needs to anticipate the short- and medium-term strategic roles of this base and to predict the technological developments likely to occur in the next five years and beyond.

Phil is happy to go to Algeria for a few days, with its mild temperatures at this time of year, particularly as he knows he won't be staying for long! This first inspection goes well. He is highly organized, with a very efficient assistant, and he manages to obtain all the information he requires to write his report.

He reaches Paris on November 5, delighted with his visit and impatient to see Victoria again. He arrives directly at her apartment, just before dinner. Phil is surprised by the atmosphere at the apartment. There are lots of people there, glass in hand, some sitting and others standing, some white and a few black.

"I've organized a musical evening in your honor", Victoria explains, "Tonight in my studio, with some jazz musicians I met recently. They play bebop. Do you remember? We danced to bebop when you took me to the ball at the Badvington airbase to celebrate the liberation of Paris[10]. We're going to have a party. I've invited all my painter friends. Isn't it great?"

Phil is frankly not thrilled. He would rather be on his own with Victoria, but he doesn't want to be a kill-joy.

"Music? Brilliant! Will we be able to dance?"

"Definitely! We can't annoy the neighbors in my studio because there aren't any!"

Victoria has been able to get hold of beer, wine, and even Champagne. Everyone is drinking and smoking and the air soon becomes opaque. The dress code is very relaxed and some of the outfits are a bit bizarre. Phil tries to talk to one of the guests, a man in his mid-twenties with long hair and a checked jacket that descends almost to his knees. His casual pants, which are also checked, are short, revealing immaculate white socks. He has an umbrella permanently affixed to his left arm. He's a "zazou", one of the group of jazz fans that have shocked the French middle classes. But Phil has been out of France for several years and knows nothing of the zazou craze that has survived the war, taking the piss out of everything, from the Germans to the Vichy regime and the Resistance! When the race laws came into force, some of them even

<hr>

[10] *See volume 1 "A French Pilot in Gaitford" chapter 18*

started wearing a yellow star, like that worn by Jews, but with "zazou" written on it, to express their derision. Several of the guests are dressed in the same style.

"That's a very original outfit you and your friends are wearing. Are you going to put on a clown show for us?" Phil asks naively.

The man looks surprised and says "Are you from Mars or something? Who are you anyway?"

"I'm a colonel in the air force."

"A colonel in the air force! Aviation is a waste of time" concludes the zazou, who rolls his eyes heavenwards and leaves Phil in a state of astonishment.

Phil can feel that he doesn't quite fit in with this crowd. He can't even talk to Victoria, who is busy welcoming the guests. She seems perfectly at ease in the middle of these creatures, doesn't seem to notice time passing and pays Phil little attention. Fortunately, the musicians soon arrive and everyone goes up to Victoria's studio for the jazz party. Victoria finds the time to come and see Phil, to explain that several well-known musicians will be playing tonight.

Four musicians take to the stage, with an accordion, double bass, guitar and percussion. The band leader is the accordionist, Joe Privat, otherwise known as the "White Gypsy", who plays a mixture of bebop and Manouche jazz. He is a bit on the chubby side, with slicked-down hair and sideburns extending to below his ears. He starts by playing a short melody to warm up, after having placed a cap on his head and lit up a cigarette, which rapidly goes out but remains clamped in his mouth. He begins by thanking Victoria for the invitation, speaking in slang with a strong Parisian accent. Then he presents his fellow musicians, concluding with "Victoria told me we have one of her mates here tonight. A colonel who commanded a big bomber base in England. Where is this colonel? I don't like the military myself, but I'm prepared to make an exception tonight. Come on, show yourself, flyboy!"

Phil is embarrassed and Victoria comes to his rescue.

"Here he is. His name is Colonel Destivel. He's very modest and he didn't want a fuss made about him, but it's a bit late for that now. What are you going to play for him Joe?"

The accordionist replies "Something special, very swing, perfect for a bomber colonel flyboy. This is Atomic Swing, boom boom! It was composed after the explosion of the first atomic bomb."

It is, effectively, very swing, and Phil discovers that the accordion adapts very well to jazzy rhythms. He can't really see the direct link between the melody and the explosion of a bomb, but never mind!

Joe and his band continue to play. A few couples start to dance the bebop, but the lack of space discourages the others from dancing.

After three quarters of an hour, Joe gives his musicians the signal to finish their set. He thanks Victoria and, dog-end in hand, plants a huge smacker on her cheek. After a short pause, another two recent arrivals prepare to play. They are also in their mid-thirties. The first is a guitarist who looks to be of Manouche origin. He is very dark and has a small moustache. His hair is shiny and impeccably combed. He is wearing a jacket over an immaculate white shirt, with no tie. The other man, who is taking his time to tune his violin, has a refined appearance, with his hair perfectly combed back from his face. The gypsy then speaks.

"Victoria, you asked us to play something special for one of your military friends who is here tonight. Is that the man you are trying to spoil? That man over there? Very good. Stephane and I spent the whole morning rehearsing to please you my dear! Here is an original interpretation for all of you, but especially for you, Sir, and of course for Victoria, for whom I have a very soft spot, as you know."

The violinist begins playing first. He plays the first few notes of the Marseillaise softly, with much sensitivity. Colonel Destivel applauds, but rapidly stops because the piece does not continue in the way he thought it would. The guitarist plays a few powerful chords and then accompanies the violinist with brio, as he plays the rest of the Marseillaise in a very jazzy swing style. Phil is initially shocked and then completely fascinated by the dexterity of the guitarist, who plays with only two fingers on his left hand.

Victoria arrives and takes Colonel Destivel by the hand. Phil follows her lead and the two of them dance a joyful wild bebop to these patriotic tones. The musicians and the two dancers are met with thunderous applause at the end of the piece.

Victoria explains to Phil that these two artistes, Stephane Grapelli, an Italian, and Django Reinhardt, a pure-blood gypsy, are rapidly becoming known in jazz circles in Paris. Phil enjoyed it, but he can't help thinking that his superiors would be less than delighted to see a colonel dancing to the national anthem revisited and transformed into jazz.

The musicians then continue their concert, which is much appreciated by the audience. When they stop for a moment to cool off a bit and have something to drink, Phil goes to talk to the gypsy.

"I can see that your left hand has been burnt. You have scars and only two of the fingers are mobile. That's a bit like what happened to me in '44. I spent several months in an English hospital and everything was put right by an operation on the tendons and a skin graft. Wouldn't you like to have surgery on your hand? I could help you. I know some very good surgeons on the other side of the Channel."

"Thanks, that's very nice of you, but I manage very well with my two fingers now. It works perfectly! I really don't want the quacks to get their hands on me!"

Phil doesn't insist, even though he thinks that it must be much easier to play with four fingers than with two. Stephane and Django continue their concert until noises from the floor below disturb them. Victoria asks Phil to go and see what is going on.

At the front door, Phil finds Peggy speaking in broken French to two policemen and an inspector.

"I'm Colonel Destivel!" he says "Is there a problem Inspector?"

"Colonel! Hmm! We'll see about that. Can I see your papers please?"

Fortunately, Phil has his papers in the back pocket of his pants. He hands the inspector his civilian and military papers. The inspector examines them carefully and his tone softens.

"I'm sorry Sir but the neighbors have complained about the noise and one of them told me that there was even a caricature of the Marseillaise."

"Noise! I'm sorry. We're upstairs and we thought that the neighbors wouldn't hear us up there. I'll tell the musicians to stop. As far as the Marseillaise goes, I don't see what you mean. The neighbor must have misheard."

"I'm prepared to overlook this incident, but the noise will have to stop. Agreed?"

"Of course. I'll see to it immediately."

The policemen leave and Phil goes and explains the situation to Victoria. It is late and she has to ask the musicians to stop playing. They understand because they encounter this problem all the time. You have to play in cellars these days to avoid upsetting people!

It is really late by the time everyone leaves. Victoria takes Phil to her bedroom. She will tidy up her studio tomorrow or another day. She is absolutely exhausted and asks Phil to undress her. He doesn't need to be asked twice. He first takes off her shoes and stockings. Her plump naked thighs excite him. He caresses her knees and then moves upwards to her panties, which he adjusts slightly to admire her abundant blond pubic hair. He helps her to remove her cardigan and her blouse and, for a moment, contemplates her white silk bra, which pushes up her breasts. He gently undoes the bra and strokes Victoria's breasts and nipples. Phil's soft hand and sustained attention to her most intimate zones wake Victoria up. She feels the desire in her belly and she clenches her buttocks. She rapidly releases Phil's manhood from its constraints and is not disappointed. The pleasure that follows is rapid but intense, despite the late hour.

Late in the morning, Phil renounces his dreams and returns to consciousness just as Victoria, in a white dressing gown, arrives in the bedroom pushing a trolley loaded with two very English breakfasts. The meal would not be out of place in a prestigious hotel, with freshly squeezed orange juice, tea, scones, fried eggs, toast and marmalade.

Victoria and Phil have had great difficulty meeting up over the last year or so. This morning, they are like two adolescents, frisky and laughing. They finally get dressed and go to find Peggy, who has been looking after the twins all morning. After the twins have had their nap, their parents, arm-in-arm, take them for a walk in the *Jardin du Luxembourg*. It's a nice day and the trees are dressed in their fall colors. Phil's two days of vacation are magnificent and it is not until the evening of the next day that Phil leaves to return to his other children and his mother, as if he had just left the plane that brought him back from the inspection in Algeria.

He walks home, suitcase in hand, thinking again about the musical evening that Victoria had organized in his honor. He is amazed by the ease with which she interacts with people, which has enabled her to make such original friends, talented artists that he would have no chance of meeting without her. Most of his friends are air force officers, great comrades, but very different from the people he met last night. If he and Victoria live together, he will undoubtedly start moving in very different circles. But would Victoria like his friends? That's far from certain!

23

MORLEAU, FRANCE, START OF NOVEMBER 1945

Françoise had jumped for joy a month ago, when William had come to tell her that he had found Georges' treasure. She had immediately asked what there was in the hoard. William had taken 10 gold bars out of his bag and had added that that was just a small part of what was there. It was impossible for him to bring it all back. It was too heavy and voluminous and they would have to go back.

The next day, they left early, by bike, with saddlebags and backpacks, making sure that they didn't go up to the hiding place together so as not to attract any attention, although the site was generally deserted. Françoise's eyes almost popped out of her head when she saw the remaining treasure: gold bars, gold coins and jewelry. Euphoric, they left loaded up with their loot, struggling to pedal under the weight of all the precious metal. Impossible to move the lot in one go. They'd had to make several journeys.

In the evening, tired but radiant, they had waited until the children were in bed to carry out an inventory of their loot, which proved to be considerable! There were 92 gold bars, each weighing about two pounds, 1532 Napoleonic twenty-franc coins and jewelry, lots of jewelry, with priceless large diamonds and rubies that made Françoise salivate with desire.

They had hidden the lot in the cellar, in wooden crates that they covered with old newspapers. The next day, William had dug a large hole in a remote part of the garden, in which they had buried most of the treasure, leaving only 100 gold coins, a few gold bars and the jewelry in the house.

They had gotten the jewelry valued to split the hoard into two essentially equal parts. They had split the jewelry into four batches, each of which was entrusted to a different jeweler for estimation. This strategy forced them to make four bus trips to Autun, Beaune, Chalon sur Saone and Dijon. They encountered no particular problems during their travels. They had to conclude that good old Georges had been blessed with excellent taste in his choice of jewelry! Nothing but valuable precious stones, of several carats, great purity and beautiful color. Lots of money in sight if they can sell them!

The parliamentary elections on October 21 had left Françoise perplexed. Too busy with the loot, she hadn't had the time to think about it and missed having a husband to counsel her. William was no substitute in that situation. She had wanted to talk to her friend Henri, the former mayor. But, finally, she had run out of time and she hadn't voted. She feels that she has let herself down because she has been campaigning for years for women to have the right to vote.

It is now the start of November. Françoise and William are now in a position to share out their treasure, more than a month after its discovery. Françoise has had to lie to justify William's presence in her home. She says that he is an American cousin who was injured in Japan during the war and is spending a month convalescing and learning French in Burgundy. Their complicity over the last few weeks has made them firm friends.

Once the loot has been split, Françoise talks to William about the future.

"What are you going to do now? I'd be happy to keep you here for a while, but tongues will eventually start to wag. Do you see what I mean?"

William doesn't know what to say. If someone in France or elsewhere discovers that his papers are faked, he will probably find himself a prisoner of war, with the worry that he might be sent to Russia.

"Yes, I know I can't stay for long, but I don't know where to go. It's not easy for me. Maybe I will try to go to South America and start again there! What do you think of that?"

Françoise thinks for a while. William's destiny is not entirely unlinked to her own. If he is captured and interrogated, he will probably talk about her and their complicity. And that is when the problems will begin.

"Personally, I think you should go back to Germany with just a few gold coins. You can come back for the rest later. You can tell them that you lost your papers. Do you think that your parents might still be alive?"

"Go back to Germany! I really don't want to do that! But it's true that I would like to know what happened to my parents, even if I don't hold out much hope!"

"Think about it for a bit before you decide. Germany isn't far. I've decided to pass my driving test and buy a car. Then I could help you take your gold home. Once you've got proper papers, I'm sure you'll be able to find a job easily in your own country, as a journalist perhaps, or as an English or French teacher. So many people died in Germany. Language teachers must be in great demand!"

"I'll consider it carefully and I'll tell you what I decide tomorrow."

Françoise's desire for William to leave soon is simply a matter of prudence. In truth, his presence doesn't bother her at all. The children like him and Agnes has learnt some English with him. He spends his time playing ball in the garden with the boys, and teaching the older one chess. He found some stilts in the cellar and showed the children how to use them. Everyone was doubled up with laughter. They don't think about Georges much anymore, and he is beginning to be confined to oblivion! The unexpected fortune, a gift from the heavens, has completely changed Françoise's life. She now sees a much brighter future for herself.

The next day, after dinner, when they are alone, William tells Françoise that he has come around to her way of thinking. Two days later he leaves, with his false American papers, disguised as a photographer from the Washington Post. He heads to Strasbourg, with the objective of crossing the Rhine. Some gold coins hidden in his bag will enable him to survive in Germany until he has real papers and manages to find work. The two friends are both emotional on parting. They say that they hope to see each other soon and swear that, whatever happens, they will never speak to anyone else about what has happened.

Françoise feels very lonely after the departure of her friend. But, a few days later, she receives a letter that amuses her.

Dear Françoise,

You may remember me. We met at the Meknes air base. You were there to sort out some money problems and we had dinner at my place afterwards. You gave me your address in Burgundy so that I could contact you. I don't know if you have returned from Algeria, but I thought I would give it a try anyway. I've been back in Paris since July and I would be delighted to see you again. Let me know if you come to Paris. I live with my son and my grandchildren in the 15th arrondissement....

Marguerite Destivel (Maggy to friends)

This letter brings a smile to Françoise's face. She had been surprised by Maggy's character when she had eaten at her house in Meknes. How strange to want to control her son as if he were still a teenager!

24

PARIS, FRANCE, NOVEMBER 1945

Since her return from Morocco, Maggy has been writing to all the people she got along with whilst she was there. She has written more than twenty letters, a laborious task, because writing is not one of her strengths. The effort has kept her occupied for some time, but she now feels like a burden has been lifted from her shoulders.

It is Sunday, and Maggy has invited her cousin Fernand to lunch. She is very fond of this first cousin, who was widowed about ten years ago. As children, they had spent several vacations together at Maggy's parents' house close to Orleans, and they have continued to see each other regularly over the years ever since. Their relationship was interrupted only by the war and they have been seeing each other regularly again since Maggy's return from Morocco.

Fernand is something of a gourmet. His wife was an excellent cook and Maggy always goes to great trouble when he comes to lunch. Fernand is naturally of a cheerful disposition and makes everyone laugh during the meal. Paul, Claire and Phil all have a good time with him. After the coffee and brandy , Maggy and Fernand decide to go for a walk along the *avenue de Breteuil*. Phil has always wondered if his mother and Fernand weren't more than just cousins when they were younger, but he has never dared to ask Maggy.

As they walk towards *les Invalides*, they chat about their youth. However, after a few minutes, Fernand takes on a mysterious air and lowers his voice as if about to tell Maggy a secret.

"Maggy, there's something I must ask you. Not this week, but last week, on Thursday afternoon, I saw Phil on the arm of a pretty young woman with two babies, walking around the *Jardin du Luxembourg*. They seemed to get on very well, if you see what I mean. Is your Philippe planning to get married again? Tell me about it."

Maggy is absolutely astonished.

"You must be mistaken. Phil was in Algeria on a mission at the time. He didn't get back until Friday night."

"No, I'm sure of what I saw. Phil was only a couple of yards away from me. I was sat on a bench reading the *Figaro*. He didn't see me, but I saw him at close range. I'm sure it was him. I followed them. They were holding hands and they kissed several times. At the end of their walk, all four of them went into number *14 bis, rue Guynemer*, which runs along the edge of the *Jardin du Luxembourg*."

Maggy is furious about what she has just heard, but she doesn't want her cousin to see that.

"I don't know anything about it. I'll ask him. Thank you for letting me know. Even if he is grown up now, I still like to know what he is up to!"

Maggy manages to control herself and immediately changes the subject. She is deep in thought when she returns home. She could, of course, interrogate her son straight away, but he probably wouldn't say much. Now, what she really wants to know is who this woman and these children are. She understands that her son must remarry, but he can't choose just anyone! He needs a real companion who can run his house and fill the shoes of the wife of a colonel, possibly even a general soon. It wouldn't be a bad thing for his future wife to have a bit of money too. One very important thing is that the future wife must like her. If Maggy decides to carry on living with Phil and the children, her future daughter-in-law must not stir up trouble for her or want to send her to live in a home!

Maggy constructs the ideal future wife for Phil in her head and wants to know whether the woman who was seen with her son matches what she wants, not only for him, but also for herself! The address of this person is engraved in her memory: *14 bis rue Guynemer.* But how can she find out more?

After a couple of days of careful reflection, Maggy decides to pull out all the stops. At ten in the morning, she arrives at *74 bis rue d'Aboukir,* in the second *arrondissement* of Paris. She goes up to the first floor directly and rings the doorbell of the Leduc Agency. She has decided to pay a private detective to obtain the answers to her questions, no matter how much it costs.

She explains the situation, in detail, to Mr. Leduc, the former police inspector who founded the agency. She hands him a photograph of her son and indicates the address of the building that Phil and this woman entered after their walk. The detective thinks for a few seconds and says "Your problem should be fairly easy to solve if the address you have given me really is the address of the woman concerned. Come back in a week. In the meantime, can you pay something in advance? Half of the final amount."

Maggy finds the bill a bit steep, but, resigned, she takes an envelope full of bank notes from her purse and, laboriously, extracts the amount demanded.

On leaving the agency, Maggy regrets having agreed so rapidly.

"How stupid am I? I've got an address. I could have tried to find out more before rushing to a private detective and handing over a tidy sum from my savings."

The next morning, Maggy can't take any more and decides to carry out her own investigation. At ten o'clock, she positions herself opposite number *14 bis rue Guynemer*, convinced that the lady with two babies is bound to come out to take them for a walk. It seems like an affluent agreeable place, close to the *Jardin du Luxembourg*. After about a quarter of an hour, she sees a young woman come out of the building pushing a large pram with enough space for two babies. The woman crosses the street and enters the garden. Maggy follows her and sees here sit down on one of the metal chairs along a small path, with the pram next to her.

"Shame she didn't sit on a bench," thinks Maggy, "then I could have sat down next to her and started a conversation and got a close look at her." Maggy looks at the woman carefully when she gets close. She is struck by how young she is.

"A kid who must be twenty years younger than my son! Phil's gone mad! This little bitch who doesn't look anything like a colonel's wife!' thinks Maggy.

The bitch in question takes a packet of cigarettes out of her bag and lights one with a lighter.

"And she smokes! In a public park! Like a man! I must be dreaming! The world's gone completely mad" thinks Maggy, consternated. She really wants to find out more, but can't see how to go about it. She resigns herself to waiting for the detective's findings, because she doesn't want to take any risks.

It's a long week. Maggy is exasperated by her son, who seems to be perfectly natural and good-humored at mealtimes, even though he is hiding essential information from her. But she manages to behave as if nothing is wrong, because she knows that she will be in a much better position to make the necessary decisions if the information from the detective corroborates what she has discovered for herself.

Two days before the end of this week of suspense, Phil announces that he will probably go to Morocco in a few days or weeks, to inspect the air base at Agadir. Maggy wants to know the precise date of the trip, but the details have not yet been finalized.

It is today at noon that she has her appointment with the detective. Punctual to the second, she wonders what more she will learn than she has already discovered. Mr. Leduc always makes a point of being on time and, at noon precisely, he reports the results of his investigation.

"It wasn't too difficult to identify your son's girlfriend. Just a matter of greasing the concierge's palm a little. Her name is Mrs. Victoria Miller. She is English, the widow of a certain Colonel Miller, who was imprisoned in Germany but managed to escape from the prisoner of war camp at which he was being held in 1944. He had just long enough to get his wife pregnant with twins, a girl and a boy, and then he died. Mrs. Miller arrived in France about three months ago and is renting the apartment in *rue Guynemer*."

"A colonel's wife! How old is she?"

"About thirty-five."

Maggy doesn't get it. The woman she saw was much younger. She doesn't want to talk about her own investigations, but she needs to understand.

"But my cousin, who saw them together, spoke of a much younger woman!"

"Mrs. Miller has her cousin living with her, a woman called Peggy, who looks after the children. She is, effectively, much younger. Mrs. Miller is a painter and she needs time for her art. That's why she has someone else look after her children, particularly as, it appears, she often goes out to dinner and gets back very late."

Maggy now understands her error. She mistook the children's nurse for her son's girlfriend. She is reassured to find that Mrs. Miller is 35, but not very enthusiastic about her artistic activities.

"Do you know what kind of paintings she does, this Mrs. Miller?" she asks.

"The concierge, who does some cleaning for Mrs. Miller, told me that it's abstract art, colored shapes with no particular meaning."

"Really? That's ridiculous. She must do that because she doesn't really know how to draw. I see! And you say she comes home late? Can you tell me any more about that?"

"No, Madam. You asked me to identify your son's girlfriend and I have done that. If you want, I can have her followed. It's more expensive, but very effective."

"Pay more! To what end? What more is that likely to tell me?"

"A lot! It will provide you with a precise report of the activities of this lady over a period of 24 or 48 hours, possibly with the names of the people she meets and some compromising photos. Do you see?"

Mr. Leduc is asking for a lot of money and Maggy's savings are not huge. But, if it means getting her son out of a sticky situation, it's no time to skimp and haggle! Maggy agrees and the detective says he will inform her when the investigation is complete.

25

PARIS, FRANCE, AND THE HOGGAR MASSIF, ALGERIA, NOVEMBER AND DECEMBER 1945

Victoria is excited because she has just found out that the private viewing for the exhibition in which her paintings have been included is scheduled for 6 p.m. on Saturday December 8. Three of her paintings will be on show, but she isn't happy with the last one she gave to the gallery director. She wants to try, over the next couple of weeks, to surpass herself, so that she can display a more striking painting. Sat at her easel, she searches for inspiration, trying a few sketches and then starting all over again, until she is happy with her ideas. She has to get this one right.

At the start of the afternoon, there is a knock on the door to her studio. Very few people know about this door, which is accessible only via the service staircase. It's her friend Serge Andropov, who has come to visit her.

"Hello Serge. What are you doing coming up the service staircase and how did you know you could get in that way?"

"You're forgetting, my darling, that it was me who found you this apartment. I checked it out completely before suggesting it to you."

Serge is voluble and calls all women "my darling" if he finds them attractive. Serge's breath is not entirely free from alcohol vapors, as is often the case. In such conditions, Victoria would rather not find herself alone with him, as she is worried about his often cavalier advances.

"I've been sat here for the last three hours. Why don't we go for a walk in the gardens? The light is beautiful today. I want to talk about abstract art with you."

"I see! You're scared of me! But it's OK. In any case, I spent the night with a terribly passionate woman and I'm exhausted."

A little later, sat on a bench in front of the orangery in the *Jardin du Luxembourg*, Victoria and Serge have a serious discussion about the different theories underlying abstract art and the best known painters from the field, like Kandinsky, Hartung and Miro. Victoria is trying to find her place in one of the movements that came into existence during the war and is flourishing at the end of 1945. Clearly, she is not solely interested in the beauty of purely geometric forms and she finds a rich terrain for expression in the transcription of individual emotions into colors, forms and textures.

This conversation confirms Victoria's desire to shift her painting style towards more emotive representations. Ideas come flooding into her head and, after this exchange with Serge, she can't wait to get back to her easel. She has another two hours before she has to look after her children, who are currently with her cousin Peggy. Serge would rather stay for a bit longer. They stand up to say goodbye. Victoria approaches to kiss him on the cheek and he facetiously turns his face and kisses her full on the mouth. She pulls away, but knowing her friend well, she doesn't chastise him and instead laughs as she leaves.

Over the next few days, Victoria creates a new painting incorporating shapes that are almost geometric, but slightly imprecise. There are splashes of heterogeneous, bright colors, which she uses to express emotions: anxiety, but also happiness and serenity. There is also a second painting in the same vein, but with slightly better mastery of her new technique.

Jean-Louis Raqué, the gallery director, doesn't bat an eyelid as he accepts these two paintings to replace the previous ones and he encourages Victoria to continue along the same lines.

"It's really good, entirely in keeping with current trends. But you're in the nick of time, because I have to go to the printer this afternoon to finalize the texts for the visitors. I need a title for each painting."

Victoria thinks for a moment.

"The first one was inspired by the destruction of my studio in England by a German fighter that crashed into the walls. I was only a few yards away! It was horrible, but spectacular at the same time. I think 'The Final Explosion' would be a good title. I'd like to call the second one 'Rebirth in Paris.' Since I've been here with my children, I've had the impression of really starting a new life. I tried to express that with the bright, happy colors in this painting."

For the private viewing at the start of the December, the gallery director has a short biography of Victoria printed that recounts how all her paintings were destroyed in an instant by the German Junkers that crashed into her studio in England. The visitors are moved by her story, which even inspires a journalist from *Le Monde* to write an article on this new painter. Kandinsky and Nicolas de Stael, who are present at the viewing, come over to chat with Victoria and encourage her to continue her work. The gallery director has fixed a relatively high price for Victoria's paintings. The strategy turns out to be the right one, because a Swiss visitor buys them without trying to negotiate a lower price, convinced of the potential of this painter. She is excited about the reception of her work by lovers of modern art and dreams only of doing more, even better paintings.

Victoria has a nice life now, after four difficult years in a small town in England. People like her paintings and she gets lots of encouragement to continue. The money she has inherited has ensured a certain comfort and spared her from need. There has been an effervescence of culture since the Germans left. Victoria is in love with a handsome airman, who has given her the children that she had stopped hoping would ever come. Of course, the future of her relationship with Colonel Destivel remains uncertain, but life is currently offering them a moment of respite, and they are making the most of it.

Phil is supposed to be returning to France the next day, to spend two days with her before going home to *rue Lecourbe*. Victoria wonders whether she and Phil ought to talk soon about their future together.

At the same moment, Phil is asking himself the same questions, at an altitude of just under 10,000 feet, in a Siebel 204, a plane of German origin built in France by the SNCAC in 1944. He has organized a reconnaissance flight over the mountains of the Hoggar Massif, with the idea of developing the military air base a bit further away at Tamanrasset, where there is only one runway, constructed during the war and used only occasionally. Tamanrasset has become a strategic town in the south of the Sahara, a sort of gateway to Black Africa. Phil gets some photographs taken of the mountains and the adjacent plateaus. The plane is flying towards Tamanrasset-Aguenar, where it should land in about an hour. There are four people in the plane: a pilot, a navigator, an engineer and himself, as a passenger.

Phil lets his mind wander and thinks of Victoria. He can't wait to see her again, at her apartment the following evening. He asks himself if he shouldn't, at least once, invite her to lunch at his house one Sunday, to meet his family. There is, of course, the problem of Maggy, who would probably be unpleasant. But he knows how to play the diplomat and maybe if he talks to her about Victoria first she might like her?

Phil overhears the navigator talking to the pilot.

"There's a problem! The radio direction finder isn't working. I don't know where we are. I'll try to sort it out. Try to fly round in a circle so that we stay in the same region."

The pilot examines his instruments.

"Oh no! I don't like the look of this at all. The sun will be going down soon. I have enough gas for another hour, but no more!"

Phil has heard their conversation and rapidly understood the problem. If they can't work out where they are relative to beacons on the ground, they will end up going round in circles in the mountains until they have no fuel left and are forced to land wherever they find themselves. And here, in these rocky mountains, at nightfall, they have little chance of landing safely!

Phil is very anxious. Surely he can't die in a plane accident in peacetime after having survived numerous dangerous missions during the war and having already spent seven months in hospital after an accident? What will become of his children and Victoria, whom he was supposed to be seeing tomorrow? He finds it much harder to stay calm as a passenger than when he is flying the plane himself.

Phil can see the navigator getting annoyed with the radio direction finder. But he can't get it to work! They don't know where they are and it is beginning to get dark. The pilot concentrates hard and directs all his energies into avoiding the mountains, which, in this region of Southern Algeria, rise to almost 10,000 feet. He's searching for a zone that isn't too steep, to up their chances of survival if they have to make a forced landing.

The pilot can see that the tank is almost empty and he tells them that he is going to try to land on a relatively flat area that he has just identified but which, unfortunately, is not entirely free of large rocks.

The pilot slows the engines. He prefers to try to land on the belly of the plane, without descending the landing gear. The plane tips gently forward, and the descent is rapid. Phil nervously checks that his safety belt is correctly fastened and braces himself for the shock, taking short, rapid breaths. He clings on to the arms of his seat and blocks his feet under the seat in front of him. The shock arrives and is enormous. The plane bounces slightly and then ploughs into the ground at just over 100 miles per hour. The noise is deafening. The plane keeps sliding, with the risk of hitting a large rock at any minute and breaking up. They are all violently shaken, to the limits of consciousness. Phil's seat detaches from the floor and crashes into the side wall of the plane, but he is not seriously hurt. The plane finally comes to a halt after an unexpected 180-degree turn. There is dust everywhere, making it difficult to see anything inside the flight cabin, which is rapidly invaded by the smell of kerosene. With the plane finally at a standstill, the four airmen, still groggy from the shock, get out as best they can to avoid being burnt if the plane catches fire, which it might do at any moment. They are lucky though, as nothing happens, and several minutes later they return to the interior to look for the food rations and water they brought with them, together with some blankets, as it is chilly outside. They are in shock and can't believe that they made it out alive. They remain silent for a while, getting their breath back before trying to talk. The plane's radio is still functioning and the navigator sends a message to say that they are safe and sound but lost somewhere in the mountains of the Hoggar Massif. The crew members then set up camp. They force themselves to drink no more than a glass of water every three hours, because their water supplies are limited and they don't know how long it will be before they are rescued.

The night is chaotic because the site is infested with scorpions and tarantulas, which they have to chase away when they are assailed. In the early hours of the morning, they eat a rudimentary meal, hoping to see a reconnaissance plane arrive soon. The time drags by. They are afraid that they will die of thirst if they are not rapidly spotted. Towards midday, they hear a noise and see a plane some distance away that might be looking for them. They light a fire with some fuel from the plane and burn some dead wood to make lots of smoke. A few minutes later, an air force Dakota spots them and makes several low-altitude passes over their camp. They establish radio contact. The pilot of the Dakota drops some food and drink for them. The four occupants of the plane are joyful. They are safe.

A rescue convoy of two military trucks from the Saharan company based at Tamanrasset is sent to collect them. It takes two days to get there, because the terrain they have to cross is mountainous and the tracks are few in number and in poor condition. Following his rescue, Phil takes a plane that brings him back to Paris three days late. His family has been informed, but not Victoria.

When he leaves the plane, Phil has his driver take him straight to Victoria's apartment. He finds her scared to death, convinced that something serious has happened again, just like at Gaitford. Once again, she marvels at the good fortune of her companion when he tells her what happened. She doesn't want him to go straight away and asks if he can stay with her at least for one evening and one night, but Phil is aware of his family obligations.

"I would love to stay with you, but I have to look after my older children for the rest of the weekend. If you like, I can come by at lunchtime on Monday. I want to talk through a few points with you concerning our future and that of the twins.

"Yes, we will talk about all that my darling. I'm so glad you're alive. But it was a close shave, yet again!"

With that, Phil leaves for home. He walks all the way, ruminating on how best to move forward with Victoria. He can see only one solution. They should all live together, him, her, the twins, and Paul and Claire. That just leaves the problem of Maggy, which he will have to think about. But she seems to have found the solution herself.

26

PARIS, FRANCE, DECEMBER 1945

It's early Monday morning and Maggy is going to see her detective, who informed her in a letter she received the previous Saturday that he has information that will be of interest to her. Mr. Leduc has prepared a dossier for her containing two typewritten sheets of text summarizing what he has discovered by tailing Phil's girlfriend. The conclusion is clear.

"Mrs. Miller, your son's girlfriend, often goes out in the evening and comes home very late at night. Sometimes she stays out until the early hours! She goes to jazz clubs and often eats out with painters and sculptors. She drinks a lot! But she doesn't seem to take the drugs, like cocaine, often favored by these artists. She has a Russian friend whose behavior is ambiguous. Take a look at this photo taken in the *Jardin du Luxembourg* in the middle of the afternoon."

Maggy puts on her glasses and sees clearly that Mrs. Miller is kissing a man on the mouth in the photo. Her mind is made up. No point in dithering. This is not the woman for her son.

"Thank you Mr. Leduc. I have all the information I need now."

Maggy pays the bill and leaves with the dossier, determined to make rapid use of the photograph the detective has given her. She makes up her mind to act as soon as she gets home. She decides to send her son an anonymous letter, with the photo of this woman kissing another man. It might be a bit difficult for him, but at least he will have tangible proof of her bad behavior! They should break up fairly quickly after that.

Maggy prepares a large envelope, in which she places the photograph, with letters cut out from a newspaper to indicate the date and time at which it was taken. No need for anything more. The content is explicit enough by itself. She then goes to a post office in another part of Paris to mail this letter, which should arrive in two or three days' time at most. It doesn't occur to her that she may be going a bit far by getting so involved in her son's private life.

In the meantime, Phil is in his office, writing a report on his mission, when his secretary tells him that a former Royal Air Force officer is at the entrance of the ministry asking to see him. It is Captain John Luxley. Phil can hardly believe it. John always arrives when he least expects it, when he thinks that he is elsewhere. Curious to know why John is in Paris, Colonel Destivel agrees to see him straight away. They are both happy to see each other again. John explains his situation in English.

"I moved to Paris last week. I've got myself a two-year post as a mathematician at the *College de France*. I don't know if you remember, but I applied to Princeton in America. Unfortunately, they turned me down. There is a prestigious mathematics school here in France though, and they were keen to take me. I'm working with Mandelbrojt. He came to London at the end of the war for a scientific mission with the Free French forces. I think he was impressed by my time as a bomber pilot. It's the start of a new life for me. I'm getting more involved in multidisciplinary research and I'm in touch with an American mathematician called Norbert Weiner.

A little genius in the process of inventing a new discipline!"

"And where are you living? Have you found somewhere nice? It's not very easy in Paris at the moment, what with the end of the war and all."

"I love Paris! I'm renting a one-bedroom flat at the top of a building in rue Mouffetard and I've already made friends with some of my neighbors. Politics is interesting here too. Lots of progressive thinkers. More than in England. I'm practicing every day, but my French still isn't very good I'm afraid."

Phil notes down his address and says that he will invite him to lunch one day so that they can talk for longer and he can introduce John to his family. Maybe John could give Paul and Claire conversation classes in English?

On this same Monday, Phil has freed up his lunchtime to go and see Victoria. He rings the doorbell of her apartment and Peggy opens the door. He can see immediately from her somber mood that something is wrong.

"Victoria isn't here. Early this morning she had an intense pain in her leg. We called the doctor out and he saw that the leg was swollen and sent her straight to Cochin Hospital."

Phil walks to the hospital, which he knows well as his father was treated there for his heart condition. He has no trouble finding Victoria in Professor Florian's ward. Unfortunately, Victoria is in a room with three other patients, which makes it difficult to have a private conversation, but at least it's better than a large ward. She has phlebitis and has been put on anticoagulant treatment, with heparin injections to dissolve the blood clot blocking the vein.

He sees that his lover is anxious and feels lost in this rather dingy universe that is unfamiliar to her. She is asking herself how long she will have to stay here and, suddenly pessimistic, she clings to

Phil and asks him to watch over the twins if anything should happen to her. But she hasn't lost her sense of humor.

"If I die, you could always marry Peggy," she suggests. "She's pretty and she's very good at looking after children!"

"Stop talking such rubbish! Your vein will unblock itself and you'll be on your feet in no time. And seeing as you're thinking about the future, I'd like to invite you to Sunday lunch at my place soon, to introduce you to my children and my dragon of a mother. I've been wondering about her recently. She has a cousin that she has been very fond of for ages. He's a widower and she's a widow. I'm starting to think they might want to get married, even though they aren't very young anymore. They were talking about it the other day and they didn't know that I overheard. I don't think they were kidding around. My mother said she needed another six months to tie up some loose ends. I wonder what on earth she was talking about."

"Yes, I'd like to get to know your children now. And if your mother decides to go and live somewhere else, that's no bad thing after all if she's anything like your description of her!"

After three quarters of an hour, Phil has to leave, but he promises Victoria he will come back the day after tomorrow, at lunchtime. Phil has a lot of work to do. He has two reports to write: the first on the strategic value of Tamanrasset for French aviation and the second about the circumstances surrounding the accident that delayed his return by three days and might have killed him. But that evening, in his bed, worry overcomes him. He needs to know that Victoria is going to be fine.

Two days later, when he arrives at Victoria's room, the door is wide open and the room is full of doctors and students, all in white coats. He waits outside, concerned, because he can see that the white coats are massed around Victoria. He asks a nurse in the corridor what is going on and she explains that Mrs. Miller has had a fainting fit and is having trouble breathing, so they have called for the senior doctor. When the doctors leave the room a quarter of an hour later, Colonel Destivel, in uniform, identifies the oldest among them as the most likely candidate for the senior doctor. He rushes towards him to ask about Victoria.

"Mrs. Miller has had a pulmonary embolism," he explains. "It's serious and she mustn't have another one. We're going to increase the dose of anticoagulant. She's not at all well at the moment. It would be better if you came back tomorrow. She needs to rest."

Phil leaves the hospital very worried. He finds it hard to concentrate on his work and goes to see Peggy at the end of the afternoon to tell her the news. She would like to go and see Victoria, but she cannot leave the twins on their own.

The next day, when Phil arrives at the hospital ward, the nurse he spoke to the day takes him aside and ushers him into an office where she tells him bluntly, without ceremony, that Mrs. Miller died suddenly from another pulmonary embolism an hour ago. Her body has already been transported to the hospital chapel of rest. No-one can see her for the moment.

The shock hits Phil hard. Overcome, he sits on a bench in the corridor and it takes him some time to pull himself together. The nurse comes to ask if he is family, and when he tells her he is not, she asks if Victoria has any relatives in Paris. He explains that Victoria was living with her two children and her cousin in an apartment close to the *Jardin du Luxembourg* and that he will contact the cousin.

Peggy goes to pieces when Phil tells her the news. They both sob uncontrollably.

"I'll have to go back to England as soon as possible with the children," Peggy says. "Legally, they are Colonel Miller's children, even if I know perfectly well that you are their real father. Victoria told me, but she wanted it to remain a secret. The situation is complicated. What do you want to happen?"

The question is direct and surprises Phil, who has no answer. He leaves Peggy shortly afterwards.

That evening at dinner, Maggy can see that her son is suffering. He doesn't say a word, and uses the excuse of problems at work to leave the table before the end of the meal and go to his room. An hour later, Maggy taps gently on the door and finds her son in tears. She interprets his pain as a sign that he has received the photograph of his girlfriend kissing another man. She approaches him, affectionately.

"What's the matter? Is something wrong?"

"Yes, the woman I love died this morning at Cochin Hospital. A pulmonary embolism! I met her in England and she moved to Paris recently. I wanted to introduce you to her. But please just leave me now, I need to be alone."

Maggy doesn't really understand and she leaves her son alone, as asked. It's obvious he didn't get the photograph she sent. It's not worth making her son suffer even more, because, in any case, the threat presented by this woman has passed. The next morning, Maggy recovers the offending document from the post as it arrives and destroys it immediately.

During the next few days, Phil goes to see Peggy several times. She is organizing her own departure and the repatriation of Victoria's body. He feels an immense need to be at her funeral in England. It's easy to fix the date for the repatriation of the body, but Peggy can't get a date for the burial from the consulate. They tell her that the British authorities will decide what to do once the body has been repatriated. Permission for burial will be granted then, almost certainly a few days after the return of the body. Phil is depressed. He can't see how he can possibly organize to be at the funeral of his beloved and promises himself that he will go to visit her grave in the cemetery in Reading where she will repose.

Phil decides to make up for his absence by organizing, with Peggy, a final ceremony of adieu in the chapel of rest of the hospital. He invites all the friends that she had made so rapidly following her arrival in Paris.

About fifteen people attend the ceremony, many of them men, probably sensitive to Victoria's beauty and charm, mostly painters and musicians. Several of those present take to the stand to read their own poems, dedicated to Mrs. Miller and bringing tears to the eyes of the other members of the congregation. Jean-Louis Raqué, the gallery owner, pays tribute several times to her immense talent, which was about to be recognized. Her friend Serge talks about her beauty and her strong character. He even uses the word "temperament" several times, bringing a smile to the faces of his friends. Peggy thanks Victoria for the last few magnificent months that they spent together, initially in London and then in Paris, and she promises to continue to watch over the twins, whom she loves as if they were her own children. Phil speaks last. He talks about meeting Victoria on a riverbank, with fishing as the first thing they had in common. He is discreet and talks about their time together in veiled terms, as if he wants to remain enigmatic, so that only she would have been able to understand his words. His voice is broken by the end, and he is submerged by his emotions and sadness. Most of those present are in tears.

Before leaving Paris, Peggy leaves Phil her parents' address so that they will be able to write to each other. Once she gets to England, she will go and consult a lawyer and then write to Phil. This situation is very difficult for Phil. He can't see himself either raising these two babies without their mother or abandoning them to their fate in England.

Victoria's death leaves an immense hole in the life of Colonel Destivel, who feels that life has been unfair to him. At 41, he finds himself widowed a second time, after having himself miraculously escaped from several particularly serious accidents.

Six months have passed since the death of Victoria

27

MORLEAU IN BURGUNDY, FRANCE, JUNE 1946

The little bell on Françoise's gate has just rung. She leans out of the kitchen window to identify the visitor and is very surprised to see Maggy, Colonel Destivel's mother, a woman she first met two years ago and with whom she has recently been corresponding. Despite her age, Maggy is looking smart in a white dress covered with black polka dots and high heels. Françoise is taken aback by this unexpected visit, but Maggy offers an explanation when Françoise lets her in.

"I went to visit some cousins of mine near Macon and I said to myself that I would come and say hello to you on my way back. I'm sorry I didn't give you any warning. You will say if I'm in the way?"

"No, not at all. I didn't have anything planned. I was just about to start preparing lunch. You'll stay and eat with us of course?"

"That's very kind of you and I'd be delighted. My train back to Paris leaves from Chagny at half past four."

"I'll introduce you to my children and show you round the house."

In her letters, Maggy had initially invited Françoise to come and see her in Paris. Françoise had replied that things were unfortunately a bit complicated and that she couldn't easily leave the children behind. Maggy had then said that she would come and see Françoise if the occasion presented itself. But she hadn't given a date.

Françoise's children are always happy to see people arrive and they find Maggy funny right from the start. She is struck by the way they call their mother "vous" rather than the more informal and usual "tu". She finds that very "classy" and aristocratic. She is also favorably impressed by the house when Françoise shows her round.

"Oh! This is a real chateau! The tower in the corner is beautiful, like a real castle keep!"

Françoise has had all the rooms repainted and the kitchen renovated, and she has had a new electric pump installed to transport the water collected in the tank outside to the house. The gravel in the courtyard in front of the house has been replaced and a gardener has planted flowers in the flower beds. It's true that everything looks very pretty and Maggy is enthusiastic.

"But your house is enormous! How many rooms do you have?"

"Yes, it is pretty big. There are nine bedrooms, although we're not using all of them at the moment. In addition to the living room and the dining room, there is also a large office in the tower."

Françoise makes Maggy comfortable in the living room and asks the children to keep her company while she prepares lunch. Left on her own with the children, Maggy takes advantage of the situation to casually ask them personal questions about their mother.

"Your mom is very brave living on her own in this house. I mean, without a husband. It's a good job you're here. Has she been very unhappy since your dad died?"

"She's been happier these last few months," replies Agnes, the eldest. "It's not like before, when she used to cry all the time."

"Maybe she has a friend who takes her mind off things?"

"There was William before. He's her American cousin and they're friends. He used to give us English lessons, but he went back to his own country a few months ago. He's supposed to be coming to see us soon."

"Did he live in the village?"

"No, he stayed with us for quite a long time. He had his own bedroom in our house."

Agnes has stirred up Maggy's curiosity. Maggy wants to know more, but she can't see how she can continue to question the girl in this way.

Françoise calls everyone for lunch. On the way to the dining room, Maggy takes in every detail of the furniture and the décor. As she crosses the living room and the entrance hall, she sees nothing but stylish furniture everywhere, and old paintings, portraits of Françoise's ancestors, hanging on the walls. Françoise tells her the names of some of her ancestors, certain of whom were counts or viscounts. Maggy is entranced.

"I'm impressed, Françoise! You have a really beautiful house. What class!"

During the meal, Françoise and Maggy talk about their return to France, from Morocco for Maggy and Algeria for Françoise. Then Maggy changes the subject, warning her friend that she is about to tell her a secret.

"Don't laugh, but I'm going to get married soon, with a cousin who has also been widowed. There was something between us when we were young, but then we split up. Fernand had to go and work elsewhere and we both met someone else. It's a funny old world though! Me getting married again, at my age!"

"So you'll have to leave your son? How is he by the way?"

"He's doing very well. He's a colonel now, and he'll soon be a general. The kids are growing up. Paul is 17 and Claire is 16. My son and his children don't need me anymore. It's better that I go and live somewhere else. It will be easier for him when he remarries."

"Is he going to get married again then?"

"I don't think he's met anyone since he got back from England, but he's not going to live the rest of his life without a wife! I'm sure there are lots of women interested in him. When I see him leave for work in the morning, I think he looks very handsome in his uniform! He'd make a hell of a match for someone. What about you? Don't you want to get married again?"

Françoise dodges the question, indicating by a simple gesture that she doesn't want to broach the subject in the presence of her children.

Whilst they are drinking their coffee in the living room, the bell on the gate rings again. Françoise goes to see who it is and returns with someone on her arm.

"Children, look who's come to see us! You'll be very pleased!"

Françoise enters the room with William, otherwise known as Wilhelm. The children jump for joy. Françoise takes care of the introductions. Maggy tells herself that William must be Françoise's young lover, which complicates the situation and might scupper her plan.

William comes in and announces that he will be spending several days with them, without asking Françoise is if he can stay. For him, there is no question of a refusal. He's already conquered this territory!

It is soon time for Maggy to return to Chagny to catch her train to Paris. Françoise offers to run her to the station.

"I have a car now. I can take you to the station. It's not far."

"You have a car? That's great! It makes life so much easier in the country. You have more independence like that."

Maggy can't stop herself from asking more about the car.

"What kind of car is it, a Citroen?"

"No, it's a Hotchkiss. My husband and I had one before the war."

Maggy is no great car specialist, but she knows that Hotchkiss is a prestigious brand, and that pleases her. She agrees to let Françoise run her to the station, telling herself that they will have some time to themselves in the car to talk whilst she waits for her train. Effectively, they arrive at the station early and they have a quarter of an hour in which to chat. Maggy tries to find out more about William. Françoise is concerned that Maggy might think that she and William are lovers, so she decides to clear things up.

"William is my American cousin. He came to France after he was injured, to recover and perfect his French. He will be going home in a few days."

Maggy is relieved, but she asks Françoise directly if there is a man in her life. Françoise tells her that there isn't and that she thinks it's probably better that way for the moment. She recounts the episode with Georges, leaving her friend completely flabbergasted.

"He wanted to marry me but I discovered that he liked men too! Do you realize what a lucky escape I had?"

Maggy talks about her son again, praising his moral qualities.

"Over the last few months, he's been spending a lot of time managing an association that helps injured airmen and the families of airmen injured or killed on duty."

"That sounds interesting. I've never heard of this association. What's it called?"

"I think it's called *Ailes Brisées*[11]. You should join. I'll send you the precise details. I'm sure it would be useful to you."

When they part, Maggy is insistent that Françoise should come to visit her in Paris with her children.

"Come for a few days. If your children like animals, there is the zoo at Vincennes, the *Jardin des Plantes* and the aquarium at the Trocadero. And if you want to see Paris from high up, there's the Eiffel Tower. It's brilliant. Your children would love it."

Françoise thinks that it would be a bit difficult to organize, but it would be instructive for them to discover the capital during the vacation.

Maggy goes over it all in the train: Françoise is classy, she seems to be well-off, and she lives in a house that is almost a chateau in Burgundy, where she wouldn't mind spending her own vacations. She has no boyfriend, she has experience of life and her children are well brought-up. She would make one hell of a general's wife if Phil would only take an interest in her. But Maggy knows she needs to be diplomatic and not tackle Phil head-on. She needs to find a way of getting Phil and Françoise to meet. Once again, there is no room for error, but maybe the *Ailes Brisées* can help her.

---

[11] *Broken Wings*

Once Maggy has left, Françoise returns home, impatient to find out what William has been up to, as she hasn't heard from him for several months.

William tells her his story, recounting his return to Germany with no real difficulty in mid-October. He was hidden in a truck that got him over the Kehl Bridge, a none-too-solid wooden bridge reconstructed as a temporary measure, near Strasbourg.

He first went looking for his parents and learned, as he had feared, that they had been killed during the bombing of Dresden. In need of papers, he then went to see the American military, telling them about his double nationality, his war in the *Wehrmacht*, and his flight before the advancing Russian army, but saying nothing about the time he spent in France. After several interrogations and diverse checks, they had given him new identity papers. The Americans were interested in his linguistic skills and offered him a post working with them to identify Nazi war criminals, a job he accepted with relish.

Based at Nuremberg, he is currently involved in the preparation of a trial of Nazi doctors suspected of having performed horrific experiments on humans, including Roma gypsy children in particular, in the extermination camps.

"You were right to tell me to go back to Germany," he tells Françoise. "It's much better than running away to South America. It's opened up new possibilities for me in the future, maybe even in America. I'll see in a couple of years. I've managed to get a few days off and an official passport to come and see you. I wanted to collect a few gold bars. No more than five, because I'm traveling by train. That will help me in Germany, where life is very difficult at the moment."

William leaves two days later. He leaves Françoise his address in Nuremberg and promises to come back to see her soon. Françoise tells him to be careful when trying to sell his gold bars and jewelry. A few days later, Françoise and her children receive a postcard from Nuremberg confirming that their German friend has arrived safely after a rapid border crossing simplified by his professional papers.

28

PARIS, FRANCE, JUNE TO OCTOBER 1946

Phil was completely destroyed by the sudden death of Victoria in December. It had been a terribly hard blow, almost worse than he had suffered when his wife had died.

Peggy's rapid return to England with the five-month-old twins, Helen and George, had been the final straw, confronting him with a complex and depressing reality. Legally, he is nothing to his children. It would be difficult, if not impossible, to prove that he is their father. In their most recent conversations, Peggy told him that Victoria didn't want her children to be considered illegitimate and that she therefore didn't want Colonel Miller's paternity to be called into question while she and Phil were not living together as husband and wife. As Peggy is the only person who could testify to the fact that Victoria and Phil had a relationship that led to a pregnancy, Phil can't see how he could possibly make any claim at all.

Three months ago, having received no news from Peggy, he had written to her at the address in Reading that she had given him, but she never replied to his letter. Phil has decided to send her a new letter and to travel to Reading in person to see what is going on if she doesn't reply again.

Today, Maggy is returning to Paris after a few days with her cousins who live near Macon. She arrives late, after dinner, and puts off relating the story of her lunch stop at Françoise Dumaine's house, which she didn't tell Phil about before leaving, until the next day, a Saturday. She tells Phil all about it at lunch.

"I didn't say before, but yesterday I spent a few hours with Françoise Dumaine at her house near Chagny. You know her, you know. She's a widow I met at Meknes. I invited her to dinner there."

Phil, taken aback, wonders what is coming next. Does Maggy want him to marry this woman? He nevertheless asks how she was, bracing himself for the eulogy that he anticipates his mother is about to deliver.

"I had a look round her house. It's a basic sort of building, a bit dilapidated and without much land. The furniture is all old and the paintings are a bit drab. She seems to live a bit like a hermit, shut away with her three children, who seemed a bit difficult. It must be tough living in that village, where they don't even have running water. I think your association might be able to help her. It's called *Ailes Brisées* isn't it? You can give me the details. I told her I'd send them on to her. Time hasn't been kind to her, poor thing! I thought she looked old. She's starting to get gray hairs and deep lines on her forehead. Not really surprising though, with all her worries. She should dye her hair. Mind you, I get the impression that she's trying to start a new life down there. She told me about one of her neighbors, a farmer with a small-holding, who has been making eyes at her. She doesn't like him all that much, but her life is so difficult!"

Phil is astonished. He was expecting a completely different description of Françoise. It's a shame, because he remembers Françoise as a beautiful, intelligent woman that he liked talking to when he was in North Africa.

Maggy's strategy is elaborate. After careful thought, she came to the conclusion that if she painted a negative picture of Françoise Dumaine, Phil would be more surprised and charmed if he actually met her. She certainly doesn't want her son to think that she is trying to push him into the arms of this woman.

After the dark period following Victoria's death, Phil had felt the need to keep busy, to stop himself thinking too much and, therefore, suffering. He rapidly became Vice President of the *Ailes Brisées* association, and is very generous with his time, doing all he can to develop this association and make it better known.

Following Maggy's request, he gets the association to send Françoise Dumaine a letter describing its aims and the services it provides. Françoise soon joins the association and one month later, the association decides to make a financial contribution to the education of her three children, wards of the nation. They award her a sum equivalent to that she would have received for Christmas 1945 if she had already been known to them. Françoise is very grateful and volunteers to help the *Ailes Brisées* with any tasks she can perform at home. She receives a letter of thanks shortly afterwards, but no offers of voluntary work for the moment.

After the discovery of Georges' loot, which she shared with William, Françoise experienced a long phase of euphoria. This money has effectively transformed her life. But, after a few months, she starts to feel that she can't carry on living year-round in her little Burgundy village, with its very restricted social life.

At the start of August, she decides to spend some time in the capital with her children. She doesn't know Paris very well, as she has never lived there, and she stays in a hotel for a few days around the August 15 holiday to prepare for their subsequent stay.

The children like visiting the zoo, particularly the boys. Several times, she takes a taxi and asks the driver to pass through certain quarters of Paris, which she then explores on foot. This is how she discovers the quarters of *Auteuil, les Invalides* quarter, *la Muette* and *Montmartre*. But, in the end, she finds the quarter of *Saint-Germain-des-Prés* the most attractive. She soon finds an apartment to rent at *6 bis rue Bonaparte,* in a handsome 18th century building. The living room is a bit dark and looks out onto the road, but there are three quiet sunny bedrooms that look out onto a small garden.

The flat comes with a maid's room on the top floor, and Françoise intends to make good use of it by hiring a maid at the start of October. The banks of the Seine are close by, and the effervescence of *Boulevard Saint Germain* is only five minutes' walk away. Françoise extends her stay by a week to buy the basic furniture and crockery she needs. She plans to move into her new residence in mid-September.

On September 14, 1946, Françoise arrives in Paris by car, with her children. She has six gold bars in her suitcase, together with a few pieces of jewelry that she should be able to sell easily in Paris, where there are numerous jewelers. She writes a long letter to her friend William in Nuremberg, telling him that she has moved and giving him her address in Paris. She spends the first few days in a hotel whilst awaiting the delivery of her furniture.

Françoise has found herself a maid in Burgundy, a woman called Suzanne who accompanies her to Paris. Suzanne comes from Dezize les Maranges, a small village not far from Morleau, in the Saone et Loire. Suzanne will live in the maid's room on the seventh floor. The room is quite large, but a bit austere. The room is accessible only by the service staircase, it has no running water and the toilets are communal, but Suzanne is happy with her independence. Françoise is a good boss who doesn't try to exploit her. Suzanne is well paid and Françoise has organized for her to have regular working hours, which leaves her with time for herself.

Two days later, Françoise's apartment is clean and functional, even if the décor leaves something to be desired. She gets Suzanne to prepare a good dinner to celebrate their new lives.

On September 18, Françoise switches on her new Philips radio during dinner. She hears about a speech that Winston Churchill, whom she greatly admires, gave the day before at the University of Zurich. An entreaty to build a United States of Europe, federating all the countries that wish to join it, including Germany, a difficult proposition to accept after all the horrors committed by the Nazis. But she tells herself that he is probably right if we want to guarantee peace in the future.

Françoise easily finds school places for her children. Agnes will go to Hulst, a secondary school on *rue de Varenne,* and Michel will attend a small school on *rue des Saints Pères.* Romain, the youngest, is not old enough for school yet and will be looked after regularly so that his mother can have some free time.

Once the children have gone back to school, Françoise has more free time and she walks to the offices of the *Ailes Brisées* association, avenue Daniel Lesueur, in the 7th *arrondissement* of Paris, to introduce herself and offer her services as a volunteer. A secretary of a certain age asks her to complete a dossier detailing her availability and skills. When Françoise has finished, the secretary explains that they will write to her, a solution that Françoise finds only half satisfactory because she would have preferred to talk to someone there and then about what she might be able to do. She is about to leave when she hears a voice behind her.

"My dear lady, if you have some time to spare for us, I have something to offer you. My name is Lieutenant Maria and I'm on leave from the air force for the next few weeks for medical reasons. If you would like to step into my office, I'll explain."

The secretary is disgruntled and informs the lieutenant that this is not the usual procedure, but the lieutenant just shrugs his shoulders and leads Françoise into a small room at the back of the apartment that serves as the headquarters of the association.

The lieutenant must be about 25 years old. He is tall, very dark, solidly built and massive. He begins by telling her about his own misadventures.

"I'm afraid there's nothing glorious about my health problems. I jarred my spine during a rugby match two months ago and the doctor of my squadron put me on sick leave, but I'm feeling much better now. I pass the time by doing voluntary work for the *Ailes Brisées*. I'm trying to collect money from companies and I could do with some help. What's your story?"

Françoise explains that she is a war widow who has recently moved to Paris. She is interested in the lieutenant's offer. He suggests that she could help him to identify the companies that could be contacted to request a donation, to obtain the names of their directors, to find out about them, to write personalized letters to the directors and to follow up these contacts. They agree that she will help out three half-days per week. Lieutenant Maria concludes the interview by saying that he will inform the board of the association about their arrangement, but says there should be no problem. Françoise is happy with her reception as she leaves the association's offices. She will start work in a week. She likes the sound of the tasks the lieutenant has asked her to perform, because they involve a lot of contact with diverse people, and she has been deprived of human contact at Morleau.

Françoise has followed the Nuremberg trial closely on the radio. On October 16, she learns with satisfaction of the hanging of the principal Nazi leaders responsible for inflicting so much suffering on Europe, France, and her family in particular.

It's the first time that Françoise has had a regular, almost professional activity, even if she isn't paid. Etienne, as Lieutenant Maria is called, has installed her in his little office. Françoise only sees him one half-day a week, but when he is there, they talk incessantly. Etienne is very chatty and funny and he makes his office-mate laugh out loud. They are often heard guffawing in the corridor, even though the office door is closed. This jollity doesn't stop Françoise from getting on with her work, especially when the lieutenant is not there. The letters that she writes to possibly generous future donors are first read over by Etienne and then passed on to the main office of the association to be read through one last time and signed. Etienne makes very few changes to the letters that Françoise gives him to read.

One day, while they are chatting, there is a knock at the door. Someone comes in and speaks to Etienne.

"Well done, lieutenant. It was a brilliant idea to introduce concrete descriptions of the families affected by the death of an airman into the letters requesting donations. I think that moves the potential donors and makes them more likely to support us."

"I'm afraid I can't take the credit for that. It was Mrs. Dumaine's idea. Allow me to present Françoise, who comes in to help us several times a week."

Françoise turns around to see someone vaguely familiar. After a moment's hesitation she recognizes Colonel Destivel, whom she hasn't seen for four years. He rapidly figures out who she is, surprised to run into her here.

"Oh! Mrs. Dumaine! What a surprise! I thought you were still living in Burgundy."

Phil is even more surprised to see before him a woman who still looks young, pretty and elegant, with a discreetly made-up face.

An appearance very different from the image conjured up by Maggy's description not so long ago.

Françoise and Phil leave the office to chat for a while in one of the other rooms in the apartment. They talk about their respective situations. Françoise tells Phil that she has moved to Paris and says that she enjoys the work she does for *Ailes Brisées*, thanks particularly to the presence of Lieutenant Maria, whom she finds very agreeable. Phil checks all the letters she has written before sending them off. He congratulates her on the quality of her work, which is starting to bear fruit. Several company directors that they have recently written to have already made large donations to the association.

Phil comes to the *Ailes Brisées* office several times during October. He regularly hears Françoise Dumaine in animated discussions with the lieutenant through the door. Their discussions are punctuated by silences, but also by laughter, which ends up annoying him. It even occurs to him that these two might be having an affair. He knows that the lieutenant is single and that Françoise is a widow. But their relationship is strange nevertheless! The lieutenant must be ten years younger than she is, and doesn't look very elegant, with the build typical of thick-set rugby players from the South West, his region of origin. Phil if fond of Françoise and regrets not being able to talk to her on his own.

As chance would have it, the human resources director of the air force, Brigadier General Noiret, calls on Phil at the Ministry.

"My dear Destivel, we need to find a new post for Lieutenant Maria, who has just been promoted to captain," he says. "I think you know him, because he was in your group at Gaitford, and I would like to know what you think of him. Should we keep him in Paris for a while as assistant to the Major General? It's essentially an administrative post. Or should we send him to lead a squadron based at Blida in Algeria, where there will be lots of training flights? What do you think?"

Phil doesn't need much time to make up his mind.

"Maria is an excellent pilot and I'm sure he'd be an excellent squadron leader. I don't think an administrative post would suit him. I'm sure he'd be very happy to be sent to Algeria. I'd say the choice is pretty clear."

General Noiret is surprised by the rapidity of Colonel Destivel's response as he knows him to be generally more measured in his opinions. But he tells himself that, effectively, an administrative post wouldn't be ideal for a pilot who gave so much of himself during two years in England and was decorated with the Distinguished Flying Cross. Undoubtedly, he'd prefer to keep flying planes and, more generally, to exercise his profession as an airman.

Thirteen months have now passed since Victoria's death.

29

PARIS, FRANCE, FEBRUARY AND MARCH 1947

At the start of February, Maggy organizes a big family gathering bringing together her son, her grandchildren, her cousin Fernand, who has become a frequent visitor to the apartment in *rue Lecourbe,* and all the cousins living in the Parisian region. There are eighteen guests in all, invited by Maggy to strengthen the cohesion of the family and to celebrate the election of Vincent Auriol, the first president of the 4th Republic, who was nominated three weeks ago. Two tables have been placed end-to-end so that there is enough room to seat everyone. Maggy has called on the services of a caterer, who has prepared some cold cod with diced vegetables and lots of salad cream. Phil has got hold of a white wine from Meursault to accompany the fish. For the dessert, there are several bottles of Champagne to go with a particularly spectacular vacherin.

When the time comes to crack open the Champagne, Maggy gets up to give a little speech. The guests are astonished by what they hear from the mouth of their hostess, who is a bit tipsy.

"To the health of our new president, who I couldn't give two figs about seeing as I've heard he doesn't have any power anyway! But, on a more serious note, I have something very personal to tell you. I am delighted to inform you all that I'm going to marry my cousin Fernand, who you can see to my right. Don't worry, he knows all about it! We've both lost our spouses and we want to enjoy the rest of our lives, together."

Phil isn't really surprised, as he has already overheard Maggy talking about it without her realizing. He is even delighted with the prospect of seeing his mother leave his apartment.

By contrast, Paul and Claire are amazed. They hadn't imagined for one moment that you could contemplate marriage and everything that goes with it after the age of fifty!

The cousins congratulate the newly engaged couple and the bottles of Champagne arrive at the perfect time to celebrate the event. Phil feels obliged to say a few words, after raising his glass to the happy couple.

"I'm delighted for you both! I must thank Mom once again for everything she did for me and the kids during the war. I don't know what I would have done without her. I'll keep it brief, but I'd like to end by saying something that I know will make her happy. I found out a couple of days ago that I have been promoted to general. I didn't tell you until today Mom, because I wanted it to be a surprise. I know it means a lot to you, possibly even more than it does to me!"

Maggy is ecstatic. She has been dreaming of this moment for years. For her, attaining the rank of general is the height of success. The guests now take turns to congratulate their young cousin. They are proud to have a general in the family, especially one who has attained this rank at the tender age of 43. Most of them are farmers or technicians with no education beyond high school.

Two weeks later, Phil has invited his English mathematician and pilot friend, John, to lunch. John has made great progress in French since they last met, although his very strong accent, which makes Claire laugh, leaves the listener in no doubt as to his nationality. He is still happy to be living in Paris and is finding his work at the *College de France* very stimulating. The discussions at lunch are very lively. Paul is captivated by John's flying stories and his wartime work as a mathematician at the headquarters of Bomber Command in England. Claire poses a question that Maggy finds inappropriate for a young lady. She asks him if he thinks that Parisian women are pretty and whether he has a girlfriend. John says that the Parisian women are indeed very charming and elegant and that it is why he is having such a hard time choosing just one.

After lunch and coffee, Phil and John have a private conversation. The Englishman congratulates Phil on his recent promotion to general and asks him about his new job. Phil replies that, for the moment, he is continuing to inspect overseas air bases. He explains that his role is both technical and strategic. He has to anticipate possible changes in the relationship of France with the principal players in the Second World War, including Russia, a communist country increasingly seen as problematic.

At the end of their discussion, John asks Phil if he is still seeing the English girlfriend he spoke about when they last met. Phil tells him about her death and John says how sorry he is to hear this news. Finally, Phil asks if John would be willing to give his children English conversation lessons on Saturday mornings or afternoons. He adds that he would, of course, pay him for that. John doesn't agree straight away, because he is often busy on Saturdays and he wants to see if he can reorganize his day. John leaves shortly after this discussion.

Things have changed at *Ailes Brisées*. Lieutenant Maria has been transferred to Algeria, much to the annoyance of Françoise Dumaine. She loved their conversations and jokes. They had become good friends and enjoyed working together. When Etienne had told her he would be leaving soon, he had confessed, with a smile, something that had disturbed her.

"You know, I think it's probably a good thing I'm leaving. I think I've fallen in love with you a little, even though you're ten years older than me. Now I'll have to make do with the 'pajama mammas' in Algeria for consolation!"

Françoise took his words lightly, but was forced to recognize that the lieutenant, even with his heavy-set, stocky build, had a certain charm and knew how to make her laugh. Fortunately, he had behaved like a gentleman even when they were shut up together in the tiny office in which they worked. She might have found it hard to resist his advances had he made any. She is astonished when he tells her that she will now work directly with General Destivel, who comes to the association's offices occasionally.

For three weeks, she works alone, increasingly furious that Phil, whom she knows at least a little, hasn't bothered to contact her and seems to be ignoring her completely. When he turns up unannounced one afternoon, she finds it hard to conceal her annoyance.

"Good afternoon, General. Congratulations on your promotion. But I wonder whether, with all your new responsibilities, you can find any time for me. I've been working on my own for three weeks now, with lots of questions to ask you and letters for you to validate. I'm not willing to carry on like this!"

Phil is surprised by this glacial welcome and his response is cold too.

"It's true that I don't have much time for this at the moment. It's probably best that I phone you when I have a bit of free time."

The rest of the meeting is tense because Phil doesn't want it to drag on. He asks Françoise to select the most pertinent questions she needs to ask him. He will read the letters that need signing later. He organizes an appointment with her in three weeks' time, as he has no free time until then. Françoise is flabbergasted by his indifference and wonders how much time he intends to devote to the activities of *Ailes Brisées* in the future. She misses her friend Etienne and doesn't scruple to tell him so.

"I had a better way of working with Lieutenant Maria. He was here once a week, at a regular time. It was much more effective and we were able to make good progress."

Phil leaves the office a bit tight-lipped, without saying goodbye. He is actually in a very bad mood because a confidential document that he took home recently has disappeared. It presented a preliminary analysis of the potential impact of atomic weapons on conventional warfare on the ground. The French don't have the atom bomb for the moment, but their military officials realize that these weapons have changed everything and they will have to adapt.

The previous Sunday, John had finally come to give Paul and Claire an English lesson. The three of them had shut themselves up in the small room that Phil uses as his office. The lesson had lasted an hour and a half. The children had appreciated the way in which John had managed to retain their attention for the whole of this time. In the evening, after dinner, Phil had wanted to work on this document, clearly stamped with the words "confidential", but he had been unable to find it. The children had sworn religiously that they hadn't touched it. John was the only other person to have entered the room and the apartment had remained empty during the afternoon.

The next morning, Phil had felt obliged to declare the loss of this document to the security services, concealing nothing of the circumstances in which it had occurred. An investigation of John Luxley had rapidly been opened and his apartment had been discreetly searched. The missing document was not found, but there was a rough draft of a very ambiguous letter that might have something to do with it. The investigation revealed that John had lots of communist friends and that he helped to sell the left-wing newspaper *l'Humanité* on Sunday mornings. Furthermore, he was found to participate regularly at communist cell meetings. All this led to John being suspected of having passed the missing document to communists in cahoots with the Russians. Everyone knows that the French communist party adores Stalin. However, they had found nothing illegal in John's life. In these conditions, Phil had used the excuse of his children having too much homework and too many exams to cancel the lessons that John was supposed to be giving them in the future.

Phil has a lot of work to do because he is leaving for a week-long inspection in Vietnam in a few days. He is particularly excited by this voyage to a country that is very popular with the many French people who have been there, but that he himself has not yet visited.

After this inspection, he is submerged by his work and it's only a month after his last meeting with Françoise that he finds the time to come and see her in the association's offices. Françoise is not very happy and finds an excuse to leave when she sees him arrive. She really wants to pull him into line and doesn't understand how he can treat a volunteer in this manner. Phil waits for her for an hour and then decides to leave, asking himself whether it wouldn't have been better to phone her before turning up, unannounced and a week late.

Three days later, having been informed of Françoise's presence by the secretary, he phones her at the office, in the afternoon.

"I'm sorry for having been such an oaf. I haven't really behaved properly towards you since the departure of Lieutenant Maria. I've had a lot of problems. I can explain."

Phil organizes another meeting with Françoise at the association and promises that he will turn up this time.

The next time they see each other, Phil apologizes again, without going into detail, and they throw themselves into their work. It's winter but it is hot in the office. Françoise is relaxed and has taken off her jacket, as has Phil. They work efficiently for two hours. Phil compliments her on her mastery of French and good writing style. Françoise's acrimony towards the general subsides and, as he looks at her, he is struck by the natural class and discreet charm she exudes. He finds that she has a very pleasant smile. At the end of the meeting, Phil has an idea.

"By means of an apology, I'd really like to take you out to dinner one evening, if you're free. Would you like that?"

Françoise seems to hesitate for a moment, but deep-down, she is very pleased. General Destivel has an imposing presence and doesn't seem to have a woman in his life. She would be wrong to refuse, and so she accepts his invitation. Phil offers to come and pick her up from her apartment at 8 p.m. the following Wednesday. He has been assigned a car, a 15-horsepower Citroen, with a chauffeur, for his work, but he can also use it for some private purposes.

Phil has reserved a table at *La Coupole*, a brasserie on *Boulevard de Montparnasse* that is very fashionable, although this will be the first time that he has eaten there. A number of painters and writers spend much of their time there. When they arrive, Françoise is impressed because a black woman eating at a table opposite theirs waves to Phil, who barely recognizes her. It's Josephine Baker, the singer who gave a concert at the Gaitford base in May 1945, when Phil was the commander of the base. He explains that to Françoise, who finds it astonishing, and somewhat vexing that the singer had recognized him straight away. Then it's the turn of Stephane Grapelli, the jazz violinist, to come over and place his hand on Phil's shoulder whilst singing the Marseillaise.

Françoise and Phil order a whisky before dinner, which immediately loosens up their tongues.

Françoise asks Phil whether he met any pretty Englishwomen at Gaitford, but feels awkward when Phil tells her his story.

"Yes, I did meet and fall in love with someone, but it ended badly. She came to live in Paris and died of a pulmonary embolism a few months after her arrival."

"Oh, I'm so sorry! I was just joking around. I didn't realize. Please forgive me!"

"It's OK. I forgive you. You couldn't possibly know. You too, if I remember rightly, it's nearly four years since you were widowed. Wouldn't you like to find love again? Maybe you already have?"

"No, not really. There was a neighbor in my village, an engineer, who was interested in me. I found out, by chance, that he was homosexual. I hadn't imagined for a moment that he might be. Then he died in a road accident."

"People seem to drop like flies around us, but it's not our fault!"

They then speak about their children. Phil doesn't mention the twins, a secret that often keeps him awake at night. Phil asks Françoise if she is managing financially, with her children to bring up. She remains evasive on this point and says nothing about the gold and jewelry that she and William found.

They gradually get to know each other better. They have a lot to talk about and get on well. By the end of the meal, they are calling each other by their first names. When the taxi arrives at the foot of Françoise's building, Phil says goodnight and kisses her on both cheeks.

They see each other regularly in the following weeks. They go to the cinema together, an activity that they both appreciate.

Françoise vaunts the charm and talents of Gerard Philippe, a young actor unknown to Phil. For his part, Phil adores Micheline Presle and wants to take Françoise to see all the films in which she has a role. Françoise had played the piano a lot before she got married. She is particularly fond of Ravel and Satie, and she takes Phil to concerts of their works at *Salle Pleyel.*

All of this goes on behind the back of Maggy, who is busy preparing her own wedding. Phil doesn't want his mother to try to influence him one way or the other. For the moment, his relationship with Françoise is friendly and platonic.

At the end of April, Françoise invites Phil to spend a week with his children at her house in Morleau in July.

ABOUT THE AUTHOR

James de la Boullaye is a scientist by training. This professor of medicine and research scientist has, over the last few years, found great enjoyment and freedom in the writing of fictions.

www.ingramcontent.com/pod-product-compliance
Lightning Source LLC
LaVergne TN
LVHW010319200726
843507LV00010B/1284

9782955227046